Great Dates
❧ with ❧
Some Late Greats

Great Dates
with
Some Late Greats

David Finkle

PLUM BAY PUBLISHING, LLC

For permission requests, contact the publisher at the website below:
Plum Bay Publishing, LLC
www.plumbaypublishing.com

Library of Congress Control number: 2019930283
ISBN: 978-0-9988617-9-1
Printed in the United States of America

Cover design by Roberta Granzen
Interior layout by Barbara Aronica-Buck
Edited by Sally Fay

For David, Howard, Sandy and Sally

Contents

Foreword

In presenting the following manuscript, I'm asking you the reader to recognize as true a series of (almost entirely) serendipitous incidents that will strain credulity to the breaking point and possibly far beyond it, as far beyond as the other side of the grave.

I ask you to take my word that what are included here are no more and no less than events experienced by myself and others over several years. The others are men—some longtime friends, some acquaintances, at least one stranger encountered on a plane—who trusted me with their accounts but only after they had learned of mine. (Why there are no women involved, I'm reluctant to speculate. Whether their absence indicates a difference between the sexes, I'm in no position to conclude. If pressed to conjecture, I might say that men are needy in ways different from women, but I wouldn't stand by it. It's just a thought.)

I have to confess that I never recorded the men's stories as I listened attentively. I only relay them as I remember them—as accurately as possible, to be sure, and as much in their voices as possible. Their recollections are too indelible to be dismissed. They are absolutely not the sort of unexpected happenstances that I—or they—would have been able to concoct out of whole cloth. I am not convinced that anyone could, though others might deem it possible.

I readily admit that living through my experiences severely tested my credulity, as it did the credulity of those whose stories I report. I suspect when you hear about the events in as much detail as they and I are able to recount, they will test yours as well.

Indeed, they were so incredible even as they unfolded for me that I resisted passing them along in fear of exposing all of us to sustained derision. (Believe me when I confess I have never been the kind of man able to laugh easily at himself. I laugh at many things easily, but laughing at myself—I've had to accept belatedly—isn't one of them).

When I reported these experiences to friends and acquaintances whose responses I accepted as genuine, and they, to a man and woman, encouraged me to publish them, only then did I agree to commit anything to print.

Nevertheless, without further explanation, here is the manuscript for your perusal. I ask nothing more than your indulgence as I unfold these thirteen stories, mine the first and last among them. The first is the one that disposed me to hearing the rest and, as an inevitable result, to believing them whole-heartedly.

I also ask that if you choose to reject what you're about to read as a series of impossibilities in the world you know—or think you know—please withhold your scorn and simply regard the accounts as fantasies dreamed up in the kind of fertile mind I only wish I had.

—Paul Engler, August 2014

My First Story

✂ or ✂

Marilyn Monroe Is Hamlet

It began with no advance notice, as do so many things—incidents, episodes, events, developments, whatevers—in this mysterious and inexplicable life.

Not all that long ago I was walking across East Fifty-seventh Street in bustling New York City on an especially brilliant September afternoon. It was the kind of day that gave rise to the false-promising term "Indian summer."

As I knew I would, I passed the chain-link-fronted, fenced-off, unmown-grass-covered vacant lot that's what's left of a building in which I once lived. Whenever I see it—maybe once a year now, not much more often—I feel as if I'm being unceremoniously notified that my past is in the process of being obliterated.

I probably wouldn't mind so much if other Manhattan buildings where I've shelved and stacked my books and set up light (very light) housekeeping hadn't also gone the way of the dodo bird or other species that may not be extinct but are at great risk in these unpromising ecological times. But there are two more edifices in which I dwelled, well, temporarily—one on East Sixty-third Street and one on West Seventy-eighth Street—that have also been razed in my dishonor.

The erasure of the five-story building from this East Fifty-seventh streetscape—the others as well—feels as if my recollections of what it was like to live there are also meant by a spiteful deity to be deleted.

But they're my recollections. I want to keep them.

So I do what I always do. I start running through as many memories from those far-away-and-getting-farther years as I can. What follows is perhaps the most indelible memory from those days.

Just to put what's rapidly beginning to feel like melancholia, which it isn't, into context, I'll say I moved into that ground-floor East Fifty-seventh Street studio apartment shortly after I stampeded to New York City to start my brilliant career. My brilliant career in what—and as what—I had only a vague idea. Of what lay ahead of me I had no idea. And even less of an idea of what was to become of me.

At the time, a friend of mine who'd already been a local resident for an impressive (to me) spell referred to my experiences as "first-year New York." I'd tell him I'd gone here or done that, and he'd chuckle and say, "First-year New York." I resented it, because by "first-year New York," the querulous friend—a co-worker at my entry-level magazine-staffer job—really meant "naïve." Worse, he really meant "naïve and cute." I didn't enjoy being dismissed as naïve *or* cute, mainly because I was naïve—and probably "cute," too, in my way. Whatever my way was.

Today, though, the whole notion of my naïveté brings to mind memories I get a kick out of retrieving. A favorite—surely the most outlandish—is the memory of the celebrated neighbors I had then and what it meant to a boy from the sticks—for me, Allentown, Pennsylvania, was unarguably the sticks—to live in such close proximity to famous people, to live in such close proximity that I'd actually get to know them.

The neighbor who impressed me the most, however—the neighbor I most wanted to get to know so I could say I knew her and had shared a confidence or two with her—was someone who wasn't technically a neighbor. She was dead by the time I moved in. But if I'd moved in as recently as a couple decades, even just a decade, before I did, she would have definitely been a neighbor.

I'm talking about Marilyn Monroe. When Marilyn Monroe was in the city, she lived on the next block. On the same side of the street, no less. That Marilyn Monroe and I could have lived a block apart but didn't was merely bad timing.

What I thought was especially bad about it was that if we'd really lived a block apart, it would undoubtedly have been only a matter of time before we would have passed each other on the street; before we would have become nodding acquaintances and then friends—and then maybe even more.

Many people have these sorts of fantasies about prematurely deceased celebrities, but, come on, mine can't be dismissed so readily—no matter how naïve or cute I was. Dreamers separated from her by thousands of miles might have been kidding themselves, but not someone twenty-two, understanding and outrageously compassionate, who lived nearby and whose head and body weren't stuffed with booze, drugs and weird Hollywood notions.

So there you have it. The inevitability of my saving Marilyn Monroe but for a lousy chronological discrepancy of a decade or two is one of the most indelible memories of my East Fifty-seventh Street life and what I wanted from it.

And yet, one inclement October Saturday when I'd occupied the 330 East Fifty-seventh Street ground-floor studio apartment for no more than eight or nine months, I was running a few errands when a sudden squall caught me. Not entirely by surprise. I happened to have my handy-dandy collapsible umbrella with me. So what did I care?

That's when, with the suddenness of the downpour, my reverie was interrupted by the sight of a short woman standing forlornly under a canopy in a nondescript raincoat with a kerchief tied under her chin. To me in that moment, she was just a woman stuck in the rain. As I reached her, I shot a pitying glance. She returned the gaze from a pair of very big and wide eyes, eyes that seemed to say, "Protect me, protect me, you handsome, tall and protective stranger. Protect me. Take care of me."

At least that's how I saw those amazing peepers as I barreled along in my quasi-romantic, hardly uncommon mode. I knew the look was meant for me alone, because the shower had sent many would-be pedestrians into doorways and under canopies. There was no one else passing. I also had the unshakable feeling I'd seen the look before—or the eyes before. My follow-up thought was that Marilyn Monroe's eyes were very much like this woman's. In a trice—whatever short measure of time a trice is—I thought, "This *is* Marilyn Monroe. *This* is Marilyn Monroe. This is *Marilyn Monroe!*"

Then I thought, "Of course, you think this woebegone woman is

Marilyn Monroe. You have Marilyn Monroe on the brain. Given your current frame of mind, you'd think anybody who looked at you—doorman, delivery boy, barking Scottish terrier—was Marilyn Monroe. I sent the thought packing but not the woman. I figured we'd exchanged looks and hers was unmistakably a call for help.

"You look like you could use some assistance," I said. "If you're going in my direction, you can share my umbrella."

She took me up on the offer. "Thanks," she said in a voice I thought I recognized but took another couple seconds to place: It was Marilyn Monroe's wispy whisper, the hint in it of the bedroom, of the king-sized bed, of the tangled silk sheets. Again I had the any-doorman/delivery-boy/terrier-in-current-frame-of-mind thought.

As we were stepping along (I had slowed my pace to accommodate hers), I said, "You'll get a kick out of this. For a moment there, I thought you were Marilyn Monroe. She used to live on this block."

The woman turned towards me and said in a wispy whisper while giving me a look of wide-eyed innocence and allure, "I *am* Marilyn Monroe. I know I lived on this block. I used to live in that building." She pointed at the building where I'd seen her standing and shivering like a kitten in a gale.

"Sure you are," I said. "You're Marilyn Monroe, and so's that doorman over there." I pointed at a doorman who had just put a woman into a taxi cab.

"No, he isn't," she said, dropping the wispy whisper. "*I* am."

"Look, lady," I said, "You've already got my help. You don't need to pretend to be a dead woman to get me to escort you to the corner."

"That's funny," she said in Marilyn Monroe's sexy breathiness, "I spent so much of my last years on earth pretending not to be Marilyn Monroe, and now you think I'm pretending to be her. Me. You want to see my Marilyn Monroe walk?"

With that, she strode out from under the umbrella and started walking in front of me. I knew that walk. It's the walk Marilyn Monroe does when Jack Lemmon and Tony Curtis first see her in *Some Like It Hot*.

Was this the real Marilyn Monroe? Could she be? How could she be? She couldn't be. But maybe she was. Stranger things had happened to me than running into the dead Marilyn Monroe in the rain in front of her old building.

No, stranger things hadn't happened to me. Nothing that strange. I think I can say without fear of contradiction that if this was the real honest-to-God Marilyn Monroe, it was by a long chalk the strangest thing that had ever happened to me.

When she had taken eight or ten of Sugar's steps, she turned and started back to me. As she did, a woman who'd been heading our way stopped in her puddle-luscious tracks. She was wearing a plastic head covering and glasses the rain had attacked. She took her glasses off, began wiping the lenses with the damp ends of her tied head covering. She said to my Marilyn Monroe-or-not companion, "If I didn't know better, I'd have sworn you're Marilyn Monroe."

This should be good, I thought, and waited to see how my MM replied. To get a better listen, I stepped up alongside the pair.

"You know," the woman calling herself Marilyn said, dropping the *Some Like It Hot* stance and resuming the some-like-it-shlumpy posture,

"I get that every once in a while. I only wish I were, but I'm just plain old Harriet Hempwhistle. Thanks for saying so, though. It does a lot of good for a girl's self-esteem."

"I know I was wrong," the lady said. "After all, poor Marilyn is dead these many years. If I'd known her, she wouldn't be, I can tell you. I would have straightened her out just like that about those horny Kennedy boys. *Just like that.*" On both "just like thats"s she tried to snap her fingers, but they were wet and had no snap. She looked at her hand with some annoyance and said, "But don't call yourself plain, dear. You're not plain. We're all beautiful in our own special way." Then she winked at the Marilyn Monroe person, nodded at me and left.

Marilyn said, "She's right about me being dead all these years, and still the recognition never stops—present company excepted. I might as well have died yesterday. Makes me think of *Born Yesterday*. That's a part I should have played. Billy Dawn. Don't you think? Judy Holliday got it, because she did it on Broadway, but you know if they'd made that darn movie five years later, I would have played it, and *I* would have won the Oscar instead of her. She was good, though. I'm not saying she wasn't."

She took another of her breathy breaths. "Broadway, that's the ticket," she said. "You have to play Broadway to be taken seriously in Hollywood. I was never taken seriously. Not even when I married Arthur Miller. Instead, *he* was taken less seriously. Isn't that a killer?"

She was on a roll, but just then it occurred to her she wanted an actual roll—and, as it turned out not too much later, a role. Which I'm just about to get to, since it's the burden of this, um, confession(?), admission(?), recital(?), answered wish(?).

We'd reached the corner, where she stopped and pointed across the street at the local deli. We all knew it. Marilyn Monroe would have known it. I knew it had been there when she—if she were the real Marilyn Monroe—lived in the four-hundred block.

Not only did I know it, I knew the owners had hung a signed photograph of her on the wall behind the cash register. I even knew what it said: "To Max and Florie, all the best, Marilyn." I'm only slightly embarrassed to admit I patronized the deli because she had sat in its booths, perhaps in all of them at one time or another—and sometimes with Truman Capote, who had reported their tête-à-têtes in the years he wasn't drinking so much he could still down a deluxe liverwurst platter.

"I'm going over there," she said. "You'll think this is strange and you can say no. I'll understand. But would you like to come in with me?" She widened her already widened eyes. "You can wait out the rain there, at least. If you've got some time and aren't in a hurry to get somewhere."

Okay, what do you do when you meet a woman on the street in the rain and she tells you she's the back-from-the-other-side Marilyn Monroe and then invites you to accompany her into a deli?

I don't know what you do, but I know what I did. I said, "You betcha," or words to that effect. I agreed while still considering a few possibilities about this woman: (1) that she was delusional; (2) that I was delusional; and (3) that she was who she said she was and I was in the midst of a bizarre metaphysical phenomenon and that—taking into account the other street person who'd stopped us—I wasn't alone in it. I was favoring (3), because it was rare that I found myself in the midst of a bizarre metaphysical phenomenon, and I didn't want to short-change it.

When we entered the deli, a girl far too young to have been around when Marilyn Monroe was a regular or semi-regular or whatever she was, pointed us to one of the few tables and handed us menus. We sat down and faced each other. I'd taken my umbrella down and had checked my trousers to see how wet they'd gotten. Marilyn(?) had removed her raincoat and babushka and thereby surprised me further.

I must have looked surprised, because she said, "It's the hair, isn't it?" It was. She had Marilyn Monroe's features, and, of course, she'd gotten the walk down when she wanted, but her hair wasn't the billowing blond or platinum blond I might have expected. Instead, it was cropped short, rather like Laurence Olivier's had been for the filming of his 1946 *Hamlet*. In addition, what she was wearing under the raincoat was a black leotard of the sort Audrey Hepburn had popularized.

Meaning to be funny, I said, "Are you sure you're not Laurence Olivier playing Hamlet or Audrey Hepburn in anything?"

"Good," she said. "You got it."

"Got what?" I said as the young woman who'd seated us—or, to be exact, had pointed blankly at our seats—arrived to take our orders.

Marilyn asked for a buttered roll and coffee, very hot. I opted for decaffeinated coffee and a side of toast. The young woman, appearing to be slightly irritated by our small order, left.

"I got what?" I repeated.

"The Hamlet part," she replied. "That's why I've got the hair." She pointed at her cropped coiffure and at what she was wearing. "And this get-up."

"What about it?" I said, missing what evidently was meant to be an obvious point.

"Hamlet," she said. "I'm going to play it. Him."

I thought back to my three possibilities and decided we had hunkered down on (1) that *she* was delusional. She saw something of the sort on my face and said, "I know, I know. Nobody thinks I have it in me to do anything more than act in movies where I can do as many takes as I need to get it right. What they forget is that I studied with Lee Strasberg at the Actors Studio. Paula Strasberg was my personal coach. You didn't know that, did you?"

I did know that—or knew it but had forgotten it. I also remembered that during those Strasberg years, news got around that she'd even gone on stage once as an extra in *The Teahouse of the August Moon*, just so she could say she'd played Broadway.

"Well, I did study there," she continued, "and I once went on stage as an extra in *The Teahouse of the August Moon*, just so I could say I'd played Broadway. Big deal!" She raised her voice above a whisper for the "Big deal!" and lowered it again. "That wasn't playing Broadway. You don't really play Broadway until you play a real part. You know, something substantial. And what's the most substantial part ever written? That's a rhetorical question, by the way." I could see she was proud of the "rhetorical." "The answer is Hamlet. I'm going to play it. Just once. On Broadway. To prove my mettle. My m-e-t-t-l-e, not my m-e-t-a-l."

My jaw had dropped open and not just because her roll and my toast had arrived.

"You don't think I can," she said, "but you're forgetting that I've now had plenty of time to prepare, as Stanislavski says. And not just with his book, which anybody can read. But not anybody can study with him these days. No one this side can, but on that side I not only can but did. And he's some taskmaster."

She took a determined bite of her roll. "Mmm, that's good. I've now studied with him and Stella Adler and Lee Strasberg *and* Paula Strasberg—the last two, again. Not only have I gotten tips from Olivier, who the critics said I acted rings around in *The Prince and the Showgirl*, but I also got helpful hints on technique from Shakespeare himself.

"He told me what he had in mind for certain scenes, ran me through a few of them and, when we'd finished, said 'You go, girl.' I know you may not recognize the expression yet, but sometime in the future you will, and he takes credit for it. He said he used it in *Hamlet* and *Much Ado About Nothing*, but it was cut from both productions during rehearsals."

My jaw must have been dropping open farther and farther.

She said, "You don't think I can do it? Is it because I'm a woman? Women have played Hamlet, you know—Sarah Bernhardt, Judith Anderson. The two of them had some ideas for me, too. Will—Shakespeare—said to me, 'If men played women in my time, there's no reason women can't play men now.' One nice thing about Willy, he's not fixed in his ways."

About then, I'd gotten the use of my jaw back and used it to say, "How are you going to play Hamlet? Where are you going to play it?"

"You know there's a production on Broadway now, don't you, at the Broadhurst Theatre?" she asked, rhetorically I suspect.

She knew or assumed I knew that Tom Courtenay, just having success with a couple of British angry-young-man films, was doing exactly what this Marilyn said she wanted to do: prove himself in a New York theater. The publicity for him had been overwhelming.

"If he can do it," she went on, "I can do it. I'm going to replace him."

"How?" I asked.

In retrospect, I think I was somewhat short with that, but she just waved off my implied rejection.

"Easy," she said and patted my hand. "I'm going to replace him today." She looked at the clock behind the deli counter. It was closing in on 1 p.m. "I'm going to replace him now. I don't want to miss half-hour. We've got to get going."

"We?" I said.

"You're coming with me, if you can. You do want to see Marilyn Monroe as Hamlet, don't you?"

There's a question a theater lover—which I was at the time and still am—isn't asked every day.

"Uh, yes," I stammered, "but how are you going to get on stage, let alone get into the theater?"

"We have our other-worldly ways," she said, "I'll explain them on the ride over."

She was putting on her coat and then her babushka. I retrieved my umbrella. We paid the bill. That's to say, I paid the bill, as she had no money—and left, no one there the wiser as to who she was and who I wasn't. (Incidentally, I didn't know whether her lack of funds was due to her having returned from the moneyless Great Wherever or her being a star and therefore not in the habit of carrying cash.)

"Do your other-worldly powers include dematerializing here and materializing at the Broadhurst," I brashly asked.

"No," she said. "We hail a cab." With that she raised her hand and hiked her raincoat and—the rain having ceased and her leg being Marilyn Monroe-shapely—we got one immediately.

"I learned that trick from Claudette Colbert," she said, "the real one, not the one in the movie. And now I'll put my ways to work when we get to the Broadhurst. What you may not realize is that Tom Courtenay had a small injury to his foot this morning," she said when we'd settled in the cab. "It's not enough of a sprain to keep him out of this evening's performance, but he's at his podiatrist's office now and will be advised to rest this afternoon and pull back a little tonight. They're aware of this at the theater and are expecting the understudy, whom the doorman has never seen. The general manager is also out with a head cold. That's where and how I come in."

"But," I asked, "where and how do I come in?"

The cab was working slowly through the pre-matinee traffic. Blue-haired ladies and their grey-haired companions jammed the sidewalk. As we approached the Broadhurst, the blue-hairs mingled with the younger crowd, clearly agitated at learning Tom Courtenay would not be present for the matinee but that an understudy named Martin Monroe would be.

"How you come in is you buy a ticket," said the person convincing me more and more she was Marilyn Monroe. "Where you come in is, I want someone in the audience to know that Marilyn Monroe is up there. That person is you. If you're one of those people who thought they could have been the one to save me from my August, nineteen sixty-two, passing if they'd only known me instead of all the famous people I did know who did me no good, here's your chance to prove it."

"I'll buy a ticket," I said.

"Good," she said, wispily whispering. "You'll know who's up there. All that the others will see is a darn good substitute Hamlet."

The cab stopped, and again I paid. She disembarked but not before saying, "Wish me luck. No, don't wish me luck. Tell me to break a leg."

"Break a leg, not a foot," I said while I waited for the driver to hand me the change.

By the time I got out of the cab, Marilyn Monroe—make that Martin Monroe—had gone through the stage door. I stood there a moment to see if he/she/whomever would be thrown out again. Nothing. The battered metal door remained shut.

Then, as I'd promised, I went to the box office, where more than a few disappointed Tom Courtenay fans were demanding their money back. When I succeeded in reaching the second-in-line position, the complainer in front of me was giving the man in the ticket booth so much lip about coming from Allentown to see her hero and then not getting to see him that I couldn't stop myself from saying to her, "I don't know why you're making a fuss when at this performance you could be seeing Marilyn Monroe play the part."

She looked me up and down and hissed, "New Yorkers. They think they're so smart." Then she turned on her heel and walked off, still angry as a wet hen, though wet henna was more like it.

The box office man had heard my remark. "That was pretty funny," he said. "If I thought Marilyn Monroe was going to be Hamlet, I'd buy a ticket myself."

I made as if he was being extremely funny, gave him the fifty bucks via credit card and went in. Although the orchestra was far from full, more people than you might imagine had stayed. I decided it was primarily the younger ticket buyers who'd abandoned the auditorium because they had been going to the Tom Courtenay movies. The older patrons knew about him but had less invested in his exalted station. They could afford to—even wanted to—give encouragement to a newcomer. If that's what this Martin Monroe was.

Shortly after a disembodied voice announced that Martin Monroe would be the afternoon's Hamlet, the lights dimmed and the performance started. Since Hamlet doesn't appear in the first scene, all proceeded with dispatch while Marcellus and the others discussed having bumped into the ghost of recently deceased King Hamlet and were wondering what the young prince would make of the event.

I thought the young prince would probably make of his father's roaming around Denmark what I made of Marilyn Monroe's trotting across East Fifty-seventh Street: initial disbelief but eventual acquiescence and reserved acceptance. Mostly, I thought about what it would be like to see Marilyn Monroe wandering around the Broadhurst boards.

And then, there she was, bare-headed and brooding in a bosom-concealing cape at the top of scene two while Claudius and Gertrude chit-chatted with Polonius and Laertes, and none of them behaved as if they were disoriented by sharing the stage with an actor they'd never seen before.

All the preliminary court business having been covered in iambic pentameter, finally Claudius turns to address Hamlet as "son," and Hamlet responds, "A little more than kin and less than kind." It was Marilyn

Monroe's voice given a gruff edge, and it elicited nothing from the audience but continued attention.

On and on she went, chiding Hamlet's mother and new step-father,
confronting Hamlet's father's ghost, gulling Polonius and taunting Ophe-
lia, welcoming Rosenkrantz and Guildenstern, plotting with the arriving
players to catch the conscience of the king, stabbing Polonius in Gertrude's
chambers, returning from his exiled sea journey, grasping Yorick's skull,
dueling with Laertes while bodies dropped, finally dropping himself and
being wished to heaven by Horatio just before Fortinbras marches in to
promise better days.

Marilyn's performance was, to put it succinctly—but not unkindly—
eccentric. The soliloquies were enunciated perfectly and without any saw-
ing of the air that Hamlet warns about in his *Murder of Gonzago* speech
to the players. When Marilyn/Martin was meditating whether to be or
not to be, she seemed genuinely caught up in the question. I mused that
she might have been reflecting on her own experience of being and her
more recent experiences of not being.

But it wasn't only her speaking that was up to par. Her movements
were also well-grounded. She gave Hamlet a young man's confident stance
and cocky walk, which became abrupt and less certain as he took longer
and longer to complete the retributive action he claimed to be about.
When she plunged the sword through the curtain behind which Polonius
had hidden, she let out a mannish grunt. When she held Yorick's skull
and said she knew him well, her face lighted up and you could see her
remembering good times with a close friend. In the fifth-act duel with
Laertes, her swordplay was skillful. Because the set was one of those that

has many levels, she did stumble once, but she made it seem as if it was the over-eager Hamlet missing the step, not her.

In a nutshell, her celestial mentors had done their work well.

During the intermission, I circulated to see if I could discern a consensus. I heard one woman say to her friend, "The Hamlet is okay. This actor—what's his name, somebody Monroe, like Marilyn?—has a future. We'll have to follow his progress." "He even reminds me of Marilyn Monroe," her friend countered, "something about the mouth and eyes." "He *is* slightly effeminate," the first one said, "but that's okay. When Olivier did it in the movies, he was a little effeminate, too. I always thought there was a little bit of the sissy about Hamlet anyway. His speech is too hoity-toity, don't you think? Hamlet as slightly nancy is a fair interpretation."

I had to agree. Marilyn Monroe was an acceptable Hamlet. She had obviously applied herself, and her efforts paid off at the curtain call. She appeared, in time-honored theater tradition, only after all the other actors had taken their bows. When she came out from the wings and walked to center stage, the audience responded warmly, and her fellow actors also applauded her. Or him, as they had more or less been led to believe.

Marilyn herself behaved humbly. At first, that is. She kept her head bowed and only nodded slightly in acknowledgment of the clapping and the couple dozen people who had risen to give her a standing ovation. She kept up the humility act when the cast left the stage and returned and left and returned again.

It was when the cast exited after what was clearly their final bow that she remained for a few extra seconds to lift her head, flash a smile at the

audience and walk off with the *Some Like It Hot* stride she'd demonstrated
to me earlier.

The reaction from the audience was a low gasp. Patrons turned to
one another to confirm what they thought they'd just seen. They shook
their heads as if they knew what they'd just seen was something they
couldn't have seen. There were a few titters, a few murmurs. Then as
they filed up the aisles, a silence descended that seemed to imply a group
decision that they'd all been momentarily hoodwinked but that really it
was only a temporary illusion.

I waited until most people had left the auditorium before I followed
them. I wanted to stop at the stage door and greet Marilyn when she came
out. All the other actors left within twenty minutes or so, talking among
themselves about—from what I could hear—everything but the performance they'd just done. It looked as if none of them stayed in their dressing
rooms between the afternoon and evening performances.

When even the stage hands had all come out to hustle to the stage-
hands bar at the corner, I opened the door and asked the doorman sitting
on a chair just inside if he knew whether the actor who'd played Hamlet
would be leaving soon.

"You mean the Monroe kid," he said. "He already went. He didn't
even change his clothes. He just handed the cape to me and flew out the
door as if he had a train to catch. I thought it was strange, but then again,
he's an actor. They're all strange."

That was it, and I was left standing on the sidewalk in front of the
Broadhurst Theatre, thinking that very possibly I was the only one in the

world who knew—or thought he knew or something along those lines—
that he had just seen Marilyn Monroe play Hamlet. Not badly, either.
I also knew that something I'd wished for, naïvely, of course—as well
as something Marilyn Monroe had wished for—had somehow been
granted and therefore and thereafter anything I ever wanted out of life
was possible.

Archie Horgan's Story

✂ or ✂

Jesus, Meet Elvis

I was taken by some whopping surprise—especially as a lapsed Catholic—when one unusually hot May day, the living room air conditioner went on the blink and right after I yelled "Jesus Christ" (a habit I really wanted to break) I heard a soft but firm response: "Yes?"

I'd been fiddling with the controls and so was facing away. Turning to find out the source of the "Yes?"—that I more than half thought I imagined—I saw Jesus himself standing there in white robes that seemed to be freshly laundered but weren't particularly shiny. They gave off no glow, though they were draped nicely.

Neither did the halo give off a glow. There was no halo. Jesus was simply gotten up like you see him gotten up in paintings from back then, and I don't have to tell you, I was thrown for a loop. No, really. I'd been on my haunches and when I saw him, I fell against the air conditioner. I hit it but didn't really hurt my right shoulder.

At the same time, I wasn't so out of it that I was struck dumb. As I was rubbing my shoulder, my first thought—to myself, not said aloud—

was "I suppose I asked for this." Instead, what I said was, "Wow, sorry, I didn't mean to disturb you, uh, Sir."

Jesus chuckled and said something in English. He had, I don't know, a Middle East accent? He said, "You've been disturbing me like that for a long time, and you're not the only one. Mind if I sit down?"

I pointed to my favorite club chair, and Jesus—who, by the way, was bearded but still looked like a kid—sat and stretched out his sandaled feet.

"People constantly implore me by name," he said. "I'd say it's something like a million times a day. More. And they come from all over. It can get to be too much."

I figured I could get up. I did and thought about New Testament manners. I realized I should do or say something hospitable. Pointing at the air conditioner, I said, "Sorry about the heat in here. The first uncomfortably hot day of the year, and the damn—I mean, darn—I mean the thing goes belly up." Then I said, "You're not here to fix it, are you?" I don't know what got into me. Maybe I was thinking of the old gospel tune, "Fix Me, Jesus."

"Good Lord, no," Jesus said. I guess he was referring to his Father, not himself. "In my day we didn't have air conditioners. I wouldn't know the first thing about it. No, no, I'm used to the heat. I should be. I spent all that time in the desert."

"Forty days and forty nights, wasn't it?" I said.

"More or less," Jesus said, smiling. I suppose you could say it was beatific. "Over millennia, everything gets exaggerated, but I'm here for something else."

I was curious, of course, but still felt the hospitality urge. "Can I get you anything? A glass of water, perhaps?"

"Water would be good," Jesus said. "Ever since my desert stay and a few other unforgettable experiences you've heard about, I never say no to water when it's offered."

Taking that last as him referring to the Crucifixion, I excused myself, went into the kitchen, got a glass, started the tap and yelled behind me, "Would you like ice in it?"

"Ice," Jesus said. "Why not? Ice was a rarity where I come from." Then he laughed. He had a nice laugh. He said, "No, I don't mean the other place. The one down below. That would be funny, wouldn't it? No, I mean Israel. You know, Bethlehem, Jerusalem."

I brought the iced water to Jesus, who received it gratefully and sipped. I noticed that when he held out his hand to take the glass, a stigmatum was visible. I couldn't help wincing and hoped the spontaneous reaction hadn't been noticed.

"This is a treat," Jesus said after sipping.

"I'm glad you like it," I said. "It's a simple pleasure."

"Simple pleasures are best," Jesus said in a tone I took to be like the one he must have used for the Sermon on the Mount.

"I hope you won't think me, uh, disrespectful…" I said, sneaking a look at the sofa but hesitant about sitting in Jesus's presence. With a humble nod, Jesus indicated sitting was permissible. I continued, "But I'm wondering why, if millions of people every day are, as you say, calling your name, you're answering me?"

"To begin with," Jesus said, putting his glass on a table near him and folding his hands in his lap, "yours isn't the only call I'm answering. I answer many, as you might know from the frequent large-type 'National Enquirer' headlines. People see me all the time, everywhere and in the oddest places, in the patterns that spilled water makes, in the way toast is charred, in the folds of a blanket, in the frost on a window. Secondly, I'm answering you, because I'm aware you've been trying for so long to stop doing what you think of as taking my name in vain, especially as you're a lapsed Catholic and think you forfeited the right."

I nodded assent. I was wowed that my struggles were known to Jesus. "It's embarrassing," I said, "to be, you know, saying your name when I don't believe in you." Given the circumstances, I immediately realized I'd better qualify the remark. "I mean, I believe in you. I believe you existed, but I don't adhere to Christian teachings, to the catechism. Not anymore. I respect all that, I guess I should say, but I just don't swear by it. It's nothing against you, you know."

Jesus said, "I have to laugh." He did. This time it was a hearty laugh I associate with men reacting to the kind of joke they hear in a bar. "I'm not strictly Catholic, either," he said. "I just instigated Catholicism. I'm Jewish. Circumcised, the whole megillah. So one way of thinking about it is, you're just one straying Catholic calling on a non-Catholic for temporary assistance."

"I never thought of it that way," I said.

"You could consider your frequent referring to me as one friend calling on another."

"That's nice of you to say," I said, "but I'm not just calling on you when I say 'Jesus Christ.' I'm kind of swearing. I'm blaming you for whatever's getting on my nerves."

"I don't take it that way," Jesus said, "but I do understand you deem it a habit you'd like to break. I'm here to help you with that."

"That's awfully nice of you," I said, wondering how Jesus was going to accomplish this.

"Think of my being here as an answered prayer," Jesus said.

"But I don't pray to you," I said.

"Yes, you do," Jesus said. "You may think that when you say 'Jesus Christ,' you're expressing anger and/or frustration, but I hear it as a prayer. All of us—Mohammad, Buddha, Thor, Shiva, Zeus, Hera, you name him or her—understand and share these spoken, or sometimes just thought, verbal missives to us."

As he said that, he assumed another of his nice smiles, and I began to see, right there in front of me, a show of what Jesus's appeal had been to the people around him two thousand years, give or take, before this weird late morning. Jesus was suddenly radiating light every bit as intense and warming, or more so, as the light falling through my windows.

I thought of all the religious pictures I'd seen as a kid, the ones with all the gold on them. Whoever made them got it right. I said, "I appreciate your thoughtfulness, of course, Sir, but I have to say I have no idea how you're going to get me to stop saying you-know-what when I've already tried so hard on my own to stop saying you-know-what. I mean, I know you have special powers, but still."

"I can tell you in two words," Jesus said, raising his hands, palms outward, tapering fingers upward. "Behavior modification. You must know the term."

"I know it," I said, "I mean, I've heard it and kind of know what it means, but I'm surprised you do."

"Ah," Jesus said, "I'm full of surprises. Now here's what we're going to do. I'm going to ask you to repeat 'Jesus Christ' many times over until I tell you to stop—." I was about to object, but Jesus cut me off with a barely perceptible movement of his right index finger. "Except," he went on, "every time you're about to say 'Jesus Christ,' I want you to substitute another word. Any word or couple of words. Do you follow?"

I thought I did. "You mean, I should think I'm about to say 'Jesus Christ,' but instead I say 'rainy days' or 'cigarette butts.'"

"You got it in one," Jesus said and clapped his hands together. I wondered whether the gesture aggravated the stigmata but said nothing. "Or," Jesus said, "you could use another proper name, a name you think is tamer, less heretical. John Wilkes Booth. Winston Churchill. Muhammad Ali."

I nodded my comprehension.

"Are you ready to begin?" Jesus asked.

I nodded again.

"Then go," Jesus said.

Immediately I made as if I was going to say "Jesus Christ" but said, "Elementary school."

"Good," Jesus said. "Keep going."

"City ordinance," I said. "Take the 'A' train."

"Good," Jesus said, "good."

"Chicago White Sox," I said, as the words "Jesus Christ" were forming in my mouth. "Internal Revenue Service. Pasta fagiole. Sock it to me. Eastern Standard Time."

Jesus was shaking his head in encouragement. I felt I was getting firmly in the groove, that I had it knocked. I hadn't, because just then I was beginning to say "Jesus Christ" but no alternative phrase came to mind. I slipped and said what I didn't want to say. I said, "Jesus Christ."

Jesus was forgiving—of course, he was forgiving; he was Jesus. All he did was raise his thick right eyebrow.

I resumed with new fervor. "Wheat thins," I said. "Aluminum siding. Whatever floats your boat. The tieing touchdown. By the shores of Gitche Gumee."

Jesus was nodding, encouragingly.

Now I was on a roll, practically giddy with my new power. "Bessemer steel. Pull an all-nighter. Yours sincerely. Table manners."

"Elvis A. Presley," I all but shouted, confident I could use a middle initial in this instance because I knew Elvis Presley's middle name was Aaron.

I was about to move on to "Warren G. Harding," when I saw Jesus's kindly eyes shift to the right and I heard to the left of and behind me a strummed acoustic guitar chord and the sung words "Love me tender."

I followed Jesus's gaze and saw, by the window that the defunct air conditioner wasn't under, the actual Elvis Aaron Presley—full sideburns, pompadour and favorite Gibson J-200. He was also in white-and-gold performing drag so that where Jesus had an inner glow, Elvis's was all outward.

Elvis took the attention in, pointed to his studded white ensemble and said in a musical Elvis Presley inflection, "Nudie." I knew—but wasn't certain Jesus would—that by "Nudie" Elvis meant the famous Nashville costume designer. I know a lot about country music, because I like it.

But I didn't pass on that information. The only thing that occurred to me to say was, "Jesus, meet Elvis. Elvis, say hello to Jesus."

Then I practically fell over at hearing myself make those unlikely introductions. Rather than falling over, however, I was brought back to my senses when Jesus and Elvis said in dulcet unison, "We're already acquainted." Then they both began overlapping explanations for how and when they'd previously met.

Almost instantly after agreeing they'd met but hadn't had much time to get to know each other—there being so many people to say "hi" to where they were—Elvis deferred to Jesus by an I'm-just-a-humble-country-boy dip of his large head.

I motioned Elvis to sit down, but Elvis said, "I can't sit in this outfit." (The "can't" came out as "cain't.") At the same time, he dipped his head in Jesus's direction again. I remembered that Elvis was religious, more than I was, I have to confess after not going to confession for I forget how many years.

Jesus said to me, "Elvis and I first met the way you and I did. I answered a 'Jesus Christ' he thought he'd spoken in vain."

Elvis interrupted and said, "I always tried not to swear. It's a form of cruelty, and I did have a big hit with 'Don't Be Cruel.' That's a sentiment I truly believed in and always tried to stand behind. But sometimes swear words just came out. And Jesus here helped me with that. He didn't help me with the drugs and alcohol. No one could."

"But I absolved you," Jesus said.

Elvis turned to me and said, "That happened the second time we met. In the beyond. I never thought I'd get there." (The "get" came out as "git.") "But it turns out swiveling my hips and selling so many millions of records that gave people pleasure is a mighty fine dispensation." ("Mighty fine" came out as "mahty fahn.")

Jesus pointed at Elvis. "His music is much appreciated where we are," he said. "It isn't all harps there. That's an earthly misconception."

Elvis said, "But there are *some* harps. I like them. They were used in some of my movie scores."

I was listening to this exchange and, at about this point, realized I was listening to it as if it were an everyday occurrence. "Wait a minute," I thought to myself. "This is Jesus and Elvis sitting around in my living room as if we're just three good old boys." (In my head, "old" came out as "ole.")

"In a way, we're old friends," Jesus said, reading my mind.

"Holy moly," I thought, "He's reading my mind." As I thought it, I mentally capitalized the "h" in "He."

Jesus continued to read my mind. "Thank you for the capitalization on "He," but, you know, I've never known what a 'moly' is. It doesn't exist in any language. 'Molé,' yes, but 'moly,' no. Maybe the phrase was originally Mexican and began as 'holy molé.'"

Elvis said, "I always preferred to say 'Bless-a my soul.' I liked it so much, I had them put it at the beginning of 'All Shook Up.'" He hummed a few bars and played a few chords, and Jesus tapped his sandaled foot along with the beat. I noticed what I hadn't earlier: the stigmata on Jesus's clean-as-a-whistle sandaled feet.

After only about eight measures, however, Elvis stopped himself to say to both Jesus and me, "But I'm here by accident." To Jesus, he said, "You were doing the behavior modification thingie, and I got caught up in it."

"I'm sorry about that," I said to Jesus, while pointing at Elvis. "I didn't realize what I was doing when I said his name."

Elvis bowed his head just a smidge, as if he'd just been thanked by Ed Sullivan on nationwide television.

"No," Jesus said, "my fault. I said you could use proper names. Usually it's not a problem."

"Begging your pardon, Lord," Elvis said, "but it's my fault." (The "begging" came out as "beggin'.") "I mistook it as a command performance and obliged, which I was often wont to do. Maybe I best return. You know, to the back of the big beyond."

This piqued my curiosity. "How can you do that?"

"Just a simple snap of the fingers," Jesus and Elvis said, again almost in unison.

I wondered if finger-popping affected Jesus's stigmata adversely. "No, in answer to the stigmata question," Jesus said and added, "I let your first silent queries about my stigmata slide."

I was abashed but said nothing. I didn't have to. Jesus said, "People worry about my palms all the time. They needn't. The pain abated long ago and can't be revived." He went on. "But since we're all here, I was thinking we could do something together."

I reacted before I could stop himself. "What about my behavior modification?"

Again reading my mind, Jesus said, "My guess is, the behavior modification has already taken hold. Maybe we can put it to the test."

"Sounds jake with me," Elvis said, "as long as it don't require sitting ["requahre sittin'"] down."

Jesus said, "A walk around the neighborhood might do it." He turned to me and said, "There's always something irritating happening in the streets that could provoke you to say what I think you've now trained yourself not to say. We'll find out soon enough. What do you think, Elvis?"

Elvis cleared his throat and said, "Whatever you decide is best. I may be the King, but you're the King of Kings."

"Mohammad wouldn't agree with you," Jesus said.

"I know," Elvis said. "Neither would Nietzsche."

They both had a good laugh over that.

The suggestion of a turn about the West Village seemed a curious one to me. So I said, "How can you two just stroll around the Village? You'll be noticed."

"In the Village?" Jesus said. "People may think they see me in cloud formations and tea leaves, but in the Village since the sixties, they take me for just another Jesus freak, just another off-site manifestation of Jerusalem's Jesus Syndrome."

Elvis chuckled his side-of-the-mouth chuckle and said, "And they take me for one more Elvis impersonator. They always do, especially in Las Vegas. Funny thing is, I've lost a few Elvis lookalike contests there. Didn't even come in first or second runner-up. How do you like them apples?"

I knew my nabe and knew what they were saying was true. "You're right," I said. "Let's go."

We went down to the street. As it was a Sunday afternoon and a sea-sonable one at that, the streets were crowded. I'd wondered if my companions would be noticed, and, of course, they were. Many, if not all, the passers-by glanced at them—but only for a few seconds before looking elsewhere. New Yorkers can be very blasé.

After a while I got the definite feeling I was receiving as much atten-tion as the other two. Jesus noticed it, too. Reading my mind some more, he said, "It's because you're dressed casually, and they're trying to figure out why, if you're with people dressed as we are, you're not dressed up, too."

Several people—men, women and children alike—took in the three of us and said, "Hey, Elvis!" When they did, Elvis would mime playing a few bars on the guitar and say, "Hey, yourself!" When he did that, they snickered. Elvis said, "See what I mean? They think I'm an Elvis imper-sonator—probably a third-rate one at that."

No one we passed said, "Hey, Jesus!" And after a while, Elvis remarked to Jesus, "It's like John Lennon said. Rock stars are more popular than you."

"I know," Jesus said and smiled another of his beaming smiles. "I wasn't all that popular with that many people then, either."

Several amusing incidents occurred during a street fair that Jesus, Elvis and I headed into. One of the funniest was at the corner of Bleecker and West Tenth Street. Representatives of Jews for Jesus were soliciting members. One of them saw Jesus and said, "Are you Jewish?" "All my life," Jesus replied. "Mazel tov," the guy said. The curls by his ears shook. "You sure look like a good candidate to join us." Jesus said, "Thank you, my son" and kept walking. The Jew for Jesus didn't know what to make of that.

At another corner, two young women spotted each other and raced into one another's arms. One said to the other, "It's a miracle. I was just thinking how long it's been since I've seen you."

I turned to Jesus. He put up his hands and said, "Don't look at me. I take no credit for coincidences." Again, I saw his stigmata.

Passing a stand where a tattooed man of about thirty was selling CDs, Elvis flipped through the assortment and pulled a shrink-wrapped item out. "Pirated from one of my Caesar's Palace gigs," he said to Jesus and me. "No matter how hard Colonel Parker tried, he couldn't stop it."

I knew Elvis was referring to his longtime manager, Colonel Tom Parker. What I couldn't recall was whether Parker was a genuine colonel. Elvis shook the CD and said to Jesus, "Got any miracles for this?"

"I'm afraid not," Jesus said. "That's the devil's work, so to speak."

To the tattooed purveyor, Elvis said, "Pack up your sins and go to the devil in Hades."

I recognized the remark as an Irving Berlin lyric.

"It's an Irving Berlin lyric," Elvis said to the two of us. "He taught it to me. What a songwriter!" To Jesus, he said, "He's Jewish, you know."

Jesus said, "I know. He never stops reminding me."

The tattooed guy only said, "If you don't like what you see, you don't have to buy it." I noticed one of the guy's tattoos was the head of Jesus. Jesus noticed it, too. Elvis put the CD back and said to the tattooed fellow. "I was right good in my old Caesar's Palace days."

"Sure you were," the inked salesperson said.

Though I was enjoying my walk on the wild side, it was hardly accomplishing its goal: to happen upon some kind of situation where I'd be incited to say "Jesus Christ" but would reflexively say something else.

For the longest time, nothing really irritating occurred. Though the Village thoroughfares were thronged, no one was pushing me aside rudely enough for me to say—I don't know—"jackpot winnings." I stumbled over no developing potholes. I bought nothing hot to eat that burned my tongue or spilled down my shirt. I saw nothing being sold that tried my patience. I might have objected to the pirated CD that Elvis pointed out, but it was Elvis's. I was going to say, "It was Elvis's cross to bear," but I'll abstain.

Then, suddenly, an incident.

Jesus, Elvis and I had left the street fair and were passing The Corner Bistro at Hudson and Jane when its heavy front door burst open and a man looking terrified came racing out. He was followed by a larger man wielding what looked like a long carving knife.

There was a fair amount of shouting that caused the man being chased to turn around. As he did, the man following with the apparently sharp instrument reached him and appeared to plunge what he held into the frightened man's chest.

The man let out a cry that sounded like "I'm hit," though it was obscured by all the onlookers who were accumulating and behaving as people behave when something like this happens. Some scattered. I guess they were trying to get out of harm's way. Some of the brave ones tackled the man with the knife and held him on the ground. Some of them went to where the fallen man was.

Jesus and Elvis were the first ones to get there. I was directly behind them, but when I got close to the spot, I couldn't quite see what was happening. I thought I saw blood on the ground, but when I looked a second time, I saw only what appeared to be a streak of red paint. I also saw Jesus helping the dazed man to his feet.

The man was saying, "I could have sworn I'd been hit right here." He pointed to his side. He kind of looked like Jesus looked in all those pictures with Doubting Thomas. "It felt like a dull punch."

Jesus was saying to the man, "Perhaps you were, and perhaps you weren't." I wonder if he was thinking about Doubting Thomas or thinking he was doing something like he did with Doubting Thomas.

To help get the man over his shock and to distract the crowd, Elvis started playing the cherished Gibson J-200 and was singing "Bless-a my soul, what's wrong with me? My hands are shaky and my knees are weak. I can't seem to stand on my own two feet."

The man started laughing, and so did everyone else who recognized Elvis's chart-topping "All Shook Up." Some of the younger bystanders didn't laugh. They looked like the kind of jerks who don't want to encourage any Elvis impersonator, no matter how good he is.

In the distance, I heard a siren and turned to see from which direction it was arriving. A police car came up Hudson Street and stopped. A second pulled up behind it.

Two policemen jumped out of each car. The first two hustled to the assailant still held down by a couple of bruisers in leather jackets on the backs of which was the word "Stonewall" in metal studs. The second two officers hurried over to where Jesus and Elvis were standing.

Or, to be more exact, to where Jesus and Elvis had been standing. They were no longer there. Just a slightly wobbly man surrounded by a group of people that included me.

"What happened here?" one of the cops asked anyone who might answer. He'd taken a notebook and a pen from a jacket pocket.

Everyone but the disoriented man started to speak. The policeman who wasn't writing had to call the informal gathering to order. Then, one by one, the episode was recounted—as clearly as any of us could remember it. Included in the testimony were mentions that "a guy who was gotten up to look like Jesus" and a second guy—"one of those Elvis people"—had been the first ones to come to the fallen man's aid.

Several witnesses mentioned they thought they'd seen a knife and blood but then realized they hadn't. There was general agreement that what they'd seen was only red paint that at first had looked like blood. Curiously, one of the spectators produced something he'd found in the gutter—a shiny ladle with an unusually long handle.

The fallen and now revived latter-day Lazarus declared that whatever he said had to be unreliable. He wasn't even sure he hadn't blacked out from the forceful jab he insisted he'd experienced.

He said that when he thought he'd come to, he was looking deeply into a pair of very intense eyes and was hearing what he took to be an almost religious supplication. He also said he thought he'd heard Elvis Presley singing.

"But don't go by me," he said as he concluded his bleary account, "I probably dreamed the whole thing."

"Where are these two guys?" the cop taking this down asked.

"They left immediately," a few people offered, but when the cops asked where they'd gone, no one seemed to know—least of all me.

Taking that into account, the other cop said, "We don't really need them. We've got enough witnesses we can get in touch with if we want more information or corroboration." Then they escorted the victim of "the attempted knifing" to an ambulance that had arrived from Beth Israel Hospital. (The man wielding the implement had already been taken away, presumably to be jailed.)

Once the alleged crime scene was cleared, the crowd dispersed, leaving me alone to think more about what had just happened. That was when I reran the afternoon's activity in my head.

I hadn't thought of it at the time, but I suddenly remembered that when the man ran out of The Corner Bistro with the knife (?) and brought it down, I had been discombobulated enough to shout "Jesus Christ." But I hadn't shouted "Jesus Christ." I distinctly recalled I'd yelled something wholly different. I'd shouted "Leapin' lizards." It was an outburst I hadn't burst out with since I was a kid and still under the influence of my granddad's "Little Orphan Annie" generation.

For the record, I haven't taken the name "Jesus Christ" in vain again—and at the very least, I consider that development some kind of minor miracle. And oh, yeah, I've come to believe in miracles again and certainly in the body of Christ.

Marlon Chase's Story

%   or   %

Niccolo Machiavelli, Publicity Hound

Niccolo Machiavelli has a narrow face—vulpine, you might call it. It's a face shaped like an almond, the chin almost coming to a point. It's a face with a yellowish tint to it. That's not to say it appears to be jaundiced. It's suggestive of olive skin somewhere in the family past that has (or had) lightened over the generations.

He has a high forehead rising to slicked-back, vinyl-black hair. His eyes also seem black at first but there are hints of green in them, glints of green, not unlike a cat's—and like many cats' eyes, they give the impression they're withholding very high-level classified information. You look into them but get the feeling that nothing there is really intent on looking back at you. His nose is narrow as well and with refined nostril naries. They hint at careful breeding but may just be attributable to some lucky DNA combination.

His mouth, like the rest of his features, is narrow, and his lips are thin. His teeth, when he smiles a suggestive half-smile, are long and straight and do nothing to diminish his crazy-like-a-fox demeanor.

When his face is in repose, which it almost always is—or, more precisely, when it seems to be in a perpetual state of successfully willed repose—the set of his mouth implies he's entertaining a private thought superior to whatever thought you have in your head. His beard—he's clean-shaven—is dark and lends him a sinister air.

It's as if Destiny, whoever that calculating goddess is, designed the beard for him so that he was obliged to become whom he became. Were his face a watercolor, it would suggest that a faint-to-medium black wash had been applied over the lower half of it.

Yes, I'm speaking of Niccolo Machiavelli in the present tense. Of course, I'd read about him. I'd read his bestseller *The Prince* and even sections of the much longer and indisputably indulgent *Discourses*. Anyone who's ever taken a philosophy course or political science or Renaissance history class has read the screeds. Because I had, I'd seen portraits of him done during his fifteenth-century lifetime, but I have to admit, they hadn't stuck with me. I couldn't conjure a row of them in my mind's picture gallery.

Doesn't matter. He was here in the twenty-first century. He was with me in the here and now. Were my life a romance novel or a Harlequin potboiler, I might say we met cute. But my life wasn't either of those at the time I met Machiavelli. The furthest thing from it. I was between jobs in the latest of a series of job losses, none of them what I really wanted to do, although I was in my early forties and had never settled on what I really wanted to do, let alone figuring out how to promote myself as a salable commodity.

But along comes Niccolo Machiavelli, whom I met not cute, as it happens, but dangerous. It was on a New York street—well, not on it, in it. It was an apathetic Thursday afternoon in late March—around three o'clock, to be somewhat exact—and I was waiting to cross to the east side of Lexington Avenue at Forty-eighth Street, to the northeast corner, if you want me to be exact on that count, too.

The light was red, and as I stood there not quite happy as a clam, which I never am, but as close as I ever get and thinking about who-knows-what, I realized the man in front of me was not waiting. He was stepping into oncoming traffic, as if whatever was on his mind had momentarily jammed his street radar.

He was dressed eccentrically in a black leather jacket, tight-enough black leather trousers and from the back had the look of someone who could fend for himself, but that didn't affect the impulse I acted on, which was to shout at him, "Red light." At the same time, I lurched into the street, grabbed him by his black leather sleeve and pulled him back and out of harm's way.

As he turned and nearly fell against me, a maroon SUV missed hitting him by inches. It was only by the skin of his long, straight teeth that he'd avoided being flattened into Lexington Avenue roadkill.

The SUV driver—from what I could tell a bearded man in a plaid wool shirt and furious—leaned on his horn and yelled some obscenity out his window. Whatever he said was smeared by the wind, which, I suspect, was just as well. In the meantime, the leather-clad man saved from oblivion (but only in a manner of speaking, since he turned out to be someone who had never faded into oblivion) straightened himself up and looked at me with one of his piercingly neutral gazes and forthrightly said, "Thank you, grazie."

"That's all right," I said, more out of momentary embarrassment than magnanimity, "You'd do the same for me." Brushing his sleeve where my hand had been, he said, "If you knew who I am, you might not say that."

That struck me as an odd reply to what I intended as the sort of commonplace pleasantry you say in these situations, something merely meant to lighten an awkward moment. So before I attempted to quell my curiosity at the comment, I asked, "Who are you?"

"*Mi chiamo Niccolo Machiavelli,*" he said and added after a split second with a distinct Italian accent, "*Scusi.*" Then in English. "I am Niccolo Machiavelli. I think in Italian and then forget to translate." He held out his hand, and I shook it and took what had sounded like the bait.

"Niccolo Machiavelli?" I said. "Just like—"

He cut me off. "—just like the other Niccolo Machiavelli, you were going to say."

"Uh, yes," I said. "The other, uh, the one who..."

He pulled the enigmatic smile and said, looking at me so intently that I inadvertently leaned away from him an inch or so, "There is no other Niccolo Machiavelli. I am he. *Sono Io.*"

My Italian is basic, but "*Sono Io*" couldn't be more basic. He was telling me he was Niccolo Machiavelli, the Niccolo Machiavelli who, I strangely happened to know, died in 1527. That's a good one, I thought to myself and added, also to myself, "just another Manhattan crackpot."

"My full name is Niccolo di Bernardo dei Machiavelli," he said, "but no one uses the full name now, nor did they then, more often than not. I can see you are having difficulty crediting what I am saying. Understand-able. *Capisco.*"

I should say so, I thought. We had moved back onto the curb from which I'd first spotted him and were holding our one-on-one while pedes-trians jostled around us and the afternoon traffic continued, just as if it were another ordinary day. Yet just about everything with which I'd been occupying myself had gone out of my head. It would, wouldn't it, if a total stranger had just introduced himself to you as the one and only Nic-colo Machiavelli?

Mr. (*Signore?*) Machiavelli then said, his expression of amused con-tentment unchanged, "Since you just saved my life—which is an odd way to put it, considering who I am and why I am here—I owe you an expla-nation."

"Really, you don't," I said, as much to get away from him and oblit-erate what was happening to me as it was to offer a standard demurral. "I just did what anyone would do."

"Yes, you already said that," he said, "and yet you were the one who did it. The truth is, not everyone would have. Had they known who I am, it's more likely they'd have pushed me into traffic with as much might as they could gather. Now that you know who I am, perhaps you'd like to push me." He took a moment to cast his black-hints-of-green eyes up and down Lex. "I see other vehicles heading our way."

I recoiled at the suggestion, and he saw it.

He said, "Of course, you wouldn't. You're too much of a gentleman. The truth is you may be able to give me some advice."

What? Me advise Niccolo Machiavelli? I'm not often dumbfounded, but dumbfoundedness is all I can ascribe to myself at that juncture, stand-ing on the northwest corner of Lexington Avenue and Forty-eighth Street and talking to a man in a leather jacket who claimed to be none other than Niccolo Machiavelli, the renowned fifteenth-century philosopher and political troublemaker.

I guess you could say the situation was Machiavellian. Literally, and it only got more Machiavellian, because I was too tongue-tied not to accept the (Machiavellian?) invitation to hear an explanation for his being where I'd encountered him.

The explanation began—as we were repairing to a nearby eatery (I suggested a relatively public pizza place I knew) for an explanatory chat—with his saying, "I am not yet accustomed to automobile traffic. We did not have it in fifteenth-century Florence and environs, nor did they have it during the numerous time periods I have—shall I say?—visited since."

Soon enough, we were sitting at a formica-topped table with the odor of pizza wafting around us. You heard right. Niccolo Machiavelli and I were head-to-head in a pizzeria. He had already pointed out that pizza stands were not a dime a dozen where he came from but the ingre-dients were familiar to him and lent a comforting aura.

"Oh, yes," he was saying, "this isn't the first time I've returned. I have re-materialized several times. I have had to—to clear my name, as you might say." For the first time, and then only fleetingly, his eyes lost their gleam and his mouth its firm set. "You have to understand I am known and remembered for a book to which the public had no access until five years after my death. I could have no idea what the reaction would be to its publication and, needless to say, could do nothing about it. When my disseminated observations were so—how can I phrase this?—misunderstood, there was little I could do to alter the ramifications, until, that is, I realized I had the opportunity to step in. As I am doing now. Yet again."

He took a pause and, during it, reverted to his former closed expression, saying, "I am assuming, of course, that you are acquainted with at least some of my work. I find most people in this century, if they know me at all, have read *The Prince* or some part of it. Far fewer seem to have made their way through the *Discourses*."

He stopped to wait for my reply. Since I was still in something of a daze—and pondering the dizzying notion that someone, or maybe *someones,* in a previous era had also had this sort of jarring visitation—my reply was slow to come. But realizing he was waiting for me to speak, I did. "Oh, er, yes, I have. Read you. I mean, I guess I'm like most of the people you're talking about. I've read *The Prince* and sections of the *Discourses*." Then I thought I'd try a bit of humor. "But I don't think I'm prepared to take a quiz on either of them."

I learned eventually that Niccolo Machiavelli did have a sense of humor but not where his writings were concerned. He immediately made that plain. "Do I look as if I am about to test you on the contents?" he asked. "To begin, I kept *The Prince* compact for my intended reader, one of the Medici princes, whom I knew to be not much of a thinker. Not much of a reader. More of a doer. As a result, when I embarked on the *Discourses,* I allowed myself to run on and on. Were I able now, I would edit them severely."

He gave me an even more concentrated look. "By any chance, are you an editor? One of my goals while I'm here is to cajole someone into preparing a redacted version of the *Discourses*."

Again, I was caught off guard, since one of the things I'd thought about doing but never had the courage to pursue was becoming an editor. So I just said, "No, I'm not an editor."

"There is always a first time," he said. The gaze accompanying that remark was so focused I felt as if it went right through me and shot out the other side. "I am beginning to think our meeting as we did was not by chance. I suspect I was meant to walk into the street as absentmindedly as I did. I am not, I assure you, an absentminded person."

By this time, I became aware of the pizza man behind the counter in his soiled white apron and white cap. He must have been signaling me for some time that my slice was ready. I had ordered a plain slice; Niccolo Machiavelli had ordered nothing. Now, as I went to get my slice, he changed his mind and asked if I'd pick him up two garlic knots and a beverage. I got him an Orangina.

When I sat down, he nodded his thanks for the garlic knots and took a healthy swig of the Orangina. Then he resumed speaking. "You understand, don't you, that I have to do something to change the perception of me, something I have only been able to do successfully in too few of my previous reappearances? I did very well in nineteenth-century Italy. What is your phrase? They got me. But they were my countrymen, albeit a few hundred years after my initial manifestation."

The memory appeared to give him a moment's cheer, but it faded into his stern look. "More often than not, however, I am misinterpreted. I am the man who put the pejorative adjective 'Machiavellian' into the language, into many languages. I say this without boasting. Entirely the opposite. You should hear some of the accents on people trying to get 'Machiavellian' past their lips."

With that he emitted a dry laugh, a laugh that sat in his throat like a Listerine gargle. I'm tempted to say it was a Machiavellian laugh, but I'd be doing what it seemed he hoped people would cease doing.

"How would you like it if your name were reconfigured into an adjective—were twisted, I should say, into an adjective?" He asked the question without waiting for my response. "You think you'd be flattered, wouldn't you? I am here to tell you you wouldn't be. How would you like it if every petty misdemeanor that some low-grade criminal or high-grade politician committed would be proclaimed—"

He stopped. "You have not told me your name."

"You haven't asked it."

He leaned towards me. "I'm asking it now," he said, and I can't help saying that if I didn't know who he was—or claimed to be—I'd still have maintained he had said "I'm asking it now" with a Machiavellian gleam in his eye.

Without delay I told him. "I'm Marlon Chase," I said.

He repeated it after me. "Marlon Chase. How would you like it, Marlon Chase, if every time some calculating executive fired an inadequate underling, he was declared Chaseian?"

Silly me. I thought the question was rhetorical. As he saw it, I sat there like a lox for too long.

"Would you?" he demanded and poked a long, thin finger into my chest. It felt like an electric drill.

I was so startled, all I could hear in my head was, "Would I what?"

"Would you?" he said again. "Would you want to walk around and hear people utter 'Chaseian' every time someone in the boardroom subtly or blatantly undermined someone else?"

It was clear he wanted me to say no, and the truth of it is, I wouldn't want to hear "Chaseian" spewed from red faces the way people throw "Machiavellian" around. I obliged him by saying "No." He looked as if he expected more. I gave him more. I said with lots of emphasis, "No, no, I definitely wouldn't. Absolutely not. Not at all. Never."

"*Da vero,*" he said, "you would not. So I have to put a stop to it whenever and wherever I can." He pointed to the now empty paper plate on which the garlic knots had come and waved two fingers. I got him two more, while he collected his thoughts, and I collected mine.

When I sat down again, he said, "You see what I am up against. I wrote a book in which, I admit, I said that power can be accrued by playing on people's fears, but my thesis was more nuanced than that. What do I find? What filters back to me in the mystical ether in which I reside? My carefully articulated nuances are disregarded, and I am someone advocating wholesale fearmongering and violence. Over the centuries, the crudest heads of state have pursued that pathetic cul de sac."

"I see your problem," I said. He started to speak but I held up a hand. I'd realized I did have something to say. I started to say it, gathering momentum as I spoke. "And it could be a bigger problem than you realize. You're talking about nuance, but we live in a time—you're living again in a time—that isn't big on nuance. In the twenty-first century, everything is done in broad strokes." I thought for a second. "I suppose some people would say that's Machiavellian, too."

"See what I mean?" Signore Machiavelli said.

I nodded that I understood his dilemma but kept talking. An idea had occurred to me. "If you don't mind my saying so, I don't think you need an editor. Revising your writings isn't going to accomplish your goals." I halted for a moment and then said, "In my estimation."

I appended "in my estimation" because I reminded myself I was talking to Niccolo Machiavelli. Ostensibly. Part of me didn't know what in hell was going on.

Whatever was, I didn't want to be too unqualifiedly provocative. Who knew what the repercussions could be? I knew I didn't want his drill-like finger in my chest again. But I saw he was listening to me closely, and as I paused, he waved the narrow fingers of his left hand, palm inward, at me, signaling that I carry on.

I did as bid, only thinking to myself that his waving with his left hand may tip to his being left-handed. Also thinking to myself that I knew enough Italian to know that "left" is "*sinistra*" in the lilting language (lilting in the territories where he came from, not so lilting farther south), and "*sinistra*" seemed about right for his reputation.

"Even if you publish a shortened version of the *Discourses*," I said in carrying-on mode, "you wouldn't get a large enough readership to change opinions of you. In my estimation." I was still hedging my bets. "As you already said, people know you from *The Prince,* and I think you're right when you say their minds are made up. So—" I slowed the pace to emphasize my metaphorical light bulb. "—I think you have to do something very different."

His gaze became even more concentrated than it had been. The green glints were shooting in his eyes like Roman candles.

"What I believe you need," I said, "is something I don't think you had in fifteenth-century Florence or in any other epoch during which you've tried to change people's opinions about you. What you need is a publicist."

The ocular fireworks ceased. "*Che vuol dire,* 'publicist'?" he said.

"A publicist," I said, "is someone who helps change your image." I saw that didn't help. I was more explicit. "You're concerned about how people have misunderstood your books and how that has affected their regard for you. A publicist is someone who comes up with and then implements strategies to change that regard. We call it 'spin.' I don't know about fifteenth-century Florence, but now we are very image-conscious, and there are people who can reshape images very effectively. Publicists, people involved in public relations."

It looked as if he needed time to take that in. I gave him time. When he'd had enough, he said—the glints started shooting again—"To me that sounds Machiavellian."

I thought he was saying he was offended.

"I'm sorry if you see it that way," I said.

"No," he said, "I like it. I only wish I had thought of this type of person when I was writing. I could have advocated that my prince avail himself of a—*che vuol dire?*—publicist. Lorenzo di Medici would have loved that. What is your phrase? Eaten it up with a spoon? With a silver spoon."

As he spoke, a new enthusiasm began to glow in him. I saw that when I'd first met him, his affect had been one of a man who, though contained, was infused with misgivings. I took my cue from that. "It so happens," I said, "that I've heard of a publicist you might want to consult."

"No might about it," he said. He heard what he'd just exclaimed and added—here's where his sense of humor surfaced—"*Allora,* I usually promote exerting might, but in this instance I shall not. Right now, there's no might about it. I would like to consult the publicist mentioned. Why do we not contact him immediately?"

"Her," I said. "She's a woman. Her name is Joy Jolson. She has a great reputation for using the means you encourage in *The Prince* to achieve the kinds of ends you want." I thought that over. "Unless you wouldn't want to work with a woman."

"Why not?" he said. "I like women. How do we reach her now?"

"We look her up and call her," I said. I took out my iPhone and Googled Joy Jolson's phone number. Apparently, Signore Machiavelli had yet to see one of those devices, but perhaps it was his interest in reaching Joy Jolson that overrode his following the iPhone train of enquiry.

As to Joy Jolson, there's no reason why I would have ever met her, but I knew about her. Everyone knew she was an effective publicist—the old-fashioned kind, aggressive as a speeding Amtrak train. She was famous for saying, "As far as I know, I'm not related to Al Jolson, but if I have to get down on one knee and sing 'Mammy' to get what I want, I'll do it."

I can't say if she ever followed through on that particular threat, but she was known to pull off tactics equally attention-getting.

After the phone rang once, Joy herself picked up. In a voice as flaming as the curly red hair she was also famous for, she said, "Joy Jolson. What do you want done? Just tell me, and I'll do it."

Since she was clearly a get-right-to-the-point businesswoman, I got right to the point. I told her my name and told her I thought I might have a client for her. She, of course, asked who it was. I told her only that I wanted to introduce him in person and if she was as intrigued as I thought she ought to be, I'd bring him over right away.

Into the phone, she said, as if shouting from the other end of the Lincoln Tunnel, "Of course, I'm intrigued, Marlon Chase. I'm always intrigued when someone has a potential client for me that they won't tell me about first. How do you think I came by Claus von Bulow? Bring whoever it is up. I'll expect you in, what, fifteen minutes? Just enough time for me to rouge my cheeks and powder my nose."

I wondered if the Joy I'd always heard about ever powdered her nose. She didn't sound like a person who paid much care to how she looked. Evidently, what concerned her was how she got things done: her way.

She hung up, and I hung up and said to Signore Machiavelli, "She's ready to see us now."

Quick as you can say "*Ponte Vecchio*" we were in a cab. Slow as you can say the initial fifty cantos of Dante's "*Purgatorio*"—the traffic was that tied up—we were at Broadway and Forty-fourth Street, down which Joy Jolson had her cluttered publicist's warren.

On the way, Niccolo Machiavelli said little. To me, that is. Under his breath, he seemed to be repeating to himself, "una publicist, una pub-licist." He was rolling the words around in his mouth as you might roll a pearl against your tongue and teeth to see if it's convincingly gritty to be genuine.

When we were buzzed up to Joy's sanctum ("lair" might be a better description) with the business's name, "Joy to the World," on the door, the woman herself welcomed us. She was wearing one of the shapeless outfits I learned she referred to as "just another of my shmattes." Behind her—amid the piles of paper, framed posters of Broadway shows she must have handled, ringing phones and a barely surviving ficus—were three young women hunched at the computers on their desks like a trio of Uriah Heeps.

My guess is that one, maybe all, of them tended to the plant. Nurturing living things probably wasn't Joy Jolson's top priority—unless it was a living thing paying her a budget-stuffing monthly retainer. (By the way, the plant still had a "Good Luck" banner draped exhaustedly around the pot, although Joy had to have been in business on her own for at least twenty-five years.)

"Glad to see ya," Joy said, as if she were Texas Guinan rasping "Hello, suckers." To me she said, "How're ya doin', Marlon Chase? Who's your friend?" She air-kissed me from no closer than three feet and shook hands with Niccolo Machiavelli.

"Joy Jolson," I said, "allow me to introduce Niccolo Machiavelli."

Joy laughed for about thirty seconds. Her laugh echoed down the hall and bounced back like a racquetball. Then she said, "Niccolo Machiavelli. That's a good one. Né what? Joe Smith from the Bronx?"

Niccolo Machiavelli didn't begin to find this amusing. "Né Niccolo Machiavelli from Florence and surrounding areas," he said.

Waving us into the office, Joy said, "I don't care if you're the real fucking Niccolo Machiavelli come back to haunt us. Come on in."

Following her lead, Niccolo Machiavelli said, "I *am* the real fucking

Niccolo Machiavelli. I'm not here to haunt you. It looks as if my books have done enough of that. That's what I'm here about."

Joy turned around and looked at him, then looked at me, then looked at him again. She did some mental computing and said, "I get it. You're going to do a Machiavelli act. Funny idea. I like that you keep it up even offstage. Helps the acting muscles stay toned."

We reached her office, which was also decorated with papers and files, various handbags dropped here and there and, on the wall, hooks from which hung any number of floppy hats. She pointed to a couple of chairs with papers on them. "Park your carcasses. Just throw the papers anywhere."

When we had sat as comfortably as we were going to get—comfort not being Joy's primary purpose for establishing her operation—she said, "I'm hooked. When does the show open and where?"

I could see that Signore Machiavelli was perplexed at the mention of a show opening. I said to Joy, "There is no show. This is something entirely different, which is why I came to you. You may find this hard to believe—I did—but sitting in your office is not a Niccolo Machiavelli impersonator. This is the real Niccolo Machiavelli."

"Look, kiddo," Joy said, her tones hard as upholstery tacks, "you're talking to the original believe-anything girl. You know me. I've seen it all. Twice. You tell me this is Niccolo Machiavelli. I believe it." She winked a wink that could have meant either she did believe it or she didn't. Whatever she believed, she honed in on Signore Machiavelli. "What can I do for you, Mr. Machiavelli?"

Signore Machiavelli saw the wink and chose to ignore it. Instead, he began talking. He started telling her what he'd told me, but before he glided too far into his spiel, she held up her hand.

He stopped.

"Excuse me," she said. "I need to get this down. That's how we do business here." She pushed a button on an intercom and said, "Guinevere, come in here and bring your notebook." Within seconds, the obsequious Guinevere came in, armed with pad and pen. There was no seat for her. She stood in front of the closed door.

"Take this down," Joy said to her and nodded at Signore Machiavelli to get back to his discourse.

Which he did, by repeating everything he'd told me in much the same way, and at the end of which he looked at Joy as if to see whether and how she would pick up the figurative gauntlet he'd thrown down.

She was silent for a moment, although she returned his gaze—met his thrown glove and raised him one.

I wasn't certain if she was only staring him back down in kind because she was about to say she didn't believe a word of it and wouldn't deal with him if her life depended on it. Since that could have been it, I thought I should step in. "Perhaps, Joy," I said, "you don't want to represent Signore Machiavelli. It would be completely understandable."

I knew as it spilled out of my mouth, I'd said the wrong thing. It stopped the who'll-blink-first match between the two in the charged room. They ceased looking at each other and turned their headlight glares on me. It was as if they were cars coming at each other on the same narrow country road and I was the deer caught crossing it.

"Look, Marlon Chase," Joy said, "I represented Roy Cohn the whole

time he was hot stuff, and once I had a fifteen-minute telephone consul-
tation with Errol Flynn in his declining years where I straightened him
out once and for all. If I can handle them, I can handle your Niccolo
Machiavelli. I don't want to call him small potatoes, but..." She let that
trail off as she simultaneously raised her arms in a that's-where-I-stand-
take-it-or-leave-it pose.

Signore Machiavelli looked at me. "'Small potatoes,'" he quoted.

Before I could decide if I really wanted to explain the phrase, Joy
jumped back in. "As long as I get my rate and an enthusiastic letter of
endorsement at the end, I'm on board."

Signore Machiavelli must have understood the phrase "on board."
He resumed his standard expression of amused detachment and his
straight-backed posture—not a simple feat on the chairs that "hostess-
with-the-mostest" Joy provided.

For my part, I was thinking about the "rates" segment of her statement. I'd paid for the garlic knots and Orangina, I'd paid for the cab ride,
but I wasn't about to pay Joy's cushy fees—not even if I could.

What she did with the money she must have raked in, I couldn't say.
She certainly didn't put any of it on her back. (On her head maybe, with
the hats.) She didn't funnel it into the office. She surely wasn't passing it
on to her bowed-head drudges. Maybe she lived lavishly. I'd never seen a
photograph of wherever she lived. Maybe she had an apartment with gold
faucets on the bathroom basin and Jacuzzi jets in her tub.

While I was thinking that over, Signore Machiavelli pulled a wallet from
the pocket of his trousers in which he didn't keep a cellphone and held it up.
It looked fat with cash. He said, "Let us not worry about remuneration."

The display was all Joy needed to see. "I've been giving this some thought," she said, interrupting herself long enough to wave Guinevere out of the room. The young woman exited so unobtrusively it was as if she disappeared through the door.

"I've been giving this some thought," Joy said again, "and I think I know what to do. No, I don't think it. I know it. I haven't read any of your books, Mr. Machiavelli, but I don't need to."

Signore Machiavelli made as if he was going to offer a reply to this, but Joy stopped him.

"No," she said, "you've talked, and now it's my turn. I don't need to read your books, because you've told me as much as I need to know. And I know about you. More than you might guess. Would it surprise you to know that I myself have been hit with the adjective that's caused you such—shall we say—such consternation? You bet your skinny rear-end. I've been called Machiavellian—me, Joy Jolson. And guess what? I've welcomed it. Why? Because Machiavellian may bother you, but one of the things it indicates to me is that I get results. It says the end justifies the means. And that's nothing to turn your nose up at, baby."

I looked at Signore Machiavelli. I was wondering if he'd ever been addressed as "baby" before, and I wanted to see how he liked it. He didn't seem to mind. The amused-detachment expression was unchanged.

"This is something we have to get across broadly," Joy went on, "and I'm not saying it's going to be easy or fast. We do it in stages." She made a show of looking Signore Machiavelli up and down. "First thing we do is change how you get yourself up. The leather has to go or at least some of it. I think I know what you think you're doing. You're thinking if people expect you to look like a hoodlum, you might as well dress like one. Wrong. We want to dress you not like a fifteenth-century terrorist, but— pay attention to this—like someone who is theorizing intellectually about the ways of acquiring power. Intellectually. Academically. See?" She tapped her head with a pencil. "Uh-huh. We want to dress you like a professor, maybe even a slightly absentminded professor."

"I am not absentminded," Signore Machiavelli interrupted.

"You know that and I know that," Joy said, "but they—" Here, she made a broad gesture taking in the whole room as if it were filled with gawping spectators. "—they don't know that. Maybe we do want you to remain a bit hip, the kind of professor students warm to." She mused for a moment." Yes, that's good, that's good. We keep the leather jacket but put you in baggy trousers and open-necked shirts with a lowered tie. Maybe a tie left over from the fifties. Our fifties, not yours. A little too wide for today's tastes. Scuffed shoes, down at heel."

She intensified her scrutiny, tilting her head this way and that. "Your face. I like the look. We might want to rough your hair up a little. We don't want you coming across as a dandy. Glasses? For the scholarly angle? No. I don't think so. The mouth is good. Somebody else might have you do something with your mouth. Thin lips can tend to look menacing."

She thought for another moment, and again held up her hand when it looked as if Signore Machiavelli was about to say something. "Nope. I'm ruling filling them out out. No Botox. Uh-uh. You do great things with your lips, and I don't want to screw it up. The only thing I'm going to insist on is some kind of blusher. Your skin's a little sallow, and we'll get nowhere if you look as if you belong in a sick bed."

Joy was percolating. She was cooking with gas, and I could see Signore Machiavelli was coming to a simmer.

"Here's the rest of the crucial first stage," Joy said. "Of course, we have you introduce yourself or be introduced—you know, on Jimmy Fallon or with James Corden—as Niccolo Machiavelli, But then you say to whoever it is—wait for it!—you say, 'But just call me Nicky Mack.' Get it? You're not Niccolo Machiavelli, which gives some people the shudders and which no one can pronounce anyway. You're Nicky Mack. You've given yourself a nickname, something contemporary, something very, very twenty-first-century, something very, very hip, something very, very, in the vernacular, awesome. This serves the dual purpose of making you sound like one of the guys and demonstrating you're the kind of academic who can make fun of himself."

There was a knock on the door. Joy shouted, "Come in," and Guinevere did with a stack of papers. She handed them to Joy, who held them up for us to take in. "The transcript," she said to us. To Guinevere she said, "What took so long? Are you out there polishing your nails on my time?" (At the most, it had taken Guinevere, who looked as if she never polished her nails, ten minutes to complete the transcribing.)

Joy waved her away again, and again Guinevere vanished through the door. Joy said, "You gotta put the fear of God into them, you know, be like Machiavelli."

She remembered where she was and with whom. She looked at him and laughed like Tallulah Bankhead after giving the punchline to a dirty joke. "But I don't have to tell *you* that. Where were we? Oh, yes, we know where we're starting. Now you have to let me do my thing. You have to shop. For some of that stuff, try Goodwill Industries. On the way out, Hester will hand you a contract. Either one of you can sign it. She'll also set up our next appointment. We'll make it soon. We want to get this show on the road."

As if anticipating a contradiction that didn't come, she said, "Okay, okay, I know it isn't a show. It's the real thing. But we're going to turn it into a show. We're going to make it a *big* show. Before we're done we're going to convince the world that being Machiavellian is the only way to be. Machiavellian is fun. Machiavellian is profitable. Machiavellian is good. We're gonna market you as the first man to understand that fear, not love, makes the world go round. Hey, there's our slogan."

She gave Signore Machiavelli—sorry, Nicky Mack—a parting look and one of her predatory smiles and waved us off.

We signed, we scheduled, we left the office and stood in the dreary hall with walls on which the paint was peeling.

"How do you think it went?" I asked the new Nicky Mack.

"I found the person to edit the *Discourses*," he said.

"Then it looks as if you're on your own," I said. "All I need to do is point you towards a charity shop."

"No," he said, "you brought me here. You introduced me to this twenty-first-century soulmate of mine. So I'd appreciate it if you'd be present at all subsequent meetings."

He gave me what I can only call a full-fledged Machiavellian look.

I acquiesced—gladly, I should add. I wanted to see how far Joy would go. I knew no matter how far she went, Nicky Mack would march right alongside her.

And so it came to pass. Mr. Mack and I had several meetings with Joy, where the entire campaign—"Mack Is Back"—was laid out. She got the T-shirts ready to fly with the slogan "Fear, Not Love, Makes the World Go 'Round" on the front and on the back the legend "Fear Is Good. Fear Is Stimulating." She secured the rights to the Martha and the Vandellas hit, "Jimmy Mack" and, with new lyrics set to it, had it recorded by several hot chart personalities. Don't ask me who they are. Beyoncé? Kanye West? That's not my domain. I'm still listening to Billie Holiday and Billy Eckstein.

She had *The Prince* and her edited *Nicky Mack's Discourses* reprinted in spanking new editions with introductions by, respectively, Henry Kissinger and Seth Meyers. She coordinated the first television and radio interviews with the books' publication dates and with the iTunes releases. Since the North American book tour took in many cities, there were multitudes of interviews.

I didn't go on the book tour. I watched the outcome along with the rest of the world, although I do know that Nicky Mack in his plaid shirt and clashing rep tie is sanguine about it. Maybe it's the blusher, but I've talked to him on the phone, and I know what he said to me and how he said it.

"I like this attack, Marlon Chase. Shall I tell you why? It's fighting Machiavellianism with Machiavellianism. I couldn't have done better myself, and I owe it all to you. Joy says the same thing, almost."

Then he did something that startled and, I have to say, outright delighted me. Through the connecting airwaves he began singing the words to the revised "Jimmy Mack." At the top of his baritone voice, he sang, "Nicky Mack, oh, Nicky, oh Nicky Mack, we're happy you've come back/Nicky Mack, oh, Nicky, oh Nicky Mack, we're singing 'Welcome back'" and so forth and so on twice through.

The one and only, the once and once again Niccolo Machiavelli sang it with a Florentine accent—the very embodiment of how stimulating fear can be and is.

Yes, that's how the famous Nicky Mack came to be and how Joy Jolson and Marlon Chase came to be partners in one of Manhattan's most successful public relations offices with a dozen flourishing ficuses. Yes, thanks to Nicky Mack and to myself, I have finally found my calling.

So now you're going to tell me that everyone and his Aunt Tillie knows that the Nicky Mack you saw everywhere not so long ago is a big put-on. Believe that if you must, but I know better.

Anton Reynolds's Story

✀ or ✀

Mona Lisa, Smile!

"And in the work of Leonardo's
there was a smile so pleasing
that it was a thing more divine
than human to behold…"

—Giorgio Vasari, *Lives of the Most
Eminent Artists, Sculptors and Architects*

This might sound strange coming from an art historian, but I consider myself as having gone past the art-loving stage. It's something larger and more profound now and, as an example, goes far beyond standing amid the selfie-flashing crowd you see at Leonardo da Vinci's *Mona Lisa* whenever you're in the Louvre.

All the same, as fed up as I'd been for years with the Mona-Lisa-smile question, I do have the answer to the puzzler, and it should satisfy the inquiring minds wanting to know how it came to her lips. I cannot say why it's fallen to me to have received the answer. I'll simply say I was informed by the lady herself. In Paris. Not in the Louvre, but close enough to it.

I'd just left the Louvre on my annual trip, where I do a fair amount of my research and, during breaks, reacquaint myself with the contents. I was ambling along the Right Bank of the Seine, thinking about some of what I'd seen—not necessarily the Mona Lisa, although I had glanced that way again. Who can get over the phenomenon that the portrait is?

Yet, if I was thinking about it—about her, about the painting—at that particular moment, I wasn't thinking hard. I will say, yes, I've always been intrigued by her appearance but no less intrigued than thousands of other viewers at the Louvre, where I've seen her under glass as she is now, and not under glass as she was for many years before that.

Just as she's now a woman of a certain age, I, Anton Reynolds, am a *man* of a certain age. I've gone from lean and fresh-faced graduate student to portly and ruddy-nosed professor emeritus, and like the rest of us, no matter what age, I've seen countless Mona Lisa reproductions. But I have to believe I haven't been intrigued by her appearance—up close or in repros—that much more than millions the world over have been intrigued. I can only attribute attaining the explanation of the age-old Mona-Lisa-smile conundrum to my honed powers of observation joined with enormous good luck.

One person I spotted on my Right Bank walk was a woman sitting on the Solferino pedestrian bridge, or "passerelle." What I noticed initially was the way the woman's arms lay across her lap while she sat as comfortably as you can on those wooden benches. I noticed how her hands were positioned, the right hand over the left. I noticed how her dark hair, parted in the middle, fell to her shoulders. I noticed that, even though there was a slight breeze, her hair remained still.

What also struck me was how she sat facing the Louvre, with the

Seine curving away in the hazy late afternoon light, and far behind her, over a stretch of typical low-rise Paris buildings, just the very top of the Eiffel Tower.

I readily admit I'm familiar with the phenomenon whereby on leaving a museum or gallery, everything you see looks like the contents of the exhibit you just exited. I've left El Greco retrospectives when everyone I looked at was thin, attenuated, gaunt and greenish-tint pale. I've left Botero retrospectives when everyone I looked at was rosy-cheeked and top-to-bottom round. I've left Picasso retrospectives when everyone I looked at struck me as cockeyed.

Call it an occupational hazard. So it didn't seem odd that I was so dramatically reminded of the Mona Lisa as I looked at the woman sitting calmly on the sturdy wooden bench occupied with her own thoughts.

That she had a straight nose and soft brown eyes and a curved chin also seemed not unusual to me. That her shoulder-length parted hair was not unlike that of many women I see—and you see—every day, and that she was wearing a tailored oatmeal tweed suit on a late March afternoon, hardly seemed out of the ordinary.

Yet she made me think of the renowned portrait I had just seen—among many (unfairly) less-renowned portraits, landscapes, domestic and Biblical scenes. Just a fleeting impression, I said to myself. Yet something tempted me to look again without staring too openly.

But I had already strode past her. Giving in to the temptation required that I turn around. So I did one of the things you do in those kinds of situations. I made a show of pretending I'd forgotten something—or forgotten about something—and was halting in my tracks to think over whether I wanted to retrace my steps.

While thinking over what to do, I would naturally look around but without really meaning to look at anything in particular. You're preoccupied, and in that state, it's natural, as your gaze wanders, to take in—without anything registering strongly—whatever is around you.

I would take in the woman seated with her hands placed just so. If I happened to let my gaze linger on that one object—a woman who happened to be seated there—it wasn't because I was intentionally looking at her. She just happened to be where, innocently enough, my eyes rested while my mind concerned itself with something else.

Doing this, I was able to bring the woman into sharper focus and concluded within only seconds that she definitely resembled Ma'am Lisa. Only older perhaps. Although how old did the woman in Leonardo's portrait seem to be? I'd always thought she was in her thirties or maybe even early forties. But knowing she sat for her portrait no earlier than 1503 (Leonardo worked on the portrait sometime between 1503 and 1506) and that she was born in 1479, I had to accept that at the most she was in her mid-twenties.

The woman I was eyeing, however—without, I repeat, deliberately eyeing her—looked as if she were in her forties or maybe even early fifties. The more I regarded her surreptitiously—with the regard of a man thinking he was fooling someone—the more I felt that the woman's resemblance to the Monna Lisa, as the Louvre spells it, was uncanny.

As my late mother might have said of something that astonished her, I couldn't get over it. So instead of getting over the unmistakable likeness, as others might have—and had if they'd passed her before I did and thought to themselves that she resembled the renowned lady but kept going—I decided to do something rash and potentially rude.

I kept up the pretense of something disturbing me and made as if I needed to sit down on the closest horizontal surface, which just happened to be the bench on which the unidentified woman, whose identity I unrealistically thought I knew, was sitting.

Having been so bold as to do that, I figured I couldn't continue looking at her. I'd have to look around, fix my attention elsewhere for what I thought would be an acceptable minute or more. Then I could look around again and take her in as part of the nearby scene.

That way I'd also get a good sense of what someone as near to an exact double for Mona Lisa looked like from other than the three-quarter view Leonardo gave us, and in his process established a precedent for myriad portraits that followed her in the expanding history of art, as I knew it from lengthy study over more decades than I care to mention.

So there I was, seated next to Mona Lisa, gazing here and there at the astonishing Paris surroundings and the gauzy Paris sky until I judged enough time had passed for me to give her another once-over. Since I'd already given her a sufficiently long once-over, I suppose you could say I was gearing up for a good long twice-over.

It wasn't to be quite as I designed it. In my calculations I was about forty-five seconds to a minute away from that twice-over when I heard a voice—a mellifluous voice speaking in Italian, a voice with the consistency of an exotic confiture—say, "You know who I am, do you not?"

Swiftly turning to her, I said in my best Italian accent, in the most affronted tones, "Senora?" I said it as if I hadn't heard what she said, due to my having fallen so deeply into my supposed Solferino Bridge reverie. Or if I had heard her, couldn't imagine what she meant.

What I saw as I turned, attempting to keep up my inane ruse, was that, in her turning towards me, she maintained Leonardo's signature three-quarter view. She sat, as Mona Lisa always has, with her right hand over the left, the fingers of one hand visible, the fingers of the other partially hidden. What was even more noticeable was that she wasn't smiling. Well, she was smiling, but it wasn't the smile with which the world is familiar. It was far more wry.

She only held it for a second, because she spoke again. She repeated what she'd said. "You know who I am," and added, "It is no use to pretend you do not. Remember I have been looked at for over five hundred years. By millions of people. That is, my portrait has been. By now, I should know when I am being regarded. Signore, for reasons I do not understand, I am the most famous face in the world, photographed constantly. And do not get me started on digital cameras. You cannot name another personage whose face has been more familiar than mine for five hundred years. And do not say Jesus."

She went on, "He has been portrayed many times, to be sure, but no single painting of Him is considered definitive. There are many faces of the Christ. I, on the contrary, am singular. Perhaps I will fall into obscurity again, as has transpired for short periods of time in the past, but at the moment I am still the face all the world knows. I am Lisa Gherardini del Giocondo." A firmer tone that had crept into her voice then mellowed. "You recognize me."

What was I to say? I'd been found out. I'd sat silently through her declaration, but now I was obliged to speak. I had to admit I'd recognized her. I said, uncertainly but gaining traction as I went on, "I thought so, but you can understand my reluctance to assume you are who you say you are. You've been dead since sometime in the mid-to-late sixteenth century. You can see why I wouldn't be absolutely convinced it was you sitting on the Pont Solferino."

She acknowledged this. "You are forgiven. You are not the only one who stopped and tried to figure out if I could be who I appear to be. You are the only one who has had the nerve to sit down. And all I am *allowed* to do is to sit. In my pose. 'Do not move,' Signore da Vinci said. 'You are exactly right as you are.' So sitting like this has become the condition of my renewed presence. Thank heaven, it is a comfortable pose. What if he had posed me balancing on one hand?"

At that she smiled again, but again it was not *the* smile. It was broader and revealed two neat rows of even teeth. That's right. I have seen Mona Lisa's pearl-like teeth—*small*, pearl-like teeth. I never did see her ears. If they're shell-like, I can't presume to report.

"To tell you the truth," she said, "I am glad of the company. I am used to being looked at, but I am not used to being spoken to. Do you know I hung in Napoleon's bedroom for several years, and in all that time he never addressed a word to me? Not one. Not a single 'How do you come to be smiling?' Perhaps he was embarrassed. The things I saw him get up to when he thought no one was looking—standing on his toes to appear taller, tickling the maidservents. If he had had any humor, he might at least have bowed comically in my direction, but he was a humorless man."

Then she did something for which I was totally unprepared. (That

Napoleon owned her portrait, I already knew, but not the part about his never addressing the canvas, not even on his tiptoes.) She bowed comically in my direction and quickly resumed her pose.

"But that is not what you want to see or hear from me, is it?" she said. "You want to know about the smile. That is what they all want to know. Why am I smiling? What am I smiling about? Where does the slight, the even sly smile come from?"

By the time she said this, I'd done enough pretending. I couldn't do anymore. I knew it was time to fess up, and I was on the verge of saying, "Yes, yes, you got me, what's with the semi-grin?" when she said, "It amazes me no one notices I am not the only one smiling in a Leonardo da Vinci painting. There is a painting of his hanging less than thirty meters from mine where anyone can see another woman smiling the half-smile supposedly exclusive to me. I am talking, of course, about the Virgin in 'La Vierge aux Rochers.'

"But, do they look at her? No. Most of the people who pass through the Galerie d'Italie not looking here or there—even casually—just want to see me. Or if they do look at her, they see her with Jesus and the young John the Baptist and Saint Anne and think, 'Oh, she is smiling at them.' So is Saint Anne. She is smiling, too, for the sake of heaven. Look at 'La Belle Ferronniere' right next to them. She is beginning to smile as well. Yes, smiling. Hasn't anyone yet realized that Signore da Vinci liked his women smiling? In a commissioned portrait, he certainly was not going to show me frowning."

I was just about to say, "Yes, but what are you—were you—smiling about?" when she read my porous mind and said, "But what am I smiling about? At this point, I could just as well say I am smiling about all the people looking at me, taking photograph after photograph of me—often with themselves in it—and thinking how special I am, how unique. I am unique, but no more than every painting is unique—certainly every painting by a master. In every other capacity, I am not unique."

As she spoke—always remaining as she appears in whatever frame she's been put over the centuries or on whatever poster—she was becoming just another woman sitting on a bench on a bridge in the middle of Paris, a city where at that very moment many women were sitting on many benches on many bridges. So I took her point. She became less and less unique as the seconds ticked by and she continued chatting in her pleasantly conversational way.

"You could say I am nowhere near unique," she said, "and I would not give you an argument. I could not give you an argument. I am a middle-class housewife who married a modestly successful merchant older than myself and then had six children with him. A couple of them went into convents. A couple died young. I have had my ups and downs, good years and bad. Like anyone else. I lived to my seventies and died. As everyone else does sooner or later."

She looked at me with sympathy and said, "I could say I am smiling because I had a life no better than most people's but no worse, either. But that is not why I am smiling. I could say I am shown smiling because I knew I was being painted by Leonardo da Vinci and none of my other friends were being painted by him. That is not quite true. I did know some of his other subjects—or knew who they were. But that is not why I am smiling.

"Ask yourself this. Who was Leonardo da Vinci, anyway? At the time he painted me, he had a reputation. People in arts circles thought he was all la-di-da, but I had married at sixteen and led a relatively sheltered life. What did I know? He was always polite—very polite for a man with the kind of artistic bent he had."

By this time I'd started thinking that as someone who'd so long sat closed-mouthed, she was making up for lost time. She did confine herself to subdued speech—something of Sophia Loren's timbre—and though I stole a look around from time to time to see if anyone was taking this in, I saw that no one was. I satisfied myself we weren't attracting even an audience of one.

Or was I satisfied? I was sitting in the center of my idea of the most beautiful city on the planet with the most famous woman in the art world for the past half-millennium, and no one, other than myself, was there to record the occasion.

And I thought, if I were to record it—only for my personal satisfaction—I must do everything I can to make the record as good as it can be. What, I asked myself, would guarantee that? The answer came back loud and clear: I'd have to find a way to make her smile the Mona Lisa smile.

So far I'd gotten a panoply of smiles but not that one. "I'm sorry to interrupt," I said to her—and she nodded her acceptance of the interruption—"but aside from being polite, did Signore da Vinci do anything else to put you at your ease? They say he employed singers and jesters to keep those sitting for him entertained."

"Yes," she said, "that was something he did."

She merely had to confirm the fact of Leonardo da Vinci's in-the-atelier doings when, not allowing myself the time to think, I leapt off the bench. On the Solferino pedestrian bridge—with pedestrians to the left of me and pedestrians to the right of me—I started to do something so uncharacteristic of me, that had colleagues and other friends seen me, they'd have been at a complete loss for words but possibly not at a loss for deepening concern. After all, over the years I'd put a good deal of effort into my professor's professorial manner. On the other hand, I'd put suffi- ciently less effort into an exercise regimen.

Forget that. Right then and there, I began to caper as I thought a jester might but without, needless to say, a cap and bells. (O, for a cap and bells!) "Like this?" I asked after indulging about thirty seconds of this impromptu buffoonery.

"Something like that," she said but cracked no smile of any sort. Not at all did she readjust her lips—the thin upper lip, the fuller lower lip.

Yet her "something like that" suggested I was on the right track. So I kept up the mad pogoing for another minute or two. Mona Lisa may not have been smiling, but children passing with mothers or fathers or nannies pointed at me and giggled, giggled and pointed enough that I finally stopped hopping about like Danny Kaye or Eddie Murphy in one of their calculatedly physical screen comedies.

I stopped only to substitute music for jesting. Maybe that's what turned her smile on—someone warbling a tune. But what to sing? A com- edy song seemed best. Since I knew no early-sixteenth-century comedy songs (are there early-sixteenth-century comedy songs? There must be), I thought quickly and came up with one of my all-time favorite nonsense ditties, "Mairzy Doats." You know how it goes: "Mairzy Doats and dozy doats and liddle lamzy divey/A kiddley divey, too, wouldn't you?"

Adapted from an English nursery rhyme, it's not a number you hear too often anymore. Even when I was a kid and it was top of the charts in the United States, it may have never been heard on a Paris pedestrian bridge. But I thought the silliness of it just might be the musical feather to tickle Mona Lisa's funny bone and get that smile back in its proper place.

It didn't. While it attracted other pedestrians, a sizable number of whom (Americans?) sang along, it did nothing for the Mona.

So singing was out. Maybe straight-on comedy would be the thing to catch the humor of the apparently discerning housewife and mother. Aha, I thought, Shakespeare. I know he didn't begin to write his plays and verses until much later in Mona Lisa's century, and I had no idea whether when he did, his fame spread to Italy, despite "The Tragedy of Romeo and Juliet" being set in Verona. Still, I hoped the English sensibility that the Bard reflected might be acceptably close to the Italian sensibility.

I chose to recite what I remembered of Malvolio's speech when he comes cross-gartered before Olivia. I'd never seen that sequence fail to get an audience chuckling. I launched into the speech—"Some are born great, some achieve greatness and some have greatness thrust upon them…"— recalling more of the exchange between Malvolio and Olivia than I had any notion I would. To indicate the crossed garters I drew imaginary crosses down my calves with my right forefinger.

Since I got caught up in what I was doing, and so did the accumu-lating crowd watching me—some, I noticed, even looking around for a hat or another substitute receptacle into which they could throw coins—

it took me a minute or two to realize none of what I was doing had any effect on its non-smiling target.

Thinking fast, I switched to old Henny Youngman one-liners —"Take my wife, please." "There was a girl knocking on my hotel room door all night—finally, I let her out." "Those two are a fastidious couple—she's fast and he's hideous."

When she'd had enough without cracking a Mona Lisa you-know-what, she said, "I probably should let you know that although Signore da Vinci tried to entertain me, I never found singers, jesters and like divertissements truly entertaining. I was more readily amused by other, simpler things."

Now she tells me.

Sheepishly, I sat down next to her—amid, I should probably say, a smattering of applause from my dispersing audience. Flattering, in a way, but also galling, because a few of them, I noticed, were wearing Mona Lisa smiles I had put there.

But what good was that to me? Wearing one, she wasn't. She had given me a hint, though. She said she was amused by simpler things. Then I had to ask myself what she meant by simpler things. What would a woman who was born in the last quarter of the fifteenth century and who lived until the middle of the sixteenth century consider simple things?

Would she find a peddler slipping on a cow patty amusing? Would she find a milkmaid blushing at a swain amusing? Would she find a rustic thumbing his nose at an aristocrat amusing? Would she find a toddler taking his or her first steps amusing?

What if any situation along those lines amused her, what good would it do me? I wasn't about to impersonate a rustic thumbing his nose at an aristocrat, let alone a peddler slipping on a cow patty. Yet I was determined to make Mona Lisa smile that smile, moue that moue, if it was the last thing I ever did. All that effort at my age? It might be.

Wait a sec. What if I mooed like a cow? Absolutely not. I wasn't going to sit in the middle of Paris mooing like a cow. Or quacking like a duck. Or ribbeting like a frog. I don't care whom I was trying to make smile.

Sure, I was prepared to do anything in my power but not any of that. Nor was I going to admit defeat. I did some fast brain-wracking and, lo and behold, remembered that there'd been speculation the Mona Lisa's disposition could have been attributed at the time to her children—to, more particularly, the recent birth of her second son. Some have it the birth was the impetus for her businessman husband's commissioning the portrait.

Children! That could be the ticket. Mothers smile when thinking of their children, when they recall things their young children said and/or did during the day. Thinking to introduce the subject obliquely, I said to her, "Mona, Ms. Lisa, do you like children?"

Clearly, she did. Her face relaxed. Her eyes shifted in such a way I could see visions of children were running through her mind. The set of her mouth began to change. I was right, I thought. Here it comes. I'm about to get the smile. I'll be able to establish once and for all the smile's origin.

I watched her mouth closely—only to see it widen into a full-blown smile, the kind of expectant-mother smile that lights up a room. Not the smile I was after. Then she said with a tilt of her head, "Of course, I like children. I had six of them."

Liked them too much for *my* purposes, obviously. There had to be something. What simple sally would amuse a woman like her? Household follies, cooking mishaps, fashion don'ts, the behavior of pets? I tried making light of them all. I won't bother to repeat what I tried right there on the Solferino Bridge. Everything I tried was entirely in vain. All I got for my efforts was an expression that mixed indulgence with pity.

After this had gone on for—I don't know—twenty minutes, a half-hour, she held up her right hand to stop me and immediately put it back in place on her lap.

I stopped. I could see she had something to say. "You must be wondering why I have let you go on like this," she said. To tell the truth, I had been so involved with what I was doing that I hadn't wondered any such thing, but I nodded as if I had been thinking as much.

"Because," she said in earnest explanation, "I had seen it all before. What you were doing was almost exactly—gesture for gesture, pleasantry for pleasantry—what Signore da Vinci, that bearded old man, did while trying to get me to smile. As I have said, he liked his women smiling. When he had finally run out of things that failed to provide the desired response, he threw his hands up in the air. His paint brush went flying. He said, 'I have never in my life had so much trouble getting someone to smile.'

"That amused me. The famous Signore da Vinci having trouble getting me—the humble wife of a merchant, a virtual nobody—to smile. At that, I had to smile. When I did, he said, '*Cosa c'e*. There it is. The smile I want. Hold it.' I held it."

Then, to my astonishment, she smiled the very smile—and held it. She held it and reached over and touched me on the forearm. Only briefly. She withdrew it. The smile, she held until, right before my eyes, she began disappearing and all that was left of her was the smile. Then, slowly as the sun falling below the horizon, that disappeared, too.

What didn't disappear and still hasn't is the astounding and incontrovertible fact I had added to my knowledge of the history of art and to the knowledge of others—and at my age. It's a small contribution to the art history annals I've longed to make, but even if it's only a footnote, it's something after all these years.

Doug Reithauser's Story

✂ or ✂

Babe Ruth Rounds Home

You wouldn't think I'd be the one to whom Babe Ruth would reveal himself when hustling around the corner of Trenton, New Jersey's Stockton and Perry Streets. Yet, there he was, as if loping towards home after knocking a bases-loaded home run in the bottom of the ninth.

There he was—the Babe, the Behemoth of Bust, the Big Bambino, the Colossus of Clout, the Mammoth of Maul, the Prince of Pounders, the Sultan of Swat, the Wazir of Wham!—and under the weirdest circumstances. I grant you that Babe Ruth revealing himself to anyone after his August 16, 1948, death would be weird, but that he should make himself known, and to me, on the day I'd decided to take the train from Manhattan to wander around my old neighborhood, was mighty weird.

To begin with, it was already weird that I was there. I'm not even sure *why* I was there. It was a whim. It was an urge I couldn't pinpoint. Earlier that morning, I just had the feeling I wanted to walk down the street where I lived for the first nine years of my life. I wanted to sit on the stoop of the Perry Street building where I'd got bitten by the stoop-sitting bug from the time I was three or four. (I still set great store by sitting on a stoop.)

I wanted to size up the building where my dad, general practitioner Julius Levi Reithauser, had his office on the first floor, and he, my mother Hannah, my brother Arthur and I lived on the second floor. The three elderly O'Reillys, two unmarried sisters and an unmarried brother, lived on the third floor.

What had I expected to glean from perching on that stoop as I had when I was a kid playing with other kids and regarding the stretch of land I could see to the right and the left as the entire universe? Memories, of course, surfaced. I won't say, as some might, that they flooded back. What I experienced was more like a rain of memories, even more like a hail. I was pelted with stinging recollections, all of them random.

Some of them weren't even memories of things that had happened. They were fantasies about dad, or Julie, as my mother called him, and about my mom, Hahn, as he called her. I imagined him taking her, an Atlantic City girl to whom he'd been introduced and about whom he'd become serious, to see, for the first time, the office where he practiced. I imagined him coming home from the hospital the day I was born and knowing he now had a son.

When these thoughts had crowded my head to the extent that I was beginning to have not a standard headache but a head *something*, I started thinking I'd only be able to alleviate it by a method having nothing to do with ibuprofen. I stood up, shook myself off and decided I was on a fool's errand. I felt that whatever I had come for was eluding me. Taking the next train back to New York City, where my post-Trenton life was, would be the smartest, safest, most practical thing to do.

I'd barely gotten thirty feet from that old stoop with its rounded club-chair arms (that hadn't brought me much club-chair comfort over the last hour or so) when I saw a burly figure turning the corner on the run. Everything about him was rounded or round-ish, including his face. What's more, everything about him looked familiar.

If I didn't know better, I thought to myself, I'd say I was watching the revered Babe Ruth hurtling himself my way. That's a laugh, I thought—Babe Ruth coming towards me and not towards some oldtime baseball fan. Some old baseball fanatic, I thought, like my father, like Julie Reithauser. There's someone who would have appreciated the moment bigtime.

I never had much of an interest in the game, the so-called national pastime. I was so uninterested that it was tantamount to an unspoken wedge between Julie and me. On hot afternoons during the baseball season, Julie—no office hours scheduled, his morning hospital trip completed and no pressing house calls—would have two radios going, one in his and Mom's bedroom and one in the kitchen. He'd be running in his baggy boxer shorts from one to the other, changing stations to catch up with as many games as he could beam in from the local airwaves. Was there static? He'd strain to hear through it.

I'd be coming back from Traver's bookstore in the center of town with the latest entry in the *Hardy Boys* series I followed. I'd pass him on the way to my room where I could read to my heart's content. Julie had long since given up on trying to get me to share his love of the sport. If I passed him as he jogged between radios, he wouldn't say much more than

"Hi, Dougie, how's my boy?" and keep going. I'd counter with an affect-less "Hi, Dad, the games exciting?" That was as much interest as I could muster on his behalf.

But it wasn't Dad or anyone like him for whom Babe Ruth was appearing. It was "baseball's so boring" me, who was startled as the man slowed to a halt, gave me a smile that for sure looked like the smiles I knew from photographs and said, "Excuse me, pal. I'm trying to find the train station, but I must have made the wrong turn."

"I guess you did," I said.

"I must've turned left when I should have turned right after the last guy I stopped gave me directions," he said. (I'm still saying "he," because I was trying to convince myself I wasn't losing it.)

"You did, unless you're looking for the bus station," I said. "If you're looking for that, you're going in the right direction." I turned and pointed in the opposite Perry Street direction. It had slipped my mind for the moment that the Perry Street bus branch had long since ceased operating.

"No, buddy, I want the train station."

"In that case," I said, "you're definitely going in the wrong direction. I can tell you the way, since I'm from around here. As a matter of fact, I'm headed to the station myself. You're welcome to join me."

Things were getting weirder and weirder, weren't they?

"Thanks, fella," he said. "Don't mind if I do." He fell in beside me.

"Of course, if you want to run there," I said, "I can just tell you which way to go."

He said, "I already tried that, and look where it got me. Besides, I'm pretty sweaty." He wiped his face with his thick right forearm. He was wearing a short-sleeved shirt and gabardine trousers. When he raised his arm, he exposed a sizable sweat stain.

"Okay, then," I said, "I guess we're off."

"Mighty nice of you to do this," he said.

"Don't mention it," I said and then remained silent for most of the next block. But curiosity was mounting in me. I could feel it surging. After we'd proceeded a fair distance up Stockton Street, which wasn't looking any too affluent (not that it ever had), I said, "Excuse me, but I wanted to ask you if anyone has ever told you you look like Babe Ruth?"

At that, he stopped altogether, laughed and said, "I get it all the time."

"I'm not surprised," I said and started to say something else along those lines, but he interrupted me.

"But there's a good reason for it," he said, adding the Babe Ruth smile. "I *am* Babe Ruth." Anticipating my response, he said, "You don't believe me. After all, I passed away some time ago, but I *am* the Babe."

To illustrate his claim, he struck an at-bat pose, pulled his cupped hands back and swung like every Sultan-of-Swat pose and effortless swing you'd ever seen in newsreel footage. (I never said I knew nothing whatsoever about baseball. For any young American boy, it would have been impossible not to know something—if only to know what to avoid.) It would have wowed Julie: Babe Ruth miming a home-run swing not a couple hundred feet from where the old man practiced medicine, a couple hundred feet from his crackling radios. (This is before we moved and he could add a television console to his network.)

By the time he mimed his swing we'd walked far enough along

Stockton Street to reach the place where the Stockton Street Paper Company had once been housed. It had been torn down. Now it was a large empty space surrounded by a chain-link fence.

If the intention was to keep trespassers out—it was; a sign marred by graffiti said as much—the expectation had been violated. From what I could see, the fence had been cut open at three places, leaving the scruffy area available.

It so happened that as Babe Ruth offered his impromptu Babe Ruth's swing demonstration, I wasn't the only one who observed it. Others passing by may have noticed and not thought anything of it, but a bunch of kids around eight or nine did. They were the ones who'd laid temporary claim to the prohibited ground, and wouldn't you know it, they were playing baseball.

Only after the Babe completed his swing—and I'd taken in the sweet follow-through—did we realize we had company. Only then did the kids begin running up to the fence yelling "Hey, you, hey, Mister!" in overlapping appeals.

Babe Ruth and I turned. Eight of the boys pressed against the fence, while two of them wedged through the nearest chain-link opening. Those two planted themselves by us with their hands, the gloved hand and the free hand, on their hips.

"We saw you," the one closest to us said. "We ain't never seen a swing like that."

Instead of responding to the remark, Babe Ruth faced them with his hands on *his* hips and said in a mock-stern tone, "Ain't you boys supposed to stay out of that field?"

One of the boys crowding the fence said, "We s'posed to, but no one ever bothers us." "'Sides," another one blurted, "Where else we gonna play 'round here? Do you see anything looks like a real diamond?"

"I guess I don't," the Babe said. "Would you boys mind if I joined you?" As he said that to a chorus of encouraging young cries, he looked at me, winked and said, "You mind if I do? You can go ahead, if you like."

As if I was going to miss this. I said I wouldn't mind at all.

"The problem is," Babe Ruth said to the boys, "I'm a pretty big guy. I'm not sure I can get through any of these holes in the fence."

"Sure you can," one said with a kid's enthusiasm, and the others chimed in with similar reassurances. "Over here," one of them said, running to an opening a bit further along. "Bigger men than you have made it."

Running to it with the easy lope I'd seen earlier, the Babe said, "I didn't know there *were* any guys bigger 'n me." He laughed, and the kids laughed, too.

In their laughter were glimmers of suspicion that they'd just encountered a grown-up kid, a mature man who liked to play as much as they did. Anyway, it's always seemed to me that there's no sport like baseball to bring out the boy still lurking in the grown man, in someone like my baseball-crazed dad.

Babe Ruth could have been the poster man for that truism. If the boys had only known, but it was plain that they didn't. It was plain that if they'd ever heard about Babe Ruth, he didn't mean much to them these many years after their new fellow trespasser built Yankee Stadium. "You want to learn how to swing like what you just saw?" he said as the boys crowded around him. The "yeah, man"s were unison. "Okay," he said, "we'll take turns." He pointed to one of them. "You, what's your name?"

"Cliff," the boy said, lighting up at being called first, "but they call me 'Bunter,' 'cause I always bunt, and I'm good at it." His preadolescent chest swelled when he said that.

"Great, Bunter," Babe Ruth said, "but now I want to see you swing for the bleachers. It'll be good for you. When they see you come up to bat, they think you're going to bunt, don't they?" Bunter nodded yes. So they move in. Every once in a while, you hafta fool 'em. When you do, they'll never know what to do when they see you. They'll get flustered." He pointed at his round head. "You gotta fake 'em out. Now let's see your swing. Who's the pitcher here?"

"I us'ly am," two of them answered simultaneously. "Chucky," one added. "Rolly," the other one said.

"Rolly," the Babe said, "you pitch for now." Rolly visibly swelled with pride. Chucky was abashed. The swat sultan said, "Chucky, you'll take over in a few minutes." He looked them over. "Let's play ball."

The boys ran back onto the field. Rolly pitched one. Bunter swung at it. "That's not it," Babe Ruth said. He adjusted Bunter's grip on the bat—but only after handling the bat himself and throwing me a look that said he wished the boys had something better to work with.

Bunter tried again and then again. After four or five more tries, he connected with one that caused the others to chase deep to the back of the field, where someone or someones had heaped plenty of trash.

That was the Babe's signal to call the next batter and then the one after that. Some of them got into—forgive me for this—the swing of things better than others, but they were all improving their grip, their stance, their eye, their power.

Incidentally, I'm observing this from the street side of the fence. I felt like an anxious father, and by now I wasn't the only one there. It occurred to me that maybe some of the others were anxious fathers and mothers. Several other pedestrians had stopped for a few minutes each. One of them said before moving on, "Those little league coaches don't know when to stop." "Maybe he needs players for a losing team," another said to no one in particular. "Could be he's scouting ringers for a rich kids team."

Finally, only Chucky was left and what he said as he took the bat was, "You know what they call me? Babe Ruth."

So these kids had heard of Babe Ruth.

"Yeah?" the Babe said. "Why is that?"

"'Cause there was an oldtime baseball player who was once a pitcher."

"I think I heard a' him," the Bronx Bomber said.

"And he hit a home run every time he came up to bat," Chucky said with a pinch of awe.

"Every time," Babe Ruth said. "Imagine that."

"Yeah," Chucky said. "And I'm a pitcher who hits a home run every time I come up to bat." He must have noticed a look cross the Babe's face. "Okay, maybe not every time. But lots. And not many pitchers can do anywhere near that. Not even in the major leagues. Especially in the major leagues."

"Then let's see what you got," Babe Ruth said.

Rolly was pitching again. He hurled the first one. Chucky, a. k. a. Babe Ruth, pulled a long drive into what passed for left field.

"You're right, Babe, you got something there," the man himself said. "Now let's see how we can make it even hotter." The Babe had Chucky cannon a dozen or so more, and sure enough, Chucky upped his game.

By this time and after they'd all had their turn at bat, the boys were intensifying demands they'd been making all along. They wanted to see the Babe swing as he'd been instructing them to, although they didn't call him the Babe. They already had one Babe Ruth—Chucky—in their midst. They were still calling the real Babe Ruth "Mister."

"Show us how you swing, Mister," they'd been shouting. Knowing I was with him, a couple of them came over to the fence. "Mister, tell him to show us his swing," they implored.

Finally, the honest-to-God Babe Ruth finally gave in, with a shrug of his broad shoulders towards me. The gesture patently meant, "What else can I do?"

He had Rolly pitch a few and then Chucky. Knowing the force he could apply, he pulled his swing, knocking the ball in different directions so that all the boys had a chance to field it.

But they only enjoyed that for so long. They knew the Babe wasn't swinging as he'd been insisting they should. They could tell he was holding back. After only about ten minutes, they started to yell for him to give it all he had. "C'mon, Mister, we know you can do better than that," they yelled, or versions of it. They kept it up, too, until with another what-else-can-I-do shrug, the Babe agreed but told them, "Just one."

Chucky wound up and pitched the ball at Babe Ruth as fast as his ten-year-old right arm allowed. The Babe swung. The bat met the ball and went sailing high and long. It sailed over the field gaining height as it went. It sailed for a city block and then another. The boys had all turned to watch it go. They were hollering "Wow!" and "Jeez!" and "Would you watch that sucker go!" and whistling.

I was in awe myself, but now I have to talk about Trenton real estate. It's been on the slide for some miserable time. Much of it in the immediate vicinity has been torn down but not rebuilt. Only a few ramshackle, barely habitable tenements remained between the two blocks over which the ball had traveled and Trenton's main drag, East State Street, which farther along became the somewhat tonier West State Street. What hadn't been razed on the other side of East State Street at this juncture was City Hall, an edifice that looked like any City Hall in any American city—a set of steep stairs to a squatting structure with long rows of tall windows to the right and left.

It was into one of those windows that Babe Ruth's connected ball crash-landed with no center fielder to catch it.

Don't take my word for this, but I think the boys, the Babe and I heard the window shatter. I could be imagining it. What I didn't imagine were the half cut-off figures that appeared in the window frame or windows to the right and left of the window. Besides that, not one of us missed seeing three burly uniformed men run out of City Hall's main double-door and down the steps, heading for where we were standing.

Looking at me with a look I can only interpret as confidence-instilling, Babe Ruth turned to the boys and said, "Don't worry, fellas. You got nothing to worry about." He pulled something from his pocket and handed it to Bunter.

It was a baseball. From where I was pressed against the fence eight or ten feet away, I could tell it was a ball that had been walloped many times.

"You boys go on playing," the Babe said, "and don't forget what I taught you."

At that, he scrammed to the opening through which he'd pushed before. He emerged on my side, stood up and headed to me. "I gotta get out of here and fast. When those guys coming this way get here, they're not going to believe that any of these kids could have whammed a ball that far. They'll think someone else right outside that building did it, that it was just a coincidence the boys were playing here at the same time. You can corroborate that. You can tell them nothing like it happened from here. Sorry about not catching the train with you, but, wait a minute, I never got your name."

It hadn't occurred to me I'd never told him who I was. I certainly knew who he was. "Douglas Reithauser," I said.

"Reithauser," he said and shook his head. "That's a heavy load of a name to carry. How do you spell that?"

I spelled it for him. When I did, a quizzical expression took over those familiar snub-nosed features.

"I've heard that name before," he said and furrowed his brow. "That's a name you don't forget. I've autographed thousands of balls, and I never remember the names of the fans who ask. But that one I remember. I never heard any like it. The kid spelled it like you just did, all methodical like."

The quizzical look returned to his face. "And I remember where I signed it, too." He hit the side of his head with the edge of his right palm. "It was here. Right here in Trenton. Summer of 1920. I was on a tour. Signed it for a kid just about the same age as these kids here. Had to be somebody related to you, don't you think?"

He asked that as he was looking up Stockton Street. The burly trio was fast approaching. "Gotta go," he said. And did. It was as if he vanished in a cloud of sandlot dust.

Whether anyone else noticed, I can't say. The boys were intently focused on their game, making like nothing else mattered to them.

The first of the burly men came to the fence and shouted to the boys. They pretended not to hear the first and second time he called. Finally, they stopped what they were doing and looked at him. "This ball belong to you boys?" the man asked and held up the Babe-battered missile.

"No, sir," one of the boys said. Holding up his mitt with the baseball Babe Ruth gave them in its worked-on pocket, Rolly said, "Here's our ball, sir."

"Funny," a second burly man said, "a ball just came through a City Hall window. You boys don't know anything about that?"

The boys all shook their heads. Some of them muttered "No, sir," as if butter wouldn't melt in their lying mouths.

The third of the burlies looked at me, questioningly. I looked him in the eye and said, "Look where we are. Look at them. Do you think any of these kids could smack a ball from here to City Hall?"

The three of them looked at each other. "Guess not," the first one said. They nodded to each other in tacit agreement. They shook their heads and started walking back where they came from.

Watching them go, the boys started laughing among themselves. They stopped when Rolly, having removed the ball from his mitt, said, "Hey, would you look at this. There's an autograph on it. You can hardly read it, but it says 'Babe Ruth.'" "Maybe he knew Babe Ruth," another one said. "The real Babe Ruth?" another one said. Then there was a group "Wow!"

As the boys were passing it around, I started to leave for the station. I wasn't thinking of that autograph. I was thinking about the baseball the Babe had signed in 1920. I knew who that Reithauser boy was, of course. He was Julius Levi Reithauser, my father, at that time an eleven-year-old boy.

I could see him, beaming at meeting a hero, at getting him to sign a baseball. I'd come to Trenton for memories. Now I had a new one. It wasn't mine. It was Julie's. He'd never shared it with me, perhaps because he thought it would mean nothing to me, that my lack of enthusiasm at being told he'd once met the great Babe Ruth would hurt him, would tarnish the memory. He didn't want to take the risk.

But now I know. Now I have the memory, his memory. What's more, I'll have it forever.

Grant Shipley's Story

✂ or ✂

Gossip Boys

Marcel Proust?!" I blurted.

The person I was taking for Monsieur Proust—rightly, I can assure you—put a neurasthenic finger to his neurasthenic lips.

"Please. Quiet," he said. "No one must know I am here. Yet." He spoke not in French but in an impeccable, though murmurous and neurasthenically aristocratic French accent.

Luckily, I understood the accent—or understood enough of it. You can't fool me. My language courses in prep school and college—mighty fancy institutions, the both of them—stood me in good stead, especially since I'd read Proust in French. Not all of *A la recherche du temps perdu,* but enough. Has anyone ever read all of it? I assume Proust had and a few French professors.

I'd had professors who cultivated the same accent this guy was using to impress us *étudiants maudits.* "Damned students"—that's what I heard one of them mutter under his breath for us to hear during one particularly frustrating class.

I wasn't being fooled about a suddenly materialized Marcel Proust imposter. How could I be—me, Grant Shipley, who always believed in reincarnation, whose parents sometimes considered me potentially neurasthenic? Why couldn't someone, anyone, be reincarnated as himself or herself? And here it was. Happening. Marcel Proust—from his neurasthenic hair to his neurasthenic nose and neurasthenic mustache to his obviously neurasthenic feet encased in laced, fine leather shoes, patently (pun intended) custom-made for neurasthenics.

How could I be so sure of this? How could I not be so sure? I was sitting on Manhattan's West Twenty-third Street in a tea shop called Madeleine Patisserie. Would there be any likelier place for Marcel Proust to fetch up in Manhattan? Furthermore, I had just taken the opening bite out of the first of two madeleines I was having with my—what I'll call here for thematic purposes—tisane.

Under the circumstances, how could this palpable vision not be Marcel Proust? I took my time making my next remark. When I was prepared, I made it in a carefully subdued tone. I also panned my head right and left so he could see I was intent on not calling attention where attention wasn't wanted.

"How did you get here?" I asked, while trying not to appear throttled or pushy, "and while I'm at it, what are you doing here?"

Remaining upright in his white wicker seat, he said, "You have asked two questions. First things first." I wasn't surprised at his mastery of idiom. He was the uncontested master of one language. Why wouldn't he handle a second just as skillfully? "I am here because you have summoned me."

It's difficult not to look astonished when you are astonished, and

now I was that, and more. I opened my mouth to speak, but he, anticipating higher volume, once more started to raise a neurasthenically
admonishing finger. I remembered myself and when I spoke, I spoke
softly, if still in great confusion.

"I? Me?" I said. "I summoned you? *Moi?*"

Moi! I said, *moi* despite my aversion for English-speaking people
dropping French words into their sentences to gain aren't-I-amusing
points. *Moi!* That's how stupefied, how out of control I was.

"Yes, you," he said. He restrained himself from "*Toi*"—if he'd even
had the inclination. "Are you surprised?"

"I am," I said, ignoring my long-held belief in an after-life taking
place in this life.

"I will confess I had something to do with it," he said. "I have been
thinking about returning—to life, you understand—but there are condi-
tions. My return was contingent on someone thinking of me, someone
who was convinced I could rematerialize. Oh, what is the antonym of
évanouir?" His dark eyes got darker. He did a funny mustache twinge that
I don't recall from my reading about him as something he was reputed to
do. "You were thinking of me as you ate your madeleine, were you not?"

Without realizing what I was doing until I was in the middle of
doing it, I took another bite out of the madeleine I'd been holding
throughout this initial exchange and thought for a second. The truth was,
I had been thinking about him. I realized I thought about him for a split
second at the very least every time I ate a madeleine. The tart, sweet,
lemony madeleine in front of me was no different, of course. I even often
thought, What would it have been like to know him?

I said as much and appended, "But I can't imagine there's a French major or minor"—I had minored in French at Old Ivy, where I was a snarky, legacy, trust-fund kid—"who doesn't think of you every time he or she eats a madeleine. After all, every one of us has read *Swann's Way*." Okay, okay. I actually said, "*Du coté de chez Swann*." I won't deny giving into pretensions every once in a while, and when better to go whole-hog-pretentious than on meeting Marcel Proust?

"You may assume that madeleines and I go together in the minds of millions," M. Proust replied, "but apparently it happens less often these days than you think."

I don't know what startled me more, his appearance or that disclosure.

He continued, "That answers your first question. Your second question—what am I doing here?—is also up to you. I'm doing what you want me to do."

I didn't want him to do anything. It was bad enough that my thinking of him had somehow worked as a summons.

He took a sip of the tisane that had materialized along with him and then wiped the corners of his mouth with a paper napkin. The expression he made then was that of someone for whom paper napkins were not an acceptable amenity.

What were the proprietors thinking of this out-of-the-blue patron? I wondered, but when I looked over at them being busy as so many *abeilles* (bees) behind the counter, they were taking no notice.

Neither was anyone else. The five other patrons—the ones M. Proust did not want to be aware of his presence—were acting as if he wasn't there when, I'm telling you, he was.

"I don't want you to do anything," I said.

"When you were thinking about me," he asked and again the mustache twinge happened, "what were you thinking about me doing?"

I gave that some consideration and then said, "Nothing. I was thinking of you in the abstract."

He picked up one of two madeleines that had materialized alongside his tisane and raised it to his mouth. "Were you thinking about me eating a madeleine?"

That would have made sense, wouldn't it? But no, I wasn't thinking about him eating a madeleine. I was just thinking Proust-madeleine-madeleine-Proust—nothing more probing than that predictable word association.

He took a tiny bite from his madeleine, and I took another bite from mine. He was thinking I don't know what. I was thinking that I didn't know what to think.

Anyway, I spoke first. "But if you say you were thinking of coming back to life, you must have been thinking of coming back to do something."

"Not really. I never did much when I was living. Go to parties. Chat up the rich, famous and miserable. Why would I want to do much now?"

"You did plenty," I said, amazed to find myself defending Marcel Proust to *himself*. I'd only come in to read The New York Times. "You wrote like a house on fire. When you died—at only forty-eight, need I remind you?—you left behind one of the great novels of the century. Maybe the greatest. You were industry in a cork-lined room."

"Oh, that," he said. He looked as if a foul odor—something deeply mephitic—had abruptly wafted through the room. "Yes, it's a good read, but I suffered the tortures of hell doing it. And when I say 'the tortures of hell,' I now know whereof I speak. Not that I've been to hell, but word gets back from those who have been that Dante wasn't far off the mark. Only about the number of circles did he miscalculate. There are not nine. There are *thirty*-nine. I see you're trying to imagine what they're like. Don't."

He took another sip. "You might imagine I'm back here to write. Believe me, I'm not. For me, writing was not an Edouard Manet picnic on the grass. All you have to do to know I'm telling you the truth is to look at my cramped handwriting. No one having fun would have penmanship like that, and do you think it was a jeroboam of laughs keeping those single sentences snaking down the page, punctuation mark after punctuation mark—like this attenuated sentence I'm putting together right now, semicolon—until I finished what I considered a complete thought? No, that's over and done with, thank you very much, *bien merci*. No more writing for me. *C'est fini*. I'm here to do something else for someone or someones. You seem to be the one."

He fixed me with another of his intense gazes, as if he were trying to see into the deep recesses of my brain for some ardent but timid desire waiting to surface.

Now put yourself in my place. Marcel Proust comes back and offers to do anything you want him to do just because you give him a casual thought while having a madeleine with your afternoon tea. (I was drinking herbal tea, but I just throw that in.) What do you do? Your mind starts spinning, I'll tell you that much.

Mine was spinning like a gyroscope, but nothing spun centrifugally from it. I wasn't about to ask M. Proust to make me rich and famous. I was already rich—the trust fund, you know. And I had no interest in being famous. Judging from his seven volumes, even he couldn't guarantee I wouldn't be miserable along with it. There are already enough of the other rich and unfortunately famous for me not to want to be counted among them. Do I want to attend one more charity ball with a bunch of bulemic women in complicated Proenza Schouler confections? Do I want to attend galas with a handful of movie stars and their current-but-days-numbered spouses, with a group of snickering walkers, with arrivistes hoping to break into society?

I don't. So after thinking it over for a few minutes—with Marcel Proust looking at me as if he were contemplating *Du coté de chez Shipley*—I couldn't come up with anything.

I could only come up with a big fat *rien de tout*. I said, "There's really nothing I need done at the moment." That came out sounding ungrateful. Better amend it. "I suppose what you could do for me is tell me the meaning of life. You get very close in your books. But for now the pleasure of your company definitely suffices."

"My company has not always been accounted pleasant," he said. "You can ask anyone." He looked around. "Not anyone here, of course." He continued looking, and as he scanned the patisserie, he said without looking at me, "If I can't do anything for you, perhaps I can do something for someone else here. Maybe someone else needs my attention."

The someone elses here included three women sitting across the room with shopping bags by their chairs. I took them for friends having a chat, and it looked as if one was having a birthday. What appeared to be unwrapped presents and their trimmings had been pushed aside by the tea things and tiny cakes.

They hadn't ordered madeleines.

I looked at the other two patrons sitting closer to us. They were a girl and boy, whom I took to be seventeen or eighteen. They were on a settee with their tea and cakes in front of them. They were dressed as contemporary seventeen- or eighteen-year-olds dress: jeans, clunky shoes and black jackets over T-shirts with slogans on them too faded to read from where I was. They were leaning into one another, giggling.

I noticed Marcel Proust was also looking at them closely, examining them almost as if he were holding a magnifying glass. Or a lorgnette.

I wouldn't have said they were that interesting, but his interest piqued mine further. The girl wasn't the sort I'd have thought other girls her age would have considered pretty, although they surely would have regarded her as noticeable and made a point of avoiding her or be considered uncool by their judgmental friends. She had ginger hair that shot out five or six inches like springs from an old mattress. She had freckles spread across her nose and a wide mouth, on which she'd applied lipstick the color of unripe plums. She was only slightly overweight but thought herself compensating for it by wearing tight hose with runs in both legs. An opening at the ankle on her right leg revealed part of a tattooed heart.

The boy was smaller. His hair marked him as once being a tow-head, a tow-head now darkened. The hair was tousled and flopped over his forehead and ears. It was difficult to tell much about his arms in the black jacket hanging open—although his hands were busy. What could be seen below his cropped trousers suggested his legs were plump and that even at whatever age he was, he hadn't yet lost his baby fat and never would. His face was round and his eyes were wide under dark eyebrows. He had a stub of a nose and a mouth that was slightly pursed—poised as if to say something *risqué*.

In short, picture an all-American boy, then picture the opposite. That gives some idea of what he looked like—not quite decadent, but as if he had more on his mind than hewing to a strict moral code. It was a look I'd seen before but couldn't place.

M. Proust continued to observe them and his admonitory finger was up in my direction again, but I understood it was meant to keep me silent me for a different reason. He didn't want to be interrupted while watching and, it seemed, cogitating.

We sat like that for perhaps another minute, and I took the opportunity to sip more of my tisane and finish off the first madeleine. I also had time to note to myself that it was unnecessary to think about Marcel Proust while ingesting, since Marcel Proust was right there with me.

I also had the odd thought that in the future whenever I had tea and a madeleine, I might again conjure him—and again and again. Was I in for an endless series of visits from Marcel Proust and an equal number of challenges as to how to entertain him? In my current state of worried mind, did I want that? Could I avoid his sojourns by eliminating the madeleine? Could I do it by never frequenting Madeleine Patisserie again, even though it was the only French teahouse in my neighborhood and therefore a valuable asset?

The baroque thought train was halted, however, when *mon ami nouveau* (pardon my French) turned away from the boy and girl and back to me. "They're talking about people they know," he said.

I was poised to ask him how he knew that, but the finger again. "Don't ask me how I know this," he said. "You have read my turgid masterpiece. So have I—read it in many translations now—and I know gossip when I see it. I always did. You will not contradict me when I say gossip is my specialty. I'm not wrong about those two." He nodded so slightly in their direction. An onlooker—of which there were none—could have taken the movement for a neurasthenia tremor. "Look at them," he demanded.

I did his bidding. The two—whom I assumed were high school students playing hooky—were giggling again with their heads and bodies still bent conspiratorially towards each other. When they stopped the giggling, the boy resumed talking. The pursed mouth with its tinge of mischievousness was moving quickly.

That's when it struck me where I had seen the face before. This boy looked like Truman Capote. No, no, no. He wasn't Truman Capote, not in the way the man next to me was—*definitely* was—Marcel Proust. But there was a similarity between the boy with the tousled blond hair hanging over his brow and the young Truman Capote whom Irving Penn photographed at twenty-three supine on a couch and looking like a sullen angel.

I thought, How odd that Marcel Proust and a kid who reminded me of Truman Capote should be in the same room? I said nothing.

"Something is drawing me to that boy," M. Proust said, "and the girl, too."

Just as he said that, the boy and girl fell into another rapture of giggles, the decibel-level volume of which seemed to alert them for the first time to the possibility of others becoming aware of them.

They stopped giggling at that exact moment and looked around the room. They saw us looking at them, but rather than exhibit any interest in us or anything approaching embarrassment or contrition, they each assumed the sort of disdainful expression only teenagers can affect. When they had beamed their looks at us long enough to suit them, they turned back to their banter.

"I must speak to them," M. Proust said, engaging me once again.

I engaged him, too, and we sat like that—looking at each other—for the minute or less it took for me to realize his "I must speak to them" was a request for me, a command even, to approach the teenagers and invite them over for an audience.

This, of course, felt less like Marcel Proust doing for me—as he had offered earlier—than my doing for him. But he was who he was, and I wasn't going to sit there having some kind of silent face-off with him.

"Are you certain?" I asked. "You said you did not want people— other than myself—aware of you."

"I am ready now," he said and arranged himself slightly, as a monarch on a throne might. "I have the unusual sense I am now needed."

He looked to be in complete earnestness. So I rose and took the four or five steps across to the teens. I could tell they were aware of my proximity but were going to ignore me. I assumed they expected I was going to admonish them for being loud. It occurred to me that teachers must have accosted them often for disruptions. I expected they were thinking they might have to accede to teachers but not to just anyone elsewhere, certainly not parents or any adult presuming to act *in loco parentis*.

"Excuse me," I said, "I don't mean to interrupt, b—"

"You are interrupting," the girl said, interrupting me.

I was inclined to let it go at that and turned back momentarily to M. Proust, who still looked utterly self-possessed and was watching my transaction intently. I decided to forge on. "Yes, I am," I said, "and I apologize for that, but there is a gentleman here who would like to speak to you and your friend."

I indicated Marcel Proust.

The girl looked over, sized the returned-from-the-deceased novelist-essayist up and down and said to me but aimed at him, "What if we wouldn't like to speak to him?"

She put the "like" into quotes hung with moist sarcasm and was ready to go back to ignoring me when she—and then I—caught sight of the boy. He had looked over at Marcel Proust and was now staring in that direction. I couldn't tell whether it was a sarcastic gaze to match the girl's tone of voice or whether it was outright flirtation. I could tell there was something unmissably louche about it.

It was then I realized the boy was wearing very light eyeliner.

There was an even more startling revelation to come, thanks to this precocious cherub, but for the moment he turned to his friend and said, "Oh, let's. Come on, Brooke, he seems harmless."

Brooke gave out with a billowing sigh and said, "All right, Hodge-Podge. Whatever you say, but it's your funeral."

I had to laugh at the word "funeral," which was something of a mistake on my part, because Brooke looked at me and said with a slap-worthy smirk, "What are you laughing at?"

"A private joke," I said. "Now, if you'd care to join us."

She wasn't through. "I don't care to, but Hodgey-Podgey does. So we will."

They both made a big deal of picking up their teacups and saucers, madeleine plates and book bags and bringing them over to our table. Since there were two other unoccupied white wicker chairs near enough to our table, there wasn't much furniture shuffling involved.

When they were seated, she with barely concealed intolerance and he with something lascivious about the play of his features, I said, "Perhaps we should all introduce ourselves." I said who I was and started to say, "And this is Mar—" But I stopped, because as I was indicating Monsieur, he made an all but imperceptible nod that I took to mean he didn't want his name mentioned. Instead, I slurred into "—Mar, uh, my friend, and you are?"

"I'm Hodge Hewitt," the boy said. "She calls me Hodge-Podge. Hodge is a family name. I like it, actually. And she's Brooke Warshawski."

That's when Marcel Proust did something I saw as inspired—but, of course, he was celebrated for inspiration, wasn't he? He took both of them in (in more ways than one) and said, "I am delighted to make your acquaintance, *Mademoiselle* Warshawski and *Monsieur* Hewitt."

From their reaction, it was clear to me that neither of these kids had ever had their acquaintance instill anything approaching delight in another human being. I would have said the opposite. They were both so thrown at this instance of politesse—"politesse" being a concept that probably eluded them entirely until that moment—that they could only look at each other in bewilderment.

Being addressed with French honorifics also caught them with their figurative faded jeans down. "You're French," Hodge said and as he did, everything guarded and naughty about his manner dropped away.

"Yes," M. Proust said.

"That explains your clothes," Brooke said. Her guard hadn't yet fallen, although it was lowering slowly.

"I am not certain what explains yours," M. Proust said.

"But you're not speaking French," Hodge said.

"I have learned English," M. Proust said.

"I took French sophomore and junior year," Hodge said, "but I wasn't very good at it. *Comment allez-vous?*"

"*Très bien, et vous, mon cher jeune homme?*" M. Proust replied.

"Wow," Hodge said. "I never got to speak French to a real French person before." With that he leaned back triumphantly in his chair and his black jacket fell open to reveal his T-shirt, thereby exposing astonishing revelation number two. We could read the slogan on his T-shirt—except it wasn't a mere slogan. It said—I kid you not—"*Longtemps je me suis couché de bonne heure—Marcel Proust.*"

Both Marcel Proust and I recognized it instantly as the first line of "*A la recherche du temps perdu.*" Marcel Proust recognized it, of course, because he wrote it. But I did as well, because I'd read it and also used it with my many hoity-toity friends when playing "Name the First Line."

Incidentally, we could also read what Brooke's T-shirt honked— "Screw Now, Talk Later." Ignoring hers, M. Proust said to the Hewitt boy,

"That's a very interesting T-shirt. Where did you get it?"

"I found it in a bin at a vintage clothing store on Broadway. Do you like it?" Hodge asked. He turned to Brooke. "See. They like it." He turned to us. "She doesn't like it."

"What's to like?" Brooke wanted to know. "Some remark some dead French guy said. '*Voulez-vous coucher avec moi?*' That line, like, went out with the hula hoop. So lame."

Her comment sent Marcel Proust into a neurasthenic paroxysm. I thought he was going to collapse or, worse, evaporate. I went to lift his teacup to him, but he waved me off and regained enough of his composure to ask Hodge-Podge, "Do you know what the words mean?"

Hodge tightened his eyes to make us assume he was thinking and, after what he considered a sufficient pause, said, "I told you I was, like, not too good at French—something about sleeping for a long time, I think."

Brooke's curiosity had been aroused. She took another look at the T-shirt and read "*de bonne heure*" aloud to us. "Does 'heure' mean 'whore'? Sleeping a long time with some kind of whore, maybe a good whore?"

I looked at M. Proust to see if this was going to set him off again. He maintained his equanimity and said, "It means 'For a long time I went to bed early.'"

"'Went to bed early,'" Brooke said, thoroughly flummoxed. "How dull is that? Like, who wants to go to bed early? The best clubs don't get going until two in the morning."

If M. Proust was thrown by her idiotic comment, he didn't show it. He said, "The line is attributed to a child at the beginning of a long book about something you two young people might find intriguing."

"When was this book written?" Brooke wanted to know.

"In the early part of the last century."

"No wonder," Brooke said. "The dark ages." Expecting confederacy, she looked to Hodge. It wasn't forthcoming. Whereas she had only been disarmed momentarily, he was now all ears—not that under the tumbling hair we could see much of his ears.

He spoke to M. Proust. "What's, like, intriguing about the book?"

"Before I answer you," M. Proust said, "I'm going to ask you a question. Earlier, when the two of you were sitting over there, you were gossiping, weren't you?"

This nonplused our young companions, who blurted out more or less in unison, "How did you know that?"

"I am a practiced observer of human behavior. I recognize gossiping merely by the way bodies move, mouths, eyes."

Brooke said, "So what? There's nothing wrong with gossip. Everybody does it."

"Everybody does it," Hodge chimed in.

"I did not say anything was wrong with gossip," Marcel Proust said. "Gossip can be a vital component of human expression."

"Well then?" Brooke said. Complacency sat on her face like a toad on a lily pad.

"*If*," M. Proust said, making a very big thing of the "if," "it is done well."

"What do you mean, 'if it's done well?'" Hodge asked.

"I see excellence is not a quality to which you have given much thought, but it must be pursued in all things," Marcel Proust said.

Brooke was about to speak, but now it was she who received the raised-finger warning. "Let me tell you the subject of your gossip. You were talking about your schoolmates, were you not? You were talking about what they have said to you and what you have *overheard* them say about you to others. You were talking about what you know of them that others do not know and that perhaps they do not know about themselves. You were talking of petty situations. I am correct, am I not?"

Through this brief speech, Hodge and Brooke had been struck silent. The most they had done was look at each other with awe. At M. Proust's question, they looked at each other to see which of them should answer, but M. Proust waved a finger at them.

"I do not need to know the particulars. I do not want to know what Francois is doing behind the back of Francoise, when Jean-Claude has had his way with Jeanne-Claude, how Pierre has tricked his parents Pierrot and Pierette into believing his lies. At your age, all young people talk about the same things—clandestine love affairs, possible pregnancies, drug use and abuse, cheating on examinations, who likes and dislikes whom."

Hodge and Brooke were nodding their heads, solemnly. They both had the appearance of children who had been found out. Visibly scrapping up the nerve to talk, Hodge said, "But that's the fun of it. That's what gossip is."

Brooke echoed, "That's what people do when they gossip."

"That is what you think they do," Marcel Proust said, "and that is how it was no challenge for me to discern what you were doing. You think of gossip as fun, as a pastime. Sometimes—you will correct me if I am wrong—you use gossip as revenge for imagined or real wrongs." He waited for a reaction.

Hodge and Brooke shifted in their chairs but said nothing.

M. Proust went on. "You are not entirely wrong. Gossip can be an amusing pastime, but—and pay close attention to me, my young friends—for gossip to have any meaning at all, it must be raised to an art. Oh, yes, gossiping well is not only a high art, it is the best revenge." He pointed at Hodge's T-shirt. "That is what Marcel Proust knew, and that is what I know."

At the moment, Brooke had nothing to say in response, but Hodge—his round Truman Capote face suddenly alive with anticipation and possibility—said, "How do you do that? How do you raise gossip to an art?"

Marcel Proust pulled himself up, although neurasthenically, and I realized that with the question he'd just posed, Hodge had unwittingly asked for a master class in gossip.

"You must realize," M. Proust began, "that underlying the urge—I might even say the instinct—to gossip is the creditable, although sometimes discredited, desire to know about one's fellow man and woman. It is in our nature to know and understand one another in order to form a social community, a society. And what I know about society would fill volumes—seven volumes to be exact. Do you take my meaning?"

Hodge nodded yes vigorously. Brooke, who had turned away from Monsieur slightly to keep up a show of distance, was listening closely, all the same.

M. Proust continued lecturing. "To know and understand others, then, requires a broad understanding of psychology. Why do people do what they do, think what they think, feel what they feel? To gossip with any authority calls for honing other skills—how to listen well, not just for what people say but for what they reveal through what they don't say. An expert gossip must be an expert observer, always on the *qui vive*. Do you know what I mean by 'qui vive'?"

Hodge nodded no vigorously. Brooke, still turned away but only slightly less so, shook her ginger-frizzed head just the least bit.

M. Proust continued. "It means the expert gossip is always on the alert for tips, cues, clues about other people. But the most important element in a gossip's makeup is an emotional one. A gossip worthy of the name must have passion. Passion is essential in every aspect of life, and that includes gossip—the passion to pursue the activity of gossiping well. Without passion, the aspiring gossip is nothing but that basest of base beggars—a tattletale."

He looked at Hodge and then at Brooke with such command that she finally engaged him, showing as much humility as perhaps she had shown anyone since her estrogen started kicking in.

M. Proust addressed them gravely. "You would not want to be thought of as a pair of tattletales, would you?"

Hodge nodded no so vigorously I thought his head might spin around entirely. Brooke nodded less dramatically.

But it was plain she was absorbing Marcel Proust's sentiments, which he continued by saying, "A supreme gossip combines the respectable crafts of the psychologist and the sociologist, the biographer and the historian. A good gossip is the chronicler of his time."

He aimed the end of that sentence at Hodge, and I could see he realized he had a hooked auditor. Not wanting to leave Brooke out, however, he turned his gaze and said, "Or of *her* time. And writing the chronicles of an age is no small matter. Do not ask how I know. Take it on faith."

With that, M. Proust paused, and as Brooke had been the last one of the two addressed, she spoke first. "I get it. It takes a lot to be a good gossip. If it'll make you feel any better, I'll never gossip again. There's too much to learn. I'd rather spend my time doing something else, like going to beauty school and figuring out how to treat split ends. There's a future in that."

M. Proust listened to what she had to say. I couldn't tell whether he knew what split ends were, but he said, "It is your prerogative. I have been meaning to ask you if you know whether you are related to an acquaintance of mine, the Comtesse Maria Eléna Beatrice de Warshawski."

"I don't know anything about that," Brooke said. "My parents never talk about family. They don't speak to most of them. I know I have an Aunt Bea in Detroit, but I don't know anything about her."

"I only ask," M. Proust said, "because her hair was the same color and the same consistency as yours. She was considered a beauty in her youth. Perhaps you are related."

Did he mean this? Was he making it up? I wondered about his sincerity, but Brooke did not. She touched her hair. She said, "Maybe I am" and fell into a reverie. I could see the equivalent of carriage rides through the Bois de Boulogne dancing in her eyes.

Now the *maître* rounded on Hodge, who was also deep in thought. "And you?" he asked. "Do you no longer feel the impulse to gossip?"

Hodge snapped out of himself. He looked as if he were having trouble finding his tongue. When he did, he said, "Oh, no, I do, I do."

Brooke looked at him as if he had lost his marbles, shrugged and said, "Whatever."

Hodge paid her no mind but went on. "I think that all sounds excellent. I'd love to be able to do it really, really well."

"Then you must get started," M. Proust said. "I suggest the first thing you do is read the book that follows the sentence you're wearing on your chest."

"I will," Hodge said. "I will. I can find it in any book store, can't I?"

"I do not know," M. Proust said. "I have not been at a bookseller's in a while. But perhaps you can."

Hodge said to Brooke, "Come on, Brooke. We're going."

Brooke looked as if she had little time for this. "I didn't cut class to go to a bookstore," she said, "but okay."

Hodge started to get up but sat back down again. "Is there anything else I need to know?" he asked Marcel Proust.

M. Proust lifted his finger to his mouth again but this time in sober thought. His mustache twitched. "No," he replied, "I don't think so. You know enough to begin. I wish you good luck. Both of you."

This last was spoken like a dismissal.

Hodge got up again and said, "Come on, Brooke. Let's go." She obeyed him but not without heaving a sigh somehow less laden with juvenile chagrin than her earlier exclamations had been. She slung her book bag over her broad shoulder. Hodge strapped his on his back.

They headed towards the door where they turned around to look at us—at Marcel Proust more than me, of course. "Thanks, sir," Hodge shot back, and Brooke added, "Yeah. Like he said."

I looked to see how M. Proust had received the farewells. I can't say with absolute conviction, but I think I saw a neurasthenic smile flicker across his lips.

I turned back to watch Hodge Hewitt and possible Comtesse de Warshawski descendent Brooke Warshawski disappear from view. Then I turned back to pick up the conversation with M. Proust.

"As for you, Monsieur Shipley, I have a simple sentence. I am capable of them. The meaning of life is what you give it."

I lowered my head to think that over, and when I looked up again, Marcel Proust wasn't there. He was gone. Not only was he gone but gone also were his teacup, saucer and plate of the one madeleine that had remained. I looked around the room to see if anyone else had noticed anything. The proprietors and staff were still fully occupied at the counter. The three women friends were studying swatches of material. One of them was evidently planning to reupholster something.

I was sitting by myself, knowing that Marcel Proust had just been there, knowing that Hodge Hewitt and Brooke Warshawski had just been there—or thinking I knew it. Marcel Proust had appeared because I'd thought of him while sipping tea and eating a madeleine. He'd come to do something for me.

Or on second thought, had he come to do something for Hodge? After all, it was Hodge who was drinking tea and eating a madeleine and wearing the T-shirt that said, "*Longtemps je me suis couché de bonne heure.*"

How could I be sure that any of it had happened?

Perhaps I'll have to wait until I see some fabulous piece of gossip in print under the Hodge Hewitt byline. I finished my second madeleine—

nothing happened—and left. Since then, however, I think about what Marcel Proust did for me: reminded me that the meaning of life is what I bring to it. And I had the unusual thought that where life was concerned, I had taken plenty from it but hadn't yet brought much to it. I can think of worse madeleine-instigated lessons. Maybe I had conjured M. Proust, after all.

Marshall Faber's Story

※ or ※

Some Happenings at Harry's Haberdashery

"We can never tell what is in store for us."

—Harry S. Truman

When I entered the store just a few steps south of the Pearl Street Mall one Boulder, Colorado, morning in April, I noticed the name on the awning—"Harry's Haberdashery"—but paid it no more than cursory attention. I also noticed the emblazoned slogan—"The buck goes farther here"—but that didn't strike a particularly resonant chord, either.

It wasn't until I heard a dull front-door ding-dong sound and saw what I took to be the proprietor appearing through a mirrored door at the rear of the shop and saying, "Why, hello" that I did a triple take worthy of Bert Lahr in one of his comedy routines.

I might just as audibly have exclaimed "Nong-nong-nong," I was that flabbergasted. The man looked so much like President Harry S. Truman that, had I not known he'd long gone to the great White House in the sky, I would have sworn on an elaborate Torah this was the very man himself.

Of course, he was, wasn't he? "How can I help you?" he asked with a smile that creased the corners of his eyes behind small, round spectacles and deepened the lines along the sides of his mouth.

Gathering my scattered wits about me, I replied, "I need some shirts. You know, a couple dress shirts, maybe something less formal. I'm at a conference here that's going on for a few days, and the only shirt I have is the one on my back. I forgot to pack any others. I don't know how I forgot to put shirts in, but I did."

Truth is, I know how I forgot: I was preoccupied with other matters, like what a fifty-four-year-old psychologist was going to say to a group of trial lawyers about jury selection that would actually mean something to them. I'd accepted the invitation to speak without thinking and subsequently wasted too much time wondering why. I didn't want to hash over the expected material—how to read character by demeanor, by dress, by nuances of response. The conferees would already have digested those tips.

The recognizable proprietor in front of me didn't need to know all that, but I was babbling on at an unusually rapid pace because the more I looked at him—that smile he held in place as he surveyed me for, I presumed, shirt size—the more he looked like President Truman beaming at photographers during his years in office.

The former President stopped my blather by saying, "I've got what you want—sixteen, thirty-four, I'm guessing."

"Yes," I said. He knew his stuff. "Sixteen, thirty-four on the nose, but not the slim-fit kind." I know my body. "Sometimes still fifteen and a half, depending on the cut."

"I'm rarely wrong," he said. Now he was looking at my face and not my neck, chest or waist. "You think you know who I am, don't you?"

He'd caught me staring and not just returning his look as you do in ordinary conversation. I gazed around as if to check whether anyone else who could pass for staff was nearby: no one. To be on the safe side I said, "I'm going to assume you're the Harry of Harry's Haberdashery."

"I am," he said, "but that's only part of it, isn't it?" He chuckled. I pulled a blank look, as if I had no idea what he was on about. He kept smiling and said, "You think I look like former President Harry S. Truman, don't you?"

I made as if to give him a closer look and then said, "No. No, not really." I wasn't going to concede without some stalling.

He eyed me and said, "Come on now. You can't fool a fooler."

What was my alternative? I saw there was no way around this. I'd just better go along with it. I said, as if I were giving him a more thorough second look, "Wow. Hey. Yes. There is a resemblance. Now that I look at you."

As a psychologist I wasn't ordinarily this coy, but this wasn't an ordinary chat.

He chuckled again, and I noticed he chuckled more from one side of his mouth than the other. "No, that's not it. You think there's more than a passing resemblance. I've seen the expression on your face enough times on other faces to know when someone takes me for who I am. You'd be surprised how many don't. Or maybe you wouldn't, time having moved on. It doesn't surprise me anymore."

I was so dumbfounded by these remarks that for all I was able to respond, he might have been speaking Urdu.

He picked up on my half-stupor and said, opening his arms to almost their full length and pulling himself up to what I figured was approximately a five-foot-nine-inch height, "Yes, I'm Harry S. Truman. As I repeated many times, 'We can never tell what is in store for us.' In this instance, we can never tell what is in the store for us." He put a puckish emphasis on the word "in." "This time I'm what's in store for you—in this store for you and ready to serve."

I've never known what the word "twinkle" means when it's invoked in connection with the eye, but I'd have to say at that moment there was something others might have called a twinkle in his eye.

"I'm ready to serve," he went on, "in a less serious capacity than I was prepared to serve during long periods of my previous life. The great Presidents—of whom I don't include myself—were always ready to serve. I only followed their lead as dutifully as I knew how."

I continued to react as if the cat had not simply gotten my tongue but had absconded with it to some remote bag.

"You're wondering why I'm here," he said. He spread his arms again and waved them in a near circle to indicate a wide space I took to represent the greater arena often called "the here and now."

"And why I'm *here*." Now he pointed a finger at the floor to indicate the establishment in which we were both standing—him with his brown-and-white spectator shoes firmly planted on the darkly stained floorboards and me feeling as if my knees might buckle at any second. "I'll tell you why I'm here, and then we'll see to those shirts you need."

We were standing in almost the exact middle of the store, which, I've neglected to mention, was maybe twenty feet wide. On both sides of us were long display-case countertops under which standard haberdashery inventory was displayed—sweaters, socks, ties, cufflinks, tie pins, assorted watches, those sorts of things. Behind the display cases, stretching the length of the store to my left were shelves built into wood stained a mahogany shade. To my right, the shelves only stretched halfway towards the back. Immediately beyond them in niches, suits, blazers and trousers hung on wooden poles. Just beyond them was an area where shoes sat on lower shelves behind four upholstered chairs with, in front of one of the chairs, a low stool next to which was one of those old-fangled metal foot-measuring devices.

Standing at attention at several spots on the counters were half-manikins cut off at the neck and upper thigh and kitted out in the latest conservative and not-so-conservative styles. One of the broad-chested manikins wore a bold-patterned sports shirt of the sort that, I remembered, had come to be called "Harry Truman shirts." (Check the December 18, 1951, cover of Life magazine.) On the far end of the counter to my right was a tray holding a half-dozen flacons of men's cologne. Whether or not it was due to one or more of those colognes, the room had a distinctively woodsy—I think that's how the perfume trade would put it—aroma that included what I took to be a few less woodsy Oval Office notes.

I've also neglected to mention how—all right, I have to go along with it—President Truman was dressed. In addition to the brown-and-white spectator shoes, he was wearing loose, light-colored Sansabelt gabardine slacks and one of those Harry Truman shirts—the pattern featuring replicas of travel decals, the kind that at one time were regularly slapped on steamer trunks. I would have testified that at least one of the repeated decals said "Potsdam." He also wore spectacles that magnified his blue eyes.

All in all, he was informal yet dapper, which is nothing less than he might be expected to be, if you recall snapshots of him, which maybe too few people do recall anymore.

"From my study of history," he said, as he pointed at the chairs at the rear of the store and led us to them, "and, in particular, the history of the American Presidency—I came to believe that it takes about forty years for the more definitive verdict to come in on any President's administration."

He motioned me into one of the worn but still plush seats and took the one next to it, smiling as he did so. "As it neared the fortieth anniversary of my death," he continued, "I decided I wanted to ascertain what my reputation had amounted to and so opted to make a return visit. You know we can do that."

I didn't know, although I didn't bother to say so.

He gave me a look of benign reassurance, something I remembered from his repertoire as recorded in newspaper and television coverage when I was a kid. "And so I decided to return as the owner of a men's clothing store. I had what I considered a few good reasons. First, I'd had a haberdashery store in the late teens, early nineteen-twenties, as was well known. I'd enjoyed it immensely, although it didn't go so smoothly. Immediately after the First World War—that darned fracas—my partner Eddie Jacobson and I did well enough, but business quickly fell off. The next thing we knew, we were bankrupt and in debt, not something that pleased Bess or her mother, Mother Wallace. Now, there was a woman for you.

"I wanted to have a second chance to make it go right. More than that, though, I reckoned a store has customers coming and going. So, rather than walking around polling people in the streets—despite my enjoyment of a daily constitutional—I'd let them come to me somewhere I could quiz them while using less direct methods.

"Why did I choose Boulder, you might ask, when I could have gone back to Kansas City—even to 104 West Twelfth Street in Kansas City, where the Truman and Jacobson Haberdashery was located? Simple. I thought I was likely to encounter more tourists and therefore have a wider range of responses in a town like Boulder. Was I right? Was I wrong? It doesn't matter."

He shrugged his shoulders with one of the most assured shrugs I'd ever witnessed.

"Now to those shirts. Later I'll find out more specifically where you stand on me as President. So far you haven't made an obscene gesture and walked out. So I'm going to go ahead and imagine you're not harboring a severely negative attitude."

He rose with the spring of a man younger than whatever age he was.

(Although in my profession you learn to size people up for age and temperament, I have no idea how you gauge heavenly years. And, yes, as someone who hadn't as yet come to any conclusion about the after-life, despite accounts of near-death experiences from several patients, I assumed he'd returned from heaven or something like it rather than any other locale. For a moment, it did cross my buzzing mind that he might have been assigned some less hospitable zone as a result of his decision to drop the atom bomb, but I rejected the thought as not mine to speculate on. Leave that to a power much higher than that of the split atom.)

Mr. President was heading for the shelves where shirts in my size were stacked. "Let's look at the dress shirts first," he said, with me following. "You look like the type of man who'll want a white shirt, maybe a blue and—I'll bet on it and be a winner—one of my fine tattersall shirts."

He was pulling out several to match his assumptions when the front door opened to the accompanying ding-dong I'd heard when I entered the unlikely emporium. A couple came in whom I'd place in their mid-to-late twenties.

The haberdasher-President set the shirts on the counter where I was standing and said, "Why don't you look through these while I see to the new customers?"

I nodded I would, as he stepped spryly from behind the counter and went towards the newcomers with the gait of a confirmed walker. "Why, hello there," he said. "How can I help you?"

I have to admit that my need for shirts to cover the upcoming conference on the University of Boulder campus abruptly took second place to my interest in whatever action I might be privy to between Mr. Truman and the two twenty-somethings. So while I pretended to sort through the selections in front of me, I kept cheating towards the front of the store.

It took me no time to see that neither the man nor the woman appeared to recognize anything about the salesman confronting them. They were in cut-off jeans and T-shirts—the man's advertised Dollywood—and seemed more concerned with each other. They had the look of people taking a temporary time-out from an argument, the vestiges of which were exchanged glares.

The woman said, "My husband needs a tie for a wedding we're going to."

"I've got what you need," President Truman said. "Right this way." He pointed to the counters in which he had ties laid out. "What color do you think? It depends on the suit and the shirt, of course. You know, if you buy a shirt, the tie is free. All you have to do is answer a little quiz question. If you tell me who the thirty-third president of the United States was and buy a shirt, you have your pick of any tie on this top shelf."

The husband, who had been hanging back a few feet, moved up when he heard that and was about to say something, when the wife, who was a few inches taller than he, said to him, "I don't need to iron any more shirts. You want a tie, and that's that." Then she turned to Truman and said, "He doesn't want a shirt. He wants a tie. We only need to look at ties."

The husband flushed somewhat and said, "For a few extra bucks, I can have a shirt and a tie."

"Your buck goes farther here, and that's a clue," the former President said.

"We don't need to spend a few extra bucks," the wife said to Mr. Truman, although she obviously meant it for the husband. "We're already spending too much on the hotel."

The husband wasn't going to be stopped. "Jack Kennedy," he said and gloated.

"Close but no cigar," Mr. Truman said.

Glaring at her husband, the tie-hunting wife said, "Will you shut up?" She turned to Truman so abruptly that she must have hurt herself.

"So what happens now that he missed it? Does the price of the tie go up?"

"Of course not," HST said. "Harry Truman."

"What?" the wife said.

"The thirty-third President of the United States," the President said. "Harry S. Truman."

"Before our time," the wife said.

"I've heard of him," the husband said.

"To hear you tell it," the wife said to the husband, "you've heard of everything and everybody." Then she pointed at what appeared to be a tie and said, "That one. We'll take that one."

Truman opened the door behind the shelf and asked, "This one?"

"No," the wife said, "the one next to it with the red, white and blue stripes. That'll do."

Truman began to take the tie out.

"Hey," the husband said. "Don't I have a say in this?"

"You've already had your say," the wife said. "You said, 'Jack Kennedy' and almost got us into trouble." She looked over where I was and caught me tuning in. "Color-blind," she said to me, pointing at her husband with a pudgy thumb.

I pretended I'd been paying no attention by returning to the shirts piled before me. So I was only peripherally aware that the couple who maybe honeymooned in Dollywood—futilely, it would seem—paid for the red-white-and-blue-striped tie (with no shirt) and left to the sound of the front-door ding-dong.

Continuing to pretend I'd taken none of that in, I looked at Truman. He was quick-stepping towards me but turned on his spectator-shoe heel

when the ding-dong went again and a boy I took to be about ten came
in.

"Why, hello, young man," our one-time President said. "What can
we do for you today?"

I wondered if that was the Presidential "we" he was invoking or
merely the merchant's.

"I need something for my father," the boy said. He was wearing a
school uniform and thick glasses. "His birthday is tomorrow."

"It would help me," Mr. Truman said, "to know two things—what
your dad likes to wear and how much money you're prepared to spend."

The boy produced a credit card and said, "I can charge as much as I
want."

"You have a credit card?" the President said. "You're a lucky fellow.
We didn't have credit cards in my day, you know. I still don't know about
the advisability of credit cards. I'm glad to extend credit without the use
of cards."

"It's not mine," the boy said. "It's my dad's. I borrowed it."

"I see," the President said. "You want to purchase a tie on your
father's money. I'll tell you what. We're having a father's birthday special
today. I'm going to ask you a question, and if you answer it correctly, you
win a shirt and a tie, and you don't have to use your dad's credit card at
all. How does that sound?"

With all the free goods on offer, what I wanted to know was, how
does Truman account to his suppliers? But there were enough other-
worldly goings-on where I was standing—and with whom I was elbow-
rubbing—that I decided inventory reckoning was the least of it.

"Awesome," the boy said. "I hope it's an easy question."

"It's as easy as I can make it," the old-time President said. "Here goes. Complete the name of the thirty-third president of the United States. He was Harry S. blank. You fill in the blank."

From where I was, which wasn't that far from either of the quiz participants, I could see the lad screwing up his eyes behind his glasses. "Um, give me a minute," he said. "I'm thinking."

"Take all the time you want, young man," Truman said.

"Um-uh," the boy stammered and finally emitted, "Taft." It came out sounding more like "Taft?"

"No," the one-time President said, "that's William Howard Taft, and a poor President he was, too, but you get a second guess."

Again the boy—no hint in his manner explaining why he'd be wearing a school uniform on a Saturday (a class trip planned for later, perhaps?)—scrunched up his eyes behind the glasses and said but very slowly, "Truman?"

"A darn good guess, young man," the pleased proprietor said. "For getting the second guess right, you have your pick of a tie or a shirt, but if you can tell me something about President Truman, you get the tie *and* the shirt."

The boy's eyes showed nothing. His thin lips tightened more thinly.

"What years was Truman the President?" the President asked.

"I don't know," the boy said after some nose-crinkling consideration.

"But if you were to guess," Truman said, "what would you say?"

"Way before I was born," the boy said. "Maybe around nineteen seventy?" The President shook his head no. "Nineteen twenty?" the boy sputtered but with uncertainty written all over his flushed face.

"No," the President said, "but you still have your pick of a tie or a shirt."

The boy hesitated and then said, "I guess I'll get a tie. That's what all my friends get their dads."

"Good. I hope you send your friends here, too," the returned President said. "I can use the business."

The boy was peering into the showcase but said, "I will, and I better tell them to bone up on the Presidents, huh?"

"Not a bad idea," Mr. Truman said and went about the job of getting the boy the right tie. I missed much of the transaction, because the front door opened again to the familiar ding-dong.

A woman entered who I'd say was in her mid-seventies and maybe more. Aside from wearing a tailored suit, she wore a stylish fedora with a long feather. Mr. Truman also noticed her and let her know he did with a raised finger intended to signal he'd get right to her.

While he finished with the boy, she began to look around. By then I had decided on three shirts I wanted, but I was perfectly content to take my time letting the otherwise-engaged proprietor know.

Within a minute, the boy in the school uniform left, swinging the "Harry's Haberdashery" bag and looking mighty satisfied with himself. As he did, the President turned his attention to the lady with a smiling "And what can I do for you today?"

The woman was fingering suits on the suit rack. "My husband needs a new suit for the summer," she said. "He refuses to shop for himself, which is why I'm here. I thought I knew all the stores in Boulder where proper menswear is sold. None of this casual-Friday stuff. I don't believe in it. If you're at work, you dress to look as if you're working and not as if you're hanging out at the nineteenth hole."

As she said that, she fixed for a lingering few seconds on the President's short-sleeved shirt with its celebration of travel to foreign climes. Then she tugged on the sleeve of a suit she must have favored. "I like this one," she said. "Three-piece. A good three-piece summer suit is hard to find these days."

In answer to this, the President said, "Then I have glad tidings for you. Today you get a three-piece summer suit for the price of a two-piece suit. You just have to answer correctly an easy question."

The woman took no time to think this over and said, "I did not come in here to be quizzed. If I find a suit my husband agrees to try on and buy, I'm prepared to pay full price."

"So you're not prepared to name two major events that took place during the years Harry S. Truman was President of the United States?"

"Truman!" the woman said as if a drunken sailor had just hurled an obscenity at her. "I shudder at the mention of the name. When he was in office, I couldn't even look at pictures of him."

"Then you wouldn't recognize him," the President said, clearly amused.

The woman said, "I wouldn't recognize him if he were standing in front of me. I'd know Thomas Dewey in an instant. The papers said he won, and I still believe it. Dwight D. Eisenhower. There was a man you could look at. Life was worth living when he was in office. Now if you don't mind, I'd like some of the details on this suit, so I can send my husband in to try it on. His name is Granger—Rufus Hallowell Granger. The third. He's retired but I see to it he still upholds certain sartorial standards."

The former POTUS jotted down a few things on a business card he retrieved from a tray by the cash register and then insisted on seeing the woman to the door. Were I in his place, I would have shown her the door, but good.

He didn't operate that way. When he opened the door for her to pass through, she stopped and said, "I'm still surprised you're here. I thought I knew every store of this type in town."

The President said, "I'm only here recently."

"The store looks as if it's been here forever," the woman said with more than a hint of admiration in her piccolo voice.

"I'm glad you think so," the President said. "The honest truth is I took great care with that. You see, I know a good deal about trade."

He closed the door behind her and, as he returned, apologized for having kept me waiting, which is hardly how I saw it.

I supposed, however, that I'd better buy the shirts I'd selected—as he'd predicted: a white, a blue and a tattersall. He said that for my patience, I'd earned the right to have three for two, if I named his two Vice Presidents.

That was a poser.

As he was watching me through thick lenses with his piercing blue eyes, I was just about to say I thought he'd asked me a trick question, when once again the door opened, and in walked three teenage boys, chewing gum and manipulating Game Boys. Right behind them were two women in their thirties carrying shopping bags. And yet more followed them. In a matter of a few minutes, the store was cluttered with shoppers.

President Truman had his hands full.

I checked my watch. It was nearing lunchtime, and I was due at the University of Boulder campus five, ten minutes to the north, but I decided some of these customers were the lunch crowd mixing with locals and tourists. What might come to pass was too good to miss.

I picked up the shirts I had almost paid for so I wouldn't have to remain stuck where I was and began loitering with intent—the intent to overhear as much as I could.

("Alben Barkley," that's who Truman's one veep was. There weren't two vice presidents under Truman. When he completed the deceased Franklin Delano Roosevelt's fourth term, he had no replacement. But where in my left-handed man's brain that piece of near-trivia came to me from—not to disparage Barkley, of course—I have no idea. Probably from the same place where Barkley's last words were housed, uttered just before he collapsed on the floor of the Senate. He said he'd rather serve in the Senate than sit in the seats of the mighty. My father quoted the words all the time. I *can* say that if I'd wandered into a haberdashery that Barkley ran, I wouldn't recognize him.)

Holding the shirts under my arm, I floated around the store as if to scope out other merchandise, but that wasn't what I was actually doing. I was positioning myself as much as I could near enough to the President and whomever he was serving to discover the ins and outs of their reaction to him.

One sixty-ish woman with a Jewish afro said, as she examined cufflink sets, "You remind me so much of someone. I only wish I could think who it is. It's not Eddie Cantor. It's not Henny Youngman. It's not George Carlin." As Truman attended to her, she kept making the same comment more or less, sometimes adding, "It's coming to me" or "It's on the tip of my tongue." Once she said, "I know it's a comedian or a character actor. That much I'm sure of."

When Truman said he had a question for her that would get her a free tie pin to go with the cufflinks, I was sure the question would be the giveaway to who he was. The question: "What President was born in Independence, Missouri?" The woman looked him straight in the eye—well, straight in the spectacles—and said, "Ooh, I know it. It's on the tip of my tongue."

"Give up?" Truman said after going "tick-tock" a few times.

"I give up," the woman said.

"Harry S. Truman," Harry S. Truman said.

The woman brightened, "Of course, Harry S. Truman. I knew I knew it. I loved him. He was a great President, not as great as the man he followed, of course, but a nice President. 'The buck stops here,' he said."

"Yes, he did," Truman said. "I remember that, too."

"Yeah, right?" the woman said and then said she'd better hurry or she'd be late to meet her friends for lunch. She bought the cufflinks without the tie pin thrown in and left not giving Harry S. Truman more than a friendly parting glance. It wasn't a glance of recognition. It was a glance of a transaction well made.

While I circulated during that half-hour, the cufflinks-no-tie-pin lady was the closest to having some recollection of the man who sat in the White House (or in Blair House during renovations) from April 12, 1945, until January 20, 1953.

I did notice a few people look at Truman on entering and whisper something in the ear of a companion, whereupon they'd both look at him with more concentration. I had the impression a few of them twigged to the proprietor's true identity and were willing to let it go at that, but most of them grimaced in dismissal and went about their business. Some of them got to field questions that at one time would have passed for gut tests in American Civ classes but weren't so easy at this later date.

Every so often, Mr. Truman would catch my eye—he knew what I was up to—and give one of his devil-may-care shrugs. Rightly or wrongly, I took them to mean he was learning what he wanted to know about his durability in the hearts and minds of the citizenry, and that he was taking it in the confident stride he'd refined on those thousands of constitutionals for which he was famous.

I also got the impression that what he was taking on board jibed with what he'd ascertained on however many other days he'd been carrying out his post-Presidential study.

At one point, a middle-aged couple came in, looking somehow forlorn. Since I didn't want to be too obvious about my eavesdropping, I stood away from them where I only caught snatches of their conversation. I was able to put together that they were looking for a sweater for a son in some sort of trouble at school—or who they worried was about to get himself into some trouble, who was going to drop out or fail his courses.

"That stinks," I heard President Truman say and then less than a minute later, "I'm going to speak plainly to you, which my better half often tells me I do too much, but I know no other way." I heard the husband and wife—both of whom wore clean but simple clothes they wouldn't have purchased had they access to a large budget—murmur a few sentences, while casting their eyes downward. Truman then said, "If you don't seek help now from the proper school authorities, you'll be doing your son a bigger disservice."

They nodded, as if they agreed with him but weren't sure they could follow through on the advice. Trying to cheer them up, Truman gave them a free-sweater question. Having heard a number of these no-brainers by now, I recognized this as by far the easiest—"Harry S. Truman was once President of the United States, true or false?"

"True," the couple said in unison. The man said, "My father didn't vote for him, but my mother did. The woman said, "From the pictures I've seen of him, you look a little like him."

"I've been told that," Truman said.

The President wrapped the sweater for them, but when he handed it to the woman, the husband said, "We can't take it for nothing. They're the goods you're selling. I'm a farmer, and where would I be if I gave my crops away?"

Truman insisted they'd won the sweater "fair and square," but the man and the woman both refused. Truman saw what I saw, which was that this was a matter of pride for them—as well as gratitude for the suggestions he'd made about their boy.

After a few minutes' back-and-forth, the President understood where they were coming from and said he'd accept half of the sweater's retail price. Money changed hands, and they left, slightly less stoop-shouldered than when they'd arrived.

By now the lunch rush was thinning, and Mr. Truman came towards me again. I knew he was thinking I'd been there longer than anyone else and deserved his consideration, but I waved at him that I was content to wait while he saw to other customers.

He turned to a man I'd estimate was in his early twenties. The fellow had on blue jeans and a sweatshirt with a hood. Not looking at anything in particular, he stood just inside the door with his hands in the sweatshirt pouch.

Had I given him any thought, I might have said he looked furtive. I might have said he looked nervous. I might have said he had a look that was both furtive and nervous. On the other hand, he didn't look unlike many young men of his age who have god-knows-what on their mind as they shamble through their day.

This was a professional opinion, although I wouldn't have offered it without giving it further thought. But I wasn't being asked.

So it wasn't until he moved a few more steps into the store and pulled out a pistol—what I had no way of knowing was the readily available Glock 17—that I got the import of a furtive-nervous look about which, as a professional, I should have been more suspicious.

In a quavering voice, he told us all that no one would get hurt as long as everyone remained quiet and the proprietor turned over all the money in his cash register. Then, still watching us and pointing the gun back and forth in an all-encompassing horizontal arc, he retreated towards the front door, turned the "Closed" sign so it faced outward and quickly bolted the door.

As he did this, there was a disturbing hush among the—I counted—eight of us, nine including the President, standing as still as the manikins on the counters. All of us, that is, except the proprietor-President, who started walking towards the young gunman.

"Stay where you are, or I'll shoot," the fellow said in his trembling voice, and the thought that raced through my head was there are some situations in which you only hear clichés, and take it from me, in my office I've heard my share of clichés over the years.

"I can't do that, young man," the President said. "I have lived a life knowing that any minute someone could point a gun at me. I know that when your time is up, your time is up. Mine has been up for quite a while now. As a matter of God's honest truth, this isn't the first time my life has been threatened, but it may be the first time for my customers. Let me tell you it's a darn scary thing. So I'm going to have to ask you to hand me the gun."

He continued advancing and was now only about six feet from the young man, who kept the clichés coming, if not yet the bullets. He blurted, "Stop where you are, or I'll shoot."

The President stopped then and said, "I'll tell you what. If you put the gun away and answer a question I put to you, I'll outfit you so you can go out and get yourself a proper job. What do you say to that?"

Evidently, the statement was so unexpected that the young man was thrown. It seemed clear to me—and likely to the others, who were quiet as statues—that the prospect of a job obtained through professional appearance was something the young man found worth thinking over. Which he was doing. At the moment, he appeared to forget about the gun.

His hand was still shaking noticeably as he inadvertently began lowering it, but he recovered himself and raised it again, saying, "What's the question?"

Mr. Truman smiled and said, "During the administration of President Harry S. Truman, what major international conflict took place?"

The young man took no more than a split-second to say, "That's it? That's the question? Nothing to it. The Korean War, although it was never officially designated as a war. It was called 'a police action' to avoid the President needing to get Congress to make a declaration of war. From the reading I've done, it was pretty obvious Truman did exactly what needed to be done in the circumstances."

The hush that had filled the store suddenly altered. It felt as if the young man had thrown us all as much off guard with his reply as he had when he first produced the weapon.

"I got it right," he said, "didn't I?"

"Yes," the President said, "you did."

"I know I did," the young man said. "Ask me anything about Truman, and I'll get it right. I know a lot about him—and other Presidents, too. I'm big on Presidents. Go on, ask me anything."

He was so cock-sure in this small victory that he must have flexed his hands, because suddenly his gun—also cocked and still pointed at the Harry's Haberdashery owner—went off. We all gasped, and one of the three women screamed. We'd been watching the young man revel in his success, but instantly we turned to look at the President.

Although the gun had been aimed at him, he was standing unharmed. Most likely, the young man's flexing hand had shifted just enough for him to miss his declared target. Possibly, there was another explanation, because the mirror on the door directly behind the President had shattered.

The young man was so alarmed that he dropped the gun like a hot potato—or like a hot pistol, which it very well might have been. (Hot, in a couple senses of the term.) When he did that, the President walked over and picked it up.

The young man immediately put his hands in the air, which none of the rest of us had thought to do earlier.

"There'll be no need for that, son," Mr. Truman said. "I'll just put this away." He referred to the Glock 17, of course. "And then we'll take care of finding some nice clothes for you."

He was walking behind one of the counters where he pulled out a white linen handkerchief and started rubbing the pistol—to remove fingerprints, it appeared.

While he did that, he went on to the young man: "Now you'll do me the favor of apologizing to the customers." He indicated all of us. "Then you'll go to the back of the store and get a broom and dustpan and pick up the pieces of that mirror while I see to these customers' purchases. Then while I outfit you, you'll tell me how you came to know so much about the Presidents of our great country, and I'll tell you how I came to know so much about them."

Perhaps anticipating the main questions the rest of us might have been about to ask, the ex-Prez said, "I know you won't try to run out the back entrance, because if you do, I have my ways of finding you. We're not that far here from Boulder Police Headquarters, and Detective Ginnie Piddock there is a good buddy of mine."

With that, the one-time Commander in Chief pointed the young man to the back of the store. The young man obliged. While he disappeared and then when he returned—broom in one hand, dustpan in the other—the President saw to our needs and, having turned his "Open/Closed" sign around again, he accompanied us to the door. To each of us, he made a few reassuring remarks about what we'd just witnessed and how he had everything under control.

I hung back until the last, and nodded when he said to me, "My experiences have taught me that I must be ready for all contingencies."

We shook hands and he closed the door behind me. I heard the ding-dong faintly. I gave him one last look through the door's window and saw him heading towards the young man, who was waiting patiently by one of the worn club chairs.

A new customer brushed past me on his way in.

And that's how I met and shook hands with President Harry S. Truman.

But before I drop the subject, two last things:

First thing, a question (good for no free items): Was Harry S. Truman ever the object of an assassination attempt?

Answer: Yes. On Wednesday, November 1, 1950, two Puerto Rican nationalists approached Blair House, where the Trumans were temporarily housed. The men exchanged fatal gunshots with security guards. The President, napping upstairs, escaped harm.

Second thing, an answer to what I was going to say in that auditorium full of trial lawyers about whom I'd been so apprehensive: I'd focus on psychological ways of disarming hostile witnesses and defendants— figuratively and sometimes, if it should become necessary, literally.

Ted Prentiss's Story

or

Jane Austen Meets Her Match in Three Minutes

"I might establish a dating service," Jane Austen said to me, a guy who's always had trouble approaching women, "but then again, it is just an idle thought."

Yes, it's *that* Jane Austen speaking, *the* Jane Austen.

Why shouldn't she be? She had every right to, and I had every right to respond, whatever my romantic history—or lack of it. Not only that, but she wasn't proving to be noticeably modulated in her address, as I might have expected she would be. Her speech was clipped, close attention paid to final consonants. Her tone was emphatic, though not all the way to harsh.

To be exact, I was registering this shortly after we had embarked on an entertaining exchange at the Barnes & Noble branch on Manhattan's Union Square. I was there looking for—then at and on—the Paul Auster shelf, or partial shelf, which ought satisfactorily to explain: (1) that I wasn't there looking for Jane Austen or thinking about her at all, and (2) why I had to make my way around a woman in a smocked dress and delicate tea-cozy-like cap as I worked along alphabetically.

If I weren't the type of person who has to know what other people are reading or contemplating reading (that I could recommend or recommend against), I might not have even noticed Miss Austen as anything other than someone standing between me and my destination.

But I *am* that type. Since it's easier for me to bury my nose in a book rather than go out on Saturday night, talking about books is just about the only situation in which I'd start a conversation with a woman.

So when I'd found the Austers—but before removing the one I wanted from the row of them—I cast a sidelong glance at what the person to my left was reaching for and saw it was *Pride and Prejudice*.

Thinking to be witty, I said to her even while not yet looking squarely *at* her in my reticent fashion, "It is a truth universally acknowledged that a single man in possession of a good fortune—" (Just to be clear, I'm a single man but not in possession of a good fortune.)

But before I finished quoting, she stopped me in my verbal tracks. Standing as tall as she could, which wasn't tall at all, and fixing me with penetrating hazel eyes, she said, "I do not intend to be rude, Sir, but I find no satisfaction in being quoted back to myself. By now I have heard myself quoted far too many times to consider it refreshing or droll."

That is an attention-getting remark, of course, and caused me to take a closer look at the woman. I saw someone who resembled drawings of Jane Austen I'd seen, wearing clothes resembling clothes she might have worn.

I thought to myself, however, that someone told she looked like Jane Austen—or even had she not been told she looked like Jane Austen—

could undoubtedly find more than one Manhattan boutique where eigh-
teenth- or early nineteenth-century outfits with contemporary tweaks
might be purchased. Any woman wanting the Laura Ashley appearance
can have it. There still are Laura Ashley outlets, aren't there? Maybe there
aren't anymore.

"Funny," I said, "you do remind me of what I think Jane Austen
looked like. You've certainly captured the period."

"There is a simple explanation for that," she said, while avoiding con-
tractions and methodically adjusting one of the curls peeking from under
her dainty cap and then returning to the book she'd pulled out. "I am
Jane Austen. Though you may have difficulty believing me, I see no reason
to deny it."

I must have been looking doubtful, because she added, "I see you
do not believe me, but here I am and not by choice. I am here by force.
They grew tired of my complaining."

At that, my expression must have shifted to completely befuddled.

"It seems my constant complaints about how my writings have been
travestied over the years caused untold vexation among the others." She
pointed a gloved right forefinger upward. "I was sent here to do my ful-
minating where it might have an effect. Here where authors have been
commissioned to finish my unfinished scribblings. Where authors have
been commissioned to write books in my style. Where authors have been
commissioned to write uncalled-for sequels and, for all I know, what are
called 'prequels,' to my few humble novels. Frankly, I am not interested
in Elizabeth Bennet as a child or a suburban matron."

Chagrin crossed her face like clouds covering the Royal Crescent at

Bath. "Do you know there are even books in which I have been appropri-
ated as a character? More than once as a common detective? You can imagine how humiliating that is."

Not being Jane Austen, I wasn't convinced I could imagine how
humiliating that is, but I nodded as if I could and said, "I can tell you I
occasionally write fiction, but in your case I would never deign to be that
presumptuous."

"Then you are one of the few," she said and slapped the book she
held against her free palm. "Do you know that *Pride and Prejudice* has
even been turned into a *comic book?*" She put the words "comic book"
into verbal italics, as if she found the phrase belittling—humiliating—
and would never have used it in any other context.

She accompanied the italics with the sort of face-distorting expression you make when you've just swallowed something unexpectedly sour.
It made her handsome (rather than pretty) face a thing of no great appeal.

"I did not know that," I said, hoping the emphasis I put on "not"
evidenced at least a modicum of sympathy and polite horror. On the other
hand, I was thinking I would like to see a *Pride and Prejudice* comic book.
I figured that would indeed be something to behold.

She said, "The residents of the other realm were tired of hearing these
sorts of diatribes." She waved her arm vaguely in several directions. The
shawl she had arranged over her shoulders stirred slightly. "So here I am,"
she said, "looking at my own books to confirm that they remain intact,
that they are not sullied as a result of the treatment accorded them for so
long now, and counting."

She fixed me with a look as if—despite my denial—I could be the next literary pirate, or perhaps she was regarding me as a convenient stand-in for whomever might be the next ungrateful poacher. I tried to look as innocent as I could of clod-like trespassing on intellectual property.

She patted me on my large hand with her small gloved one and said, "You must forgive me. Already you see how hot-tempered I become on the unbecoming subject. Where I have lately been, anything excessively hot is sent packing, at least temporarily. But now that I have ascertained my books are safe in themselves, perhaps I can relax."

I said I thought that might be a worthwhile idea.

"As you may know," she ventured, "relaxation in Bath where I spent the years eighteen hundred one through eighteen hundred five was frequently done at the spa or in the assembly rooms. I see no spa here, nor do I see anything resembling an assembly room."

We were walking out of the Austen-Auster aisle, and she was gazing around. By then, I'd completely forgotten why I was there, and said, as I looked down the escalator at the level immediately below, "Perhaps I do see something reminiscent of an assembly room."

She followed my gaze and, getting a glimpse of the café, saw where many book-buyers had—well—assembled. She said, "So it does. Perhaps you will join me for tea.

Tea with a figment? I don't think so. Tea with an actual living-and-breathing person? Why not? I said, "I would be delighted, Miss Austen."

"And you are...?" she said, extending a gloved hand again.

"Oh," I said—shaking the proffered hand and noting it might be small but the grip was as strong as her grip on consonants—"I'm Ted Prentiss. Theodore."

"Mr. Prentiss," she said. "Normally, I wait to be introduced, but I know no one here to introduce us."

I nodded my understanding in what I realize now was how I thought an early nineteenth-century gentleman might nod. Had I been wearing a hat, I probably would have tipped it. (I wasn't and how kempt my hair appeared was questionable.)

So began our tete-a-tete—her tete, bonnet-covered; my tete, uncovered—and it wasn't long before she made the remark about launching (my word, not hers) a dating service.

Over our herbal (the "h" is pronounced) teas, for which I insisted paying, we'd been talking about what she might do while back this side of the eternal divide. Since she'd returned, she said, she'd had enough time to conclude she couldn't put a stop to the writing that traded on her name, but she'd also come to understand that she was here for the duration, which meant she was here until she made some contribution or other or attained some goal—she wasn't certain which or what.

Since she seemed to be looking for suggestions, I—never at a loss for suggestions—made a few. The several I came up with, however, she'd already considered and rejected.

The most obvious, almost needless to say, was writing more novels. About that possibility, she was brisk, even brusque. "I have said what I had to say," she said. "I might have completed *Sanditon* while I am here, but, as you may know, it has already been unceremoniously finished for me."

With little pause, she said, "And I will not be launching a detective service, as some of the fabulists have had me do. Stuff and nonsense. If I poke into people's lives, it is not the sordid aspects. It is decidedly not a universal truth that people with a murder case to be solved are in need of Jane Austen. I examined lives from an entirely different perspective, which I would have considered something I need not explain."

Whenever she finished a statement about herself, Miss Austen—I wouldn't have dared address her by her given name, nor did she address me by mine—had a habit of aiming at me, and perhaps anyone with whom she was conversing, a direct gaze. It was as if she was challenging me, or whomever, to challenge her.

I wasn't inclined to do so but instead considered a few more suggestions.

While I was deciding which one to mention first, she made her dating-service remark—"I might establish a dating service, but then again, it is just an idle thought."

"Not a bad one," I said, wondering how she'd come to know such things existed as an outgrowth of nineteenth-century match-making. "Dating services are big now, especially online—if you know what that is." As someone so reluctant to date, I don't know why I was going on like this.

She nodded that she did know and gave the notion some thought while looking around the room. I saw her gaze light on the mural placed high on the Barnes & Noble café walls. In them are depicted caricatures of famous authors as if taking tea together, or something stronger, at the same watering hole. Among them are Virginia Woolf, Mark Twain and William Faulkner. Not among them is Jane Austen.

Nothing in her expression indicated her reaction to the playfully contrived mural. She merely shook her head—so that the curls appearing from under her bonnet stirred placidly—and addressed the idea of a dating service. "I do not think so. I was able to arrange matches in my fiction. I even had Emma Woodhouse come a cropper at the endeavor, but in life it is a different matter." For a moment, her eyes lost their shine. "At the dating game, I never did well for myself, did I?"

She seemed to be asking that of herself rather than of me. So I remained mum about both her hard romantic luck—and mine—and changed the subject by saying, "What about writing a book on manners? That's something we have a great big lack of these days."

She tilted her head in thought and crossed her feet in front of her. I hadn't noticed this before, but she was wearing delicate-looking slippers with flowers embroidered on the instep.

Before she could respond to the book on manners idea, I said, "Or if you don't want to write, you might want to establish a finishing school for independent young women who nevertheless like the idea of honoring traditions thrown out with the bath water—no pun intended—during the early feminist movement years."

"Yes, the feminist movement," she mused. "I have heard of that. Discussing where it went wrong, Betty Friedan has alienated almost as many of the others up there as I have. I am surprised I do not see her here as well." She looked around in what I took to be jest and then held the position for an instant, while slowly saying, "Or that contentious Andrea Dworkin."

Turning to face me again, Miss Austen hesitated for what I'd estimate was no more than another split second. It was long enough, though, for me to wonder what had caught her obviously keen eye. I looked in that direction, too.

I saw a man approaching us. Not us, exactly, but looking for a place near us. There were a few available tables and chairs, and he was clearly aiming to sit at one of them.

He was, to put it in a word, handsome. In two words—one hyphenated—he was what no one in an Austen novel would have called "drop-dead handsome." In twenty-five words or more, he was tall, had wavy hair, a bold jaw and an athletic gait. He had a prominent nose of the kind not thought of as refined enough for the twenty-first century but would have been more than acceptable in a Joshua Reynolds or Thomas Gainsborough portrait. He was wearing clothes designed to look simultaneously expensive and subtle—a tweed jacket I imagined came from Ralph Lauren's Seventy-second Street mansion as might have the gabardine slacks, lawn-green cashmere sweater and suede slip-ons. No, the shoes could have been bespoke—Jermyn Street, John Lobb, perhaps.

Looking close enough to my image of Fitzwilliam Darcy and perhaps to Miss Austen's image as well, he was holding a book. As he got near, I could see it was—of all unlikely tomes—Sir Walter Scott's *Guy Mannering*.

Guy Mannering was published in 1815, two years before Jane Austen originally died. So Miss Austen would have been aware of the best-selling Sir Walter Scott—who in his poem, "Marmion," wrote "O, what a tangled web we weave, when first we practice to deceive!" And Sir Walter Scott would have been aware of her. (Don't ask how I know any of this, but English majors sometimes retain relatively useless information.)

Whether Miss Austen had been able to discern the title of the book the man was carrying our way I can't say, since aside from the quick-as-a-hummingbird's-wing hesitation, she had returned to our conversation and was not looking at anything or anyone but me.

Nevertheless, I had no doubt she was aware of the man. Nor did I doubt she was aware I'd caught her fleeting notice of him. She gave nothing away, nor did she allow that she paid any special attention to him when he stopped at the table next to us and asked in a chamois voice that sounded as if it could have belonged to a wee-hours radio deejay, "Do you know if anyone is sitting here?"

There was no evidence that anyone had previously staked out the table—no folded newspaper, no book or books, no coffee cup or plate with a partially eaten biscotto on it, no reading glasses, nothing.

If I could tell as much, so could he. I let it ride and answered, because it was clear Miss Austen wasn't about to, "Doesn't look that way."

I'm saying I answered. I'm not saying he looked at me while I said it. He was looking at the silent Miss Austen, who happened to be directing her gaze somewhere in the middle distance and below mural level.

"Well," the Sir Walter Scott reader said and pulled one of the chairs out, "if someone is sitting here, I can always move when he or she returns."

That remark—which did have something in it of the inane— prompted Miss Austen to say, without shifting her attention, "That is true. You can always move."

I admit I'm frequently slow on the uptake. It's been a lifelong problem. But the tone in Miss Austen's voice—cooler even than she had heretofore been in our chat—hipped me that something was up. I guessed it was connected to this third party but also felt I didn't know her nearly well enough to ask what was bothering her, if "bother" was the correct assessment.

In any case, I didn't get the opportunity to ask because we were again interrupted by the newcomer at the next table. "Do either of you know anything about this book?" he asked, holding up *Guy Mannering*.

Before I could respond, Miss Austen said, "He's a fine writer," then paused for only a second, before adding, "if you have a fondness for that kind of book."

I could tell she meant her answer to be a conversation stopper, but I could see in the gentleman's ice-blue eyes that he had more to say. Ignoring her curt comment, he said, "I picked it out, because I've always liked the name Guy."

I'll just throw in here that none of this was meant for my ears. For all intents and purposes, I didn't exist for this fellow.

I didn't hold much interest for Miss Austen at that moment, either, although their reasons for dismissing me were, from what I could tell, diametrically opposed: He was trying to engage her, and she was immersed in trying to disengage from him.

Neither was having much success.

"An affinity for the name Guy seems a questionable reason for selecting a book with which you plan to spend valuable time," Miss Austen said, again visibly—to me at least—intending to end the byplay.

He said, "I beg to differ, Ms.—" and shifted from leaning towards us (towards her; I was wallpaper) to sitting upright and squaring his broad shoulders. "Forgive me. I don't know your name."

"Miss Austen," she said, not, evidently, wanting to be rude, "Miss Jane Austen."

He put out his hand, leaving her nothing to do but shake it, and repeated, "Miss Jane Austen." He cocked his head and got a gleam in his eye. He said again, "Miss Jane Austen. Like the novelist."

"Yes," Miss Austen said, "exactly like the nineteenth-century novelist."

"Never read her," he said. I gulped audibly. To myself at least. "She's girl—er—women stuff, what they call 'chicklit,' I think. I suppose you have. Read her, that is."

"In a manner of speaking," Miss Austen said.

"Is she as good as they say?" he asked.

She replied, remaining cool as a cucumber, "I am not really in a position to opine."

"Doesn't matter," he said. "What matters at the moment is I'm Guy Hudson." He laughed so that his teeth took on the brightness of a digital billboard advertisement. "Yes, you're right, Miss Jane Austen. My name in a title is a poor excuse for reading a book."

He swiveled the *Guy Mannering* copy he held back and forth as if the heft of it might somehow reveal its quality to him or us. "You seem to know it, too. Are you recommending I don't read it?"

Miss Austen took a second or three to ponder the question. What I took to be mild disdain crossed her face. If that's what it was, I couldn't discern whether it was disdain for Sir Walter Scott or Guy Hudson or both, although if I had to choose, I'd say it was the third option.

She seemed to have taken a dislike to Mr. Hudson but said in crisp, neutral tones, "I am not in the habit of recommending or not recommending books, Mr. Hudson, and if you do not mind—"

He cut her off. "But I do mind. Please call me Guy."

"Mr. Hudson," she repeated, and I could tell she was not the sort of person who brooks interruptions kindly. (Far as I could remember, no one in her books interrupts anyone else—and that includes Mr. Bennet when harangued by Mrs. Bennet.)

"You have your book," Miss Austen went on. "If I were to recommend anything, I would recommend your reading a few pages of it to see for yourself whether you might take joy in it. And now if you do not mind, I would like to return to the conversation I am having with my friend."

Hudson took that in and said with a certain amount of hurt but also defiance in his piercing eyes, "I'm sorry to have disturbed you. I won't do it again." He turned away from us and opened the book, intently paging to, I suppose, the first chapter. He began reading with showy concentration.

Miss Austen didn't wait for that to happen. She sought to resume whatever we'd been discussing. "Where were we?" she asked but not without an hauteur I took to be residue from what had just transpired.

Where had we been? Good question. I had to think. Oh, yes, we'd been talking about the contribution she needed to make—whatever that was—before she could go back where she'd come from.

I was just about to remind her where we were, when we heard a silken voice from the next table.

"I know I said I wouldn't disturb you again, Miss Austen," Mr. Hudson said, "but I feel I must ask you if I have offended you in any way. If I have, I'd like to know what it is I need to apologize for doing?"

Miss Austen took time with her answer, while both Hudson and I waited to see what she'd say. "No, Mr. Hudson," she replied, "you have not offended me, but—"

Again Hudson jumped in. "Then if I haven't offended you," he said and his chest seemed to swell with the news, "I don't see why we can't talk—"

Need I repeat it was as if I had altogether vanished into a convenient void?

This time Miss Austen cut him off by saying—and again with somewhat chilly attitude—"I was about to say, Mr. Hudson, that you have not offended me, but if you continue in this way, you *will* be offending me. You seem not to honor my talking with a friend but rather think yourself deserving of preferential attention."

"Then you do have something against me, Miss Austen," he declared.

Had I just heard what I'd just heard? It was as if I were hit by a thunderbolt of recognition. Miss Austen had just accused Mr. Hudson of *pride,* and Mr. Hudson had just accused Miss Austen of *prejudice.* I'd landed smack-dab in the middle of a life-imitates-art pot of jam!—practically a life-imitates-art slice of life! As an inveterate reader, all I had to do to entertain myself with nearly surreal pleasure was see how the situation played out.

Hold on. I was due to meet friends—honest-to-goodness friends—at seven, but what I was witnessing could present a problem. Would I have enough time to see the battle of wits before me through to the end? If the contents of Miss Austen's acclaimed works had established a precedent, this could take months, and—I checked my watch while they eyed each other—I only had about two and a half hours.

Just then the most marvelous thing happened, something that made me realize once and for all how times change and with them how old traditions can wither and fade—even if they've been embedded in the tangy aspic of early nineteenth-century print.

Guy Hudson said to Jane Austen, "I'm going to propose something to you, Ms. Austen."

"That remains *Miss* Austen to you," Miss Austen said.

"Welcome to the twenty-first century," Hudson said, meaning to be funny.

Jane Austen turned my way with an if-he-only-knew-the-whole-of-it look.

"You know about speed dating, I'm sure," he said to her and didn't wait for an answer, he was that certain she did know. "I'm going to propose we do a little speed-dating run right here. Why?" He didn't wait for an answer then, either. "Because you're an attractive woman, and I'm an attractive man, and I think we ought to get to know each other."

"You are being uncommonly audacious, Mr. Hudson," Miss Austen said.

"I'm only asking for three minutes of your time," he said, holding up his left hand, palm out. It made me think that were I to get a glimpse of his nails, I'd see they were well-manicured. "If after three minutes you can say you don't want to see anything more of me, I promise to take my *Guy Mannering* and disappear from your life forever."

Again, he waved the book in the air.

Jane Austen thought that over. "You have broken one promise to me already," she said. "How do I know you will not break this one?"

Hudson tilted his square jaw thirty degrees higher and said, "Because this time I give you my word as a gentleman. What do you say?" With his right hand, he pulled his left jacket sleeve back and the sleeve of his sweater and went about removing his watch. He handed it to me.

"Your friend will time us," he said. He didn't look at me when he said it, but that gesture was at least an acknowledgment that I was present.

"If three minutes will purchase my freedom from you," Miss Austen said, "then I agree to the challenge. It seems a small price to pay."

I was thinking about the price of the watch I now had in my possession. It was a Rolex Submariner I clocked at between seven and ten thousand dollars. That wasn't, of course, such a small price to pay.

"We'll begin on my count of three," Hudson said, still not looking at me but fixing Miss Austen with a roguish expression. "One," he said with anticipation, paused before saying "two" and took a longer pause before saying "three."

Since I was looking at the Rolex, I noted that his "three" resounded just as the second hand passed the twelve: This Guy guy was all perfection.

As I kept an eye on the Rolex's second hand and an ear on the give-and-take, I regretted that I had no tape recorder with me with which to capture what I was hearing. That's to say, I can't recall what was said verbatim. I can only give you an approximation of what was said, but, trust me, it's a reliable approximation of all the fervor and urgency to which I was privy, as they say in Morocco-bound novels.

Here goes:

Hudson: I'm pleased to make your acquaintance, Miss Austen, but even though you've denied as much, I believe I have offended you. I will admit I can do that with women to whom I'm attracted. I suppose it's a character flaw, and I have many, I'm sure. On the other hand, I have always known what I want and have felt it serves no purpose not to act quickly on it. Anything else is a waste of time, and if I have any strong dislikes, it's anyone or anything that wastes my time or anyone else's. To that end, I made my first million before I was twenty. I founded a dot-com company that remained solvent during the first dot-com bubble burst.

Austen: Mr. Hudson, I am someone to whom a single man in possession of a good fortune means less than it might to other women. On the contrary, I believe that a man who refers to his fortune before his less demonstrable qualities is a man whose motives are to be questioned. Perhaps it is a bias, but it is one from which I have always profited. I believe that one must live by standards and strict ones at that, although I am aware that my position can be interpreted by others as unforgiving.

Hudson: If you'll forgive me, Miss Austen—I won't presume to call you Jane—I think it necessary to devote some time to the reasons why men and women do what they do and not judge them simply by first impressions. I find that impulse a sign of weakness. I mentioned my success in business for two reasons. The first is that it means I am a man with whom a woman can feel secure—not, incidentally, in a nineteenth-century way but in a more contemporary manner. My equity allows me to encourage a woman with whom I'm involved to pursue her own interests. The second reason is that I believe in philanthropy and, without calling attention to myself personally—a condition I deplore—I'm able to do something about my beliefs with some humanitarian gestures about which I shall go into no further detail.

Austen: Were I to take you on faith, Mr. Hudson, I would have to confess I may have misjudged you, but I would also have to say my attitudes, should they seem aloof, have not sprung full-blown from my maiden's mind and heart. They have been formed in response to the ways of the world I have seen around me and the responses to me of that often misguided world. I have often been misjudged myself but, I think to my credit, have never greeted misjudgment with anything but humor. I am prepared to cede, however, that what strikes me as humorous may not always show on my face. Perhaps that is a flaw of my own.

Hudson: I commend you on your confession, Miss Austen. Conceding flaws isn't common to many women of my acquaintance, I have to say. The women I know may carry on about various features on their faces that they'd like rectified by expensive plastic surgeons, but that's their faces. They never apologize for their expressions.

Austen: For my part, Mr. Hudson, I know of too few men who understand that humanitarian obligations might possibly take precedence over the attentions they pay to their own person. I do, on the other hand, admire your taste in apparel.

Hudson: Same here, Miss Austen. I like what you're wearing, too. It's maybe more demure than I usually go for, but I have to say the joining of soft clothes with a tough mind is a winning combination.

Just as Hudson uttered the phrase "winning combination" and inhaled more deeply than he had for the length of the Austen-Hudson exercise, the Rolex second hand crossed the three-minute mark.

"Three minutes," I said with a staccato tempo picked up from them.

Not that they noticed me, only the signal to stop I'd announced.

They ceased talking but remained looking at each other. Guy Hudson's strategy had worked. They had gotten through to each other—had qualified as "a winning combination." But were they thinking what I was thinking: What do they do now?

I imagined Hudson expected Miss Austen and he would go off to dinner somewhere or just take a walk or possibly a ride in whatever sleek vehicle he had parked somewhere nearby. But that couldn't be what Miss Austen expected, could it? Given the little I knew of her, it wasn't what I imagined she'd do.

Finally, Hudson spoke just as Miss Austen opened her mouth to say something. They both laughed, and it was laughter that had what I can only call a merry ring to it.

Drawing on what I took to be turn-of-the-eighteenth-century deferral, Miss Austen signaled to Hudson that he should speak first.

He did but not without an appreciative nod. "Perhaps we can talk further and at a more leisurely pace elsewhere," he said. Then he looked my way for only the second or third time and added, "If your friend doesn't mind."

Caught off guard, I made a few awkward shakes of my head to let him and her know I didn't mind. If I had minded, what difference would it have made?

At my diffident nod, Hudson rose and offered his hand to Miss Austen, who stood and said to me, "It has been a pleasure, Mr. Prentiss."

I sputtered, "For me as well, and one I hope to repeat."

"One never knows," she said and joined Hudson, who had moved off a few steps.

They turned then and walked away but not before Miss Austen looked back at me while I was still within earshot and said, "I think I know why I am here now."

Then they proceeded to the escalator. As they stepped onto it, I saw him reach for her gloved hand. She didn't let him take it. Instead she slipped her arm through his.

They descended.

I'm sorry to say that what happened after that, I have no way of knowing. When they disappeared from my view, did they vanish completely? For all I know, they might have. Did Jane Austen leave behind anything to serve as a reminder of her brief drop-by in my life? No. The only thing left behind was on the table Hudson had occupied: the paperback copy of Sir Walter Scott's *Guy Mannering*.

I chuckled to myself that just as Jane Austen had eclipsed Scott for readers at the beginning of the nineteenth century, she'd just done so again at the brightening dawn of the twenty-first.

Did Miss Austen evaporate from Hudson's life as mysteriously as she materialized in mine? Did the two of them try a relationship that didn't work out, as so many don't? Are Miss Austen and Mr. Hudson living together in the connubial bliss denied her during her (previous) lifetime?

I can't say. What I can say is that a young woman—an attractive one at that—approached the table on which *Guy Mannering* lay. She looked at it, turned to me and said, "Is someone sitting here?"

"No," I said. "I guess the guy who brought it over before he left a minute or so ago decided not to buy it. I don't see why you can't sit there."

Whereupon she sat down, and we started a conversation—a conversation we've often continued. She reads. She likes books. She doesn't seem to be on the hunt for a single man in possession of a good fortune.

Arnie Potter's Story

✄ or ✄

Toulouse On Track

So there Henri de Toulouse-Lautrec was. Big as life. Bigger. On a New York City subway car. He had to be several inches taller than when he was hanging out at the Moulin Rouge in Paris with all those flashy types and putting them in his awesome art.

Instead of "hanging out at," you'd never say anything like "wasting his time at." They say the guy tossed off something like 5,000 drawings, most of them a look at the sexy times he spent there. He was such a regular that when he showed up, they must have known what kind of suds to bring him right away. What do they call it? Absinthe? I bet that was his fave rave.

Anyway, it was Toulouse-Lautrec I was looking at, all right. There was the cartoon face, the dark beard, the thick eyebrows, what I think they called a pince-nez. He definitely had a *nez* worth pincing. It stuck way the fuck out, something Cyrano de Bergerac would have called a honker. It was a schnozz the old comic Jimmy Durante would have taken his hat off to.

"Hey, you've grown," I had said to him right off the bat. Like we were longtime buddies.

"Yes, I have shot up," he said in a thick accent that sounded like some rich guy taking a look at how the other half lived. ("Yes, I have shot up" came out as "Yayss, Ah 'ave showt oop," but I'll drop the mimicry from here on out.)

"What happened?" I said. "If you don't mind my asking."

"*Pas de tous,* Arnie Potter," he replied. His head sort of bent to the side. The angle made him look—how can I put it so it doesn't come out bad? I don't know—an angle that made him look a little funny.

"You know my name?" I said, kind of shocked. How could he have known it? Near as I could figure, he couldn't have known anyone in the car or on the entire train. He'd died—he had to have—more than a hundred years before all us subway riders had jumped on the train on an early Manhattan afternoon. In September.

"*L'affiche,*" he said.

"What *affiche?*" I asked, momentarily forgetting my question to him and trying to figure out what "*affiche*" meant. I don't know French.

"That one," he said, pointing at my lapel. "The one that says, "Arnie Potter." (He pronounced it Air-nie Pottaire, but that's the last time I'm going to go into that kind of spelling.) I looked down. Sure enough, there was the name tag I'd put on at the luncheon I'd just been at. It was one of those show business time-killers that I have to attend way too frequently. I'm an agent-manager always on the lookout for leads on new talent. The pickings had recently been as thin as a strand of spaghetti.

Anyway, I hate those things. Name tags, I mean. Not business lunch-eons, although I'm hardly a big fan of them either. I only put up with those because every once in a while I do get a lead.

But name tags. I always forget to take them off. Then I walk around like a lox with them identifying me to anyone and everyone on the street. And in the subway, of course.

I removed the fucking thing and started rolling it into a tight spiral. With another funny look through those thick pince-nez lenses, Toulouse-Lautrec watched what I was stupidly doing and then pointed at my trousers.

Something else on me must have been weird. Damn, I thought, my fly is open. I meet Henri de Toulouse-Lautrec, and my fly has to be open. But he must have seen an undone fly before. A' course, back in his day, they would have been unbuttoned, not unzipped. I know that much. He'd undoubtedly unbuttoned his own fly enough times in the presence of the Pigalle prosties he called pals.

But there was no need for him to see my barn door open. I looked down at it. It wasn't open. Well, it might have been, because I couldn't see it. It was covered by the tucked-in linen napkin I didn't remove when I raced out of the Roosevelt Hotel ballroom as if late for a flight.

"Oh," I said and snatched the damn thing away to see my fly was closed, after all. "Thanks, *merci.*" Okay, I know that much French.

I ought to say that at the beginning of this little chat, Toulouse-Lautrec's face was level with my crotch. He was, you know, seated and I was standing. The idea of him getting a gander at my boxers—if my fly had been open—wasn't something I wanted to think about. It was the second day I'd worn them. Maybe the third. I'd lost count.

The seat opposite him on the other side of the aisle was available. I sat on it with a sneaky sense that it would be impolite to continue having Toulouse-Lautrec craning his short neck upward in conversation. But even seated, he was taller than I always heard he was supposed to be. Who knows where I heard it? I don't. He seemed to read my mind. "You were wondering about my growth," he said.

I nodded like a goofball—anything to get his mind off my lapel and fly.

"As you might imagine, it's the reason for my unexpected return," he said.

I saw that a few bystanders and bysitters had begun to listen in. He wasn't taking them in. He also didn't seem to notice the stops we made and the swoosh of the subway doors when riders were coming and going.

He said, "You might have seen an article in *The New York Times* a while ago about a few doctors diagnosing my case retroactively."

I hadn't.

"*Alors,* there was such an article," he said, "and in case you're interested, we do get the *Times* where I come from. The ubiquitous institutional ads for home delivery have been wildly effective. The only hitch is the blasted local newsboy leaves the paper anywhere but on the front stoop. If it's been raining, there's no reading it that day—not until it dries out and even then there are pages you can't separate. Many of us are now reading it exclusively online.

"I needn't go on, particularly since there was no rain the day the article appeared. Apparently, they think I had something they call pycnodysostosis, some gene anomaly. Don't ask me who 'they' are. Some collective 'they,' some medical collective. You can imagine how my heart leapt up, only to discover that where pycnodysostosis is concerned, they could do nothing."

With that he gave a series of agitated taps on his drum head. I didn't say yet that when I spotted him, he was sitting in his frock coat and bowler hat tapping on a round percussion instrument balanced on his right knee. It looked like a bongo without the bong part. Just the top. It looked like a small tambourine without any jangly metal thingamabobs.

When I sat down across from him, I think I was interrupting him having a good time with himself. Maybe I should have asked him if he would like a booking. I know a few clubs that might have been glad to advertise him. But it didn't occur to me. I guess if you meet Toulouse-Lautrec in the subway, even if he has part of a bongo drum, getting him a slot somewhere isn't the first thing you think of. Maybe if he'd had a paper cup or anything like that, but he didn't.

He went on, "The *Times* article set me thinking. If they could diagnose a genetic malfunction that pertains to me, what else can they do? I should have thought of it before. That I hadn't is neither here nor there and is definitely neither here nor there in the heavenly sphere where no surgery is done, even by surgeons. When surgeons arrive, they're immediately humbled. They've believed themselves God for so long, and now they're somewhere presided over by an actual God. They shut up *tout de suite.*

"*En tout cas,* what's important is that I began to wonder what else I had wrong with me that they might be able to correct. The first things that came to mind were my thigh bones. When I was thirteen or fourteen—the years blur—I fractured both femurs. They didn't heal properly, which compounded my height-challenged status, as I've learned to say in your politically correct climate."

This disclosure got me. "So you just returned to earth?" I said. "To life? Just like that?" I snapped my fingers.

"Why shouldn't I return to life?" he said and gave out with a raspy laugh that did weird things to his face. "It's easy enough to do."

"It is?" I said, leaning across the aisle even more.

"Oh, yes," he said. "*Ouais, ouais, ouais.* Nothing to it. You just decide to return and you do. *Voila! Me voici!* Here I am." He used his bongo hand to indicate his entire taller self. "It's like you yourself might decide to spend a day or two in Rouen or Hoboken or *n'importe ou* and then go do it."

"*N'importe ou*" was lost on me. "Then why don't more people return?" I asked, wanting to get this news flash from wherever his beyond was.

"What makes you think more people don't?" he said with another raspy laugh.

I had a cat-got-my-tongue moment, which he cut into by saying, "I'm being glib. There are a couple of answers to that query. One is that many people do return. More than you think." He took a moment to scan the car and then leaned in more. "I count three in this car alone," he said, lowering his bass-baritone voice.

I looked around. I saw no one who resembled Cleopatra or Voltaire or Ulysses S. Grant and said so.

"They're not all people who were in what you call the public eye," he said.

"Then how can you tell?" I asked.

"The aura," he said. "You can't see it, but I can." At that, he waved his stubby fingers at the guy sitting right next to me. "The other part of the answer is that although it's easy to come back, not that many want to do it."

"Why not?" I blurted out.

Toulouse-Lautrec was a homely man, but like so many men and women you think of as homely, there was something about him that was kind of, uh, warm. But here I am, talking about good looks and not-so-good looks when Toulouse-Lautrec—I know this much about the art he made—wasn't making homely people look good. He was into changing how you define what's beautiful.

Anyway, when I said "Why not?" he got this different expression that made me feel like less of a doofus. "They don't come back, because they don't want to come back." He waved his hand at the car we were in again. Did I already say he had big hands? Making up for his small body? "They've left all this behind. They've moved on. There's much to be said for moving on."

"But there must be so many reasons to come back," I said. "You found one."

"True enough," he said, "but don't forget I was—if you will pardon the indulgence—a painter of the outcast, an archivist of the unconventional, a poet of the misfit. Why not return to a time and place where everyone looks like a circus act, where suffering is commonplace and humiliation epidemic, where people occupy themselves with foolishness?"

Now he pointed at *my* hand. I was still rolling the damn name tag.

I went to drop it, but it stuck to my right forefinger. With my other hand I pulled it off and stuffed it in a pocket.

We'd come to another stop and passengers were jockeying around. We had to straighten up to let them pass, but he continued. "I'm not the only one with my condition or a variation of it. You know who Cole Porter is, don't you?" I nodded that I did. I sure would've liked to be Cole Porter's agent. "Then you probably know he lived much of his life after debilitating damage done to *his* legs. Before I left, I asked if he wanted to come along. He looked at me as if I were crazy and said, 'What, and take time away from playing "Begin the Beguine" for the swanky cocktail crowd here?' I didn't give him an argument."

He shook his head. His bowler grabbed some attention. No one wears bowlers on the subway anymore. The hat was a novelty, whereas people who look enough like Toulouse-Lautrec to pass for him are hardly unheard of. Some of them shuffle through car after car begging coins for all kinds of nutty causes.

Of course, only Toulouse-Lautrec happens to look *exactly* like Toulouse-Lautrec. Even though taller.

"It worked out for you," I said, indicating his body top to toe.

"*Mais oui,*" he said, "a medical miracle. Nowadays all they had to do was break the bones again and reset them properly. It was the hospital paperwork that was a pain in the *fesse*. Now I only have to stay around for the follow-up appointments and rehabilitation."

By then we were pulling into the Delancey Street stop, where I was supposed to get off. Well, as I say, it's not every day you get to have a chat with Henri de Toulouse-Lautrec. I thought about staying on the train, but I was on my way home to get some boring agent work done.

"Well, Monsieur Toulouse-Lautrec," I said as the train was slowing down, "I get off here, but it's been a pleasure talking to you."

"I share the sentiment," he replied and extended his big right hand. I looked at it. I noticed he had charcoal and oil paint and like that under his fingernails.

"I wonder," I said, noticing the opening doors, "if you have a card. I'd like to keep in touch."

"Quite out of the question," he said. "I'm afraid that for you and me it's not *au revoir* but goodbye."

There was nothing to do but accept it. I stepped off the train, but I stood on the platform long enough to watch it pull out. I waved a hearty farewell at Toulouse-Lautrec, but he didn't see me. He'd returned to tapping the weird drum head.

I know I said it's not every day that you run into Henri de Toulouse-Lautrec, but maybe in my case it *is* every day. Because don't you know I did see him again and, believe it or not, it was the very next day. I'd say it was an amazing coincidence, but with Toulouse-Lautrec, bumping into him two days in a row was nothing compared to running into him in the first place.

Anyway, the following day I was walking down Broadway in the upper Eighties when approaching me at about twenty yards away was what I again took to be Henri de Toulouse-Lautrec. Most people on the West Side would have thought it was someone who looked like Toulouse-Lautrec but couldn't possibly be and would have just kept going. That's what everybody was doing.

I knew better. I prepared to say *"Allo,"* though my surprise seeing him again changed the closer we got. Something about his face. The nearer he got, the more obvious it was.

He was wearing the same outfit he'd been wearing the previous day, right up to the pince-nez but no bongo drum thing. Instead, he was carrying a sketchbook in his left hand. Most noticeable, however, was a blackish-greenish smudge behind the pince-nez.

There was no missing it: Henri de Toulouse-Lautrec had a black eye.

"Hello there," I said as he reached me.

"Zut alors," he said, extracting himself from a reverie. *"Encore, c'est vous."*

"You've got some shiner there," I said, coming right to the point— as I'd done the previous day when talking about his added height. He didn't say anything. "Shiner" threw him. "Black eye," I said. I pointed at it, "bruise." I figured the French don't know "boo-boo."

He raised his gloved hand to his right eye and then removed the pince-nez. *"Ah ouais, la blessure,"* he said. "The wound. I am sensitive to it." I knew he meant he was sensitive about it. I didn't correct him. "You want to know how I come by it?" he asked.

Pedestrians were hurrying past us. Some looked at him, more, I think, to assess the eye damage than with any kind of famous-painter recognition double take.

"I have this because of a drag queen, I think you call them." He thought that over as he replaced the pince-nez. "Yes, a drag queen."

"You got that from a drag queen?" I said.

"Très agressif," he said, making a fist of his right hand and swinging

it close enough to my face for me to back off.

"She—uh—he—uh—she did that to you?" I asked.

"*Non, mon ami,*" he said, "I'm on my way to do that to her." A look of triumph crossed his homely face. "She did this—" He indicated his eye again. "—with her elbow."

I tried to see the scene but couldn't. "You lost me," I said.

He crooked a gloved finger at me and said, "Step into my *atelier.*" Not wanting to hold up pedestrian traffic, he moved closer to the store window we were standing by.

I followed him. He moved closer to me. I bent over to listen to him but not as far as I once might have had to.

"Last night I decided I wanted to do some sketching," he began with that raspy voice. "I went to a drag bar in the West Village."

"That must have been an eye-opener for you," I said and regretted the "eye" part.

"Not as much as you think," he said. "Remember, I was brought up in nineteenth-century Paris. I virtually lived at *Le Moulin Rouge.* I've seen it all. I think the problem was they hadn't seen me. If you know my work—"

Recalling his devotion to beauty-definition-broadening, I interrupted him. "I do. I really, really like it."

"*Un mille mercis,*" he said and went on. "If you know my work, you know I like to get close to my subjects. But proximity has its advantages and disadvantages. One of the disadvantages was that the performers got very sweaty doing what they did, and their costumes weren't regularly laundered. *Vous comprenez?* You get my drifting?"

"Yeah, I get it," I said. "I've been around performers who have that problem." I'm an agent. Of course, I have. Way too often.

"That part doesn't always strike most viewers," he said. "It's a good thing what I did was strictly a visual art. The prices some of my works go for now would be much lower were the other senses involved. But as I was saying, in this *boite* I was sitting close, and one of the *artistes* objected to what I was doing. She jumped right off the low stage and tried to grab my sketchbook. When I pulled it back, she swung around like this"—he demonstrated—"and hit me in the eye with her elbow. It was a *très* fleshy elbow, but the bone still had an impact.

"I was holding the sketchbook with one hand and fending my attacker off with the other when someone pulled us apart. I decided it was time to leave and stepped quickly through the cheering crowd to the door and out to the street. She tried to follow me, but as I was racing away, which I can do much better now, I heard someone in the club—perhaps the owner or the manager—telling the drag queen she had an act to finish."

He chuckled again, raspy-like. "She probably thinks that's the end of it, but I don't appreciate being assaulted in the pursuit of my art. I have her stage name from *l'affiche* outside. Lotta Trash. I spent the morning finding out her real name.

"How did you do that?" I asked.

"Googled it," he said with what was becoming—to me—a Toulouse-Lautrec gleam in his eye. "And from that I got her—his—Sonny Blalock's address on—" He consulted a piece of paper he'd pulled from his jacket pocket. "—West Ninety-first Street. I'm on my way there now to—how do you say?—get my licks in."

"I'd certainly like to see that," I said. I didn't expect the response I got.

"You can if you want," Toulouse-Lautrec said. "*Venez avec moi, mon ami agréable. Vous pouvez m'aider, peut-etre?*"

I didn't know for sure what he was saying, but I got the gist of it. I thought fast. I'd been on my way to an Upper West Side shoe store I liked, but it wasn't anything I couldn't put off for a half-hour or so and still be in striking distance of my destination.

"If you don't mind," I said.

"Why should I mind?" he said. "I would enjoy the company, and I would be happy to have a witness."

So we set off up Broadway. I made a few forgettable remarks about the crazy scene but mostly kept quiet, because I was thinking, "Here I am, me, Arnie Potter, with Henri de Toulouse-Lautrec, and only he and I know it. To everyone we saw and who saw us, I could be just anybody—which I was and am, you know, a talent-agent nobody—and *he* could be just anybody—which he wasn't."

To the few comments I made along the way he didn't say much more than "*Très intéressant*" or "*Très, très intéressant.*" Most of the time he was humming a tune under his breath. Actually, it was more like a mixture of humming and whistling softly. It was a melody I was certain I'd never heard before—not on the radio, not downloadable from iTunes or Spotify.

I asked him what it was. He was jarred from his reverie. "I did not realize I was doing that," he said and thought for a moment, then resumed for another moment. "Oh," he said, "it's one of the songs Aristide Bruant sang all the time. He's still singing it, you know. Up where we are."

The name didn't mean anything to me, but I figured it must be one of the Moulin Rouge characters. I wondered who this guy's agent was. "Really? He's still singing it?" I said. It was awesome to be introduced to a repertoire I figured must've been lost for a long time.

Toulouse-Lautrec said, "The song is about a man whose mother never knew the identity of his father. Sometimes I wish that had been true of me, but it wasn't. *Dommage.*"

If ever a remark begged a question, that one did, but I could see my new acquaintance probably wouldn't want to answer it. He'd retreated into his own thoughts. What I might have done but didn't—I was still stuck on the remark about the Toulouse-Lautrec and his father problem—was ask him to finish the song and maybe even teach it to me. I wouldn't have minded being the first on my block to memorize an old Pigalle street song. That would impress the Broadway jokers I hung around with.

By the time the thought struck, however, we were just about at Ninety-first Street and Broadway. Toulouse-Lautrec had again pulled out the piece of paper where he'd written an address in the block-y hand you'd recognize from signatures on his paintings and drawings.

He stopped at the corner and held the paper in front of me. "To which direction do we go?" he asked.

I looked at it again. It said: "243 West Ninety-first Street." (It really said: "243, *La Rue 91ème.*") "We cross to the north side of the street and turn left," I said. "It'll be closer to the other end of the block."

Two-forty-three East Ninety-first Street is a five-story yellow-brick-with-red-brick-trim structure dividing a row of older brownstones. The entrance is at street level. Inside the tiled vestibule—the outer metal-and-glass door was unlocked—Toulouse-Lautrec consulted the directory with a stubby thumb and, sure enough, there was a listing for "Sonny Blalock." 5F. (No reference to Lotta Trash. Apparently she didn't get mail at this address.)

Toulouse-Lautrec was paying no attention to me at that point. He pressed the button next to 5F and looked uncertain about what to do next. He only turned to me when after about fifteen seconds had elapsed there was no response.

"Maybe he's out," I said.

The possibility had obviously not occurred to him, and he got this sorry look on his face. I was about to offer condolences. No need. At just that second, the intercom came to life and a static-y voice said, "Who is it?"

Toulouse-Lautrec was at a loss.

I figured I was here, so I might as well participate.

"A delivery for Mr. Blalock," I said.

Another two-second silence and the buzzer went. I lunged for the doorknob and pushed the door open. Toulouse-Lautrec said something to me under his breath that sounded like another "*merci*" and preceded me through. He started up the stairs.

I said, "Wait a minute, Mr. Toulouse-Lautrec." I had noticed that in his post-operative condition the artist had surprisingly little trouble walking. He even had a spring in his step. But perhaps he would find the stairs difficult. I said, "There might be an elevator."

I walked down the tiled corridor but found only a door to 1R, the rear ground-floor apartment. No elevator. I shook my head no and joined him on the stairs for the four-floor climb, which took about the same out of both of us. When I first came to New York, I lived in a walk-up in Astoria. Never again.

As we reached 5F, I began to detect an unusual odor—something sweet and musty. Kind of disgusting. Toulouse-Lautrec seemed to take it in as well and even gave a small nod of recognition.

"Unlaundered costumes," he said, more to himself than to me.

Then he pushed the square doorbell button that he once might have had difficulty reaching. A metallic ring resulted, something like the sound of a rusty nail being pulled over a row of other rusty nails. Almost before it concluded, the door swung open and a more intense spray of the stale aroma hit us.

Standing there in a frilly pink bathrobe and pink mules with white pom-poms was a bruiser needing a shave and a good rinse to remove what was left of last night's makeup. I'd seen that kind of thing before, too. I estimated the man looking at us to figure out what we wanted weighed at least two-hundred-fifty pounds. Maybe more like three hundred.

Taking in that neither of us was holding anything that could pass for a package or a bouquet of flowers, he started to say, "What do y—?" Then the glaring light of recognition hit him. "Oh, it's you," he said to Toulouse-Lautrec.

"*Oui, c'est moi,*" my new friend said and stepped towards the human sandbag. As he did, he pulled his right arm back in preparation for the planned assault.

When he did that, something took me over. Sizing up the situation,

I realized that Toulouse-Lautrec might succeed in landing a punch but that the side of beef in pink ruffles I was looking at wasn't likely to just stand—or flounce—there and take it. He'd strike back. Toulouse-Lautrec could get the sort of fracture as bad or worse than whatever had crippled him when he was a kid.

Hardly considering what I was up to, I grabbed Toulouse-Lautrec's arm when it was still poised behind his head. Simultaneously, I said to the Blalock mountain of flesh, "Do you know whose sketchbook you tried to take last night?"

"No, I don't," Blalock said in a voice that was becoming increasingly macho by the moment. "What's more, I don't fucking care."

Toulouse-Lautrec was trying to break free of my grip, but I held on.

"You might care if you realized it's Henri de Toulouse-Lautrec."

"Henri de Toulouse-Lautrec?" he said. "I don't care if he's Henry Kissinger. Get him out of here."

"Yes," I said, "he's Henri de Toulouse-Lautrec. The famous painter."

With that, Blalock looked at me and then at the squirming Toulouse-Lautrec and gave out a basso-profundo laugh that filled the hallway. "Oh, sure," he said. "He's the famous painter who died at least fifty years ago."

I was ready for this. I said, "How can he be dead when he's standing right here in front of you?" As I said that, I let go of Toulouse-Lautrec, who pulled himself up to his current higher height.

Fake eyelashes flapping, Blalock took a closer look. With his two huge paws, he pulled his robe closed. "I've seen pictures of Toulouse-Lautrec. He does look a lot like him," he said as if he was on his way to being convinced.

I decided to lay it on as thick as Blalock laid on the lipstick and rouge. "And you objected to having Henri de Toulouse-Lautrec draw you while you were performing. Do you know how many people would give their right arm for the privilege?" I was giving him a good slice of agent talk.

Blalock said, "Well, it's very distracting when you're trying to entertain and someone is right in front of you with a pad and pencil." As he was saying that, the words were coming more and more slowly and going into a higher register. Like he was on helium or something. Under the heavy unshaved morning beard which was under the the remains of heavy makeup, he was beginning to blush. "How was I to know?"

With that, he looked more closely at Toulouse-Lautrec and said, "I'm sorry. I thought you were dead."

Toulouse-Lautrec, who'd let his right arm drop to his side, said, "You're probably confusing me with Georges Seurat. He also died in his thirties, but as you see—*comme vous voyez*—I'm still here."

"Oh," Blalock said, "you're probably right. Seurat." He stroked his chin and winced at the stubble. "Well, do you want to come in?" Again, he seemed uncertain how to speak to a famous person. Probably not too many of the celebrated came to watch him perform. "I guess if you want to sketch me now, you could." The proposition excited him. "I could change into a gown."

As he was issuing the invite, he was stepping backward and making a step-right-in gesture. I signaled to Toulouse-Lautrec that he should enter. He stepped over the threshold.

Then I took a step inside the door to inhale what smelled like an explosion at a perfume factory and saw what looked a lot like a chorus girls' dressing room. I've been in a few of those, too, you can bet on and be a winner. For all I knew, the fabrics making up the curtains and various slipcovers could have come from the same bolt that produced Blalock's robe.

Insulin shots were called for. So as someone who habitually shies away from inoculations, I said to our host(ess), "I hope you don't mind if I take a rain check, but I've got some errands I need to run. I just came along to make sure that Mr. Toulouse-Lautrec found your place." I didn't quite want to leave it at that. "He's come such a long way from Paris and Montmartre and parts farther off."

It was plain that Blalock couldn't have cared if I stayed, left or suspended myself by the neck from the hallway lighting fixture. He acknowledged my beg-off with a dip of his big head.

As for Toulouse-Lautrec, he was already thinking about making his 5,000 drawings collection swell to 5,001. It looked to me as if he were scanning the room for the best place he could pose the latest example of unconventional beauty bowing in front of him.

I interrupted his perusal only long enough to say, "*Au revoir,* Monsieur Toulouse-Lautrec." I think I got that right.

He turned to me and said, "Again I must regret there will be no *au revoir.*"

He barely had time to say that before Blalock closed the door, more or less in my face. I stood there for only a moment and then retreated.

And that—right up to the current minute—was the last I saw of Henri de Toulouse-Lautrec on the sidewalks of New York. Or on the subway platforms. Or on any sidewalks or subways anywhere.

What I did see around town no more than ten days later were posters and flyers ballyhooing the appearance of a drag queen billing himself/herself as Too Loose La Dreck.

The *affiches*—see now I'm speaking French—were illustrated with the drawing of a heavy-set man in a vivid pink dressing gown sitting on a divan with one leg tucked under him and one arm resting along the back of the divan. It's very much in the style of you-know-who. And if you look very closely at the lower right-hand corner, you can see a tiny "H-T-L" monogram stamp.

And hey, before I go, shake hands with Arnie Potter, Too Loose La Dreck's new agent-manager.

Edgar Chapman's Story

❦ or ❦

Where There's a Will

The weird little man standing next to me had been muttering to himself since the play began. The sound effect was that of a storm gathering in the far distance, but since the rumbling-like mumbling didn't suggest a storm traveling all that quickly, I paid him little mind.

I was much more involved with where I was and what I was doing. It was an English June, and I was at the new thatch-roofed Globe, a theatre built in 1997 and modeled after William Shakespeare's original Globe (1599-1613) when it burned to the ground, was rebuilt and then shuttered for inflammatory political reasons (1614-1642). (I'm using the English spelling of "theatre," because it only seems right under the circumstances.)

The reason for my being there—not just in London but there on hallowed Shakespeare territory—was simple. I'm a young (all right, all right, young-*ish*) playwright with one semi-hit to my credit, and breathes there a playwright who isn't interested in Shakespeare? It's practically a requirement, no? There's another reason: writer's block. I'd been confronting it to no avail and had decided a trip to Shakespeare might do me good.

Ever since I'd heard that at Shakespeare's plays there were such things as groundlings—at all the works written for the public and not introduced at court—I wanted to be one. I wanted to be a groundling. I wanted to see for myself how Shakespeare's writing took in the groundlings, how their presence affected his manuscripts.

For those who don't know, the groundlings were the poorer theatre-lovers who paid a penny to stand on the open area in front of the stage and brave the elements, while those who could afford a few more pennies remained under the thatched roof in the seats forming the famous "O" to which the opening Chorus of *Henry V* exuberantly refers.

Stop me if you've heard all this before.

The new Globe had been in operation a few years before I was able to get there. (For its construction I had sent in a few pounds that paid for a single brick. Maybe the name Edgar Chapman is on a list somewhere; maybe it's on a brick.) But I had finally arrived, had paid my five pounds for groundling status and was standing in the hot afternoon sun, wearing a paper hat offered free for sunstroke avoidance.

It was a performance of *A Midsummer Night's Dream,* not my favorite of the comedies. *Much Ado About Nothing* has that distinction. I'd switched allegiance from *As You Like It* some years earlier.

Too much information? I'm a playwright. Naturally, I'm free with the dialogue.

Here I was, at last understanding from the reaction of the people around me—many of them pressing against the stage and locking eyes with the actors—that Shakespeare had exactly this kind of give-and-take in mind when he was putting quill to vellum.

I would have been having a great time if not for the man next to me, sputtering unintelligibly. Every once in a while, I could make out a bit of what he was saying. "Not right," he'd say. At other times, he wasn't commenting on the language or the performances but was saying the lines along with the actors. "From whence did they obtain that phrase, i' troth?" was the only time I heard an entire agitated sentence and only subliminally noted it was in iambic pentameter.

Finally, during a scene where Titania is gabbing with the fairies—Peaseblossom, Mustardseed and colleagues—my fellow groundling gave out with a sharp, "No, no, no, 't'isn't it, 't'isn't it."

Decidedly prosaic as opposed to iambic pentameter, and spoken with such vehemence, I finally turned to look at him. As I say, he was short—about five-foot-seven or eight, thin and wearing what, considering the comedy we were observing, I might call well-worn rustics' clothes—lendings, in the Shakespearean vernacular, that weren't far from what could be purchased nowadays at an Urban Outfitters.

Like many men at the turn of the twenty-first century, he had a mustache, a goatee and a gold ring in his left ear.

I leaned over a foot or so and said into that left ear, "Do you mind? I'm trying to hear the play."

"And swich am I," he said, "but I hear not the play I wrote."

"Swich," I thought. Uh-oh, I thought. I know about the Jerusalem

Syndrome where pilgrims in the Holy Land suddenly think they're Jesus or John the Baptist or the Virgin Mary—sometimes all three—but I'd never heard tell of the Globe Syndrome where Shakespeare pilgrims suddenly think they're the man himself. Now it seemed I was being brought up to date the hard way.

I did have a recourse. I was a five-pound groundling—not my weight but the price of a ticket reflecting twenty-first-century inflation. Among the many benefits of those few pounds was my ability to move away from the man. But before I departed, I thought I'd give him another close eye-balling so that if I found myself near him again, I could quickly ankle away, or if I saw him coming towards me, I could nimbly veer out of his path.

After telling me about not hearing "the play I wrote," he'd turned back to the stage. What I saw in profile again was the high forehead, the beak-y nose, the less-than-damask cheek, the mustache, the thin lips tightened in rising disgust, the goatee. I saw the gold earring, glinting in the mid-afternoon sun.

Funny, I thought to myself, this Globe Syndrome is getting to me, too. Not that I suddenly thought I was William Shakespeare and felt a pressing urge to write *King Lear*. (If only.) I wasn't thinking that. I was thinking the man at my right did resemble paintings and reproductions of paintings I'd seen of William Shakespeare.

I also thought, this is nuts. No two supposed likenesses of Shakespeare even resemble each other. Almost anyone with a narrow face or, for that matter, a broad face and a mustache and goatee or no mustache or goatee and a gold ring in his ear or no gold ring in his ear could be said to resemble what people think Shakespeare looked like.

Put a goatee and a gold earring on me and I could pass myself off as a Shakespeare lookalike. So I was just about to inch off from him, when the man turned to me and said, "Do you suppose I jest? O, I do not. The whoresons have played fast and loose with me." He had deep-set black eyes that abruptly turned to fiery coals. "Perhaps they think my death has left them free to alter what I've written as they choose."

He supposes, I thought, to con me by continuing to ladle on the iambic pentameter. I also thought, I may be a fool, but I'm not that big a fool. If he was going to take me for a fool, he'd learn to take me for a Shakespearean fool, the kind that's wiser than everyone else in his immediate vicinity.

"Look, Shakespeare," I said to myself, "you're disturbing me. I'm trying to hear your play, and you're not making it easy. If you don't want people to enjoy it, why did you write it in the first place?"

But what I thought I was saying under my breath had turned into a hiss, and the people around us were giving me dirty looks as they edged away. I turned back towards the stage, and as I did, I started sidling to the left.

He sidled right along by me. "I took my quill in hand," he hissed back at me—while irritated bystanders shushed us—"because I did indeed effect a happy end. Ne'er did I count on varlets changing what I orchestrated for the stage."

I made that adamant statement out to be something more like iambic multimeter and was at a loss as to how I might answer it.

No answer was necessary. Having unburdened himself of his

thought, he took a few deliberate steps' leave of me and resumed watching and listening to the actors with basilisk eye and gazelle ear. I could see he'd resumed muttering to himself. I, too, went back to watching the play and assumed our exchange had ended.

An incorrect assumption, because when the intermission (the interval, that is) came and I was standing in the courtyard with the other milling playgoers, I was caught off guard by my groundling friend coming on me from behind and saying, "I wrote my plays in five acts, and they present them in two. God's wounds, they do not ken the basic elements of my writing."

"Excuse me," I said, "but why are you telling me this?"

"Because you addressed me as Shakespeare. You seem to know who I am."

Me and my big mouth. I decided this had gone on long enough. "That was a joke," I said.

"I fail to see the humour in calling a man by his rightful name," he said.

I write "humour" in the English spelling, because he pronounced it in something like two and a half syllables, giving the second-syllable "u" just the merest blip of recognition.

I suppose that's how they pronounced it in the Elizabethan Age, I thought to myself facetiously but said to him, "I think this has gone on long enough, don't you? Shakespeare died in 1616. We're already in the twenty-first century."

"You are as surprised as I that I am here," he said. "I did not expect to be talking to you any more than you expected to find yourself talking to me. One moment there am I in gleeful orb, then find myself on earthly turf once more."

"You're saying you've come back from the dead," I ventured.

"I am saying I am back from the removed," he said. "I all but had it right with Hamlet's father. There is a sense of hovering o'er the land." He still seemed determined to speak in iambic pentameter. He said "hovering" as "hov'ring." If the man at my side is truly William Shakespeare, I thought to myself, perhaps he can't help himself.

The bells calling the audience to the play were clanging. I headed back to my role as groundling. My 16th-century companion headed back alongside me. "I like to be called Will," he said and held out his hand.

When someone calling himself Will Shakespeare and, from certain outward appearances could be, wants to shake hands, you do the polite thing. I held out my hand and reluctantly said who I am. I said I was Edgar Chapman. (I didn't say that my parents, Shakespeare lovers themselves and especially partial to *King Lear,* had named me Edgar after Gloucester's good son.)

We shook. He had a small hand but a firm grip. This, I thought to myself, could be the hand that wrote *Macbeth* and *The Comedy of Errors.* Unless he was left-handed. In that case he would have written *Macbeth* and *The Comedy of Errors* and *All's Well That Ends Well* and *Timon of Athens* et al with the other hand.

When we got back inside, I said, "I'm going to stand in the back here."

"What you will," he said. "I need to be closer."

I watched him slip through the crowd with agile movements until he was right at the lip of the stage. It came up to his forehead. Watching the actors return to the stage, I thought they would undoubtedly be aware of him chattering to himself and might even hear his expletives.

Apparently they did, and more. Not long after the second act began—he would have said the fourth act—the actor playing Bottom spoke a line as if directing it to the audience. This was in keeping, I had begun to see, with the original Shakespeare's notions about engaging the spectators.

Having no idea what he was letting himself in for, the actor had aimed his speech at my interval partner, who must have said something snappy in reply. The actor paused, laughed and then spoke his next line— a line that seemed to catch the other actors off guard. But only momentarily. After taking this Bottom in for a second and then casting fleeting looks towards the man calling himself Will, they continued the scene.

I noticed that throughout the rest of the performance, the actors would steal occasional glances towards where my new friend was standing, but though I could see his mouth moving in the three-quarter view I had, he didn't appear to say anything else explicitly to any of the ensemble members.

When the play finished—when Titania and Hippolytus were reconciled, when Hermia and Lysander and Helena and Demetrius were sorted, when Puck had asked indulgence and bid adieu—the audience cheered as one. Or almost as one. Will stood silently at first and then, without much apparent conviction, slapped his small hands together four or five times, turned and headed for an exit.

I headed for a different exit, hoping to get lost in the retreating crowd. No such luck. Will appeared before me, his dark eyes piercing the space between us. "You enjoyed the play?" he asked.

"Very much," I said. "I hope you won't mind my saying it's not my favorite of your comedies, but I think this is a good production." I didn't know if I was joking or being sincere.

"It's not my favorite, either," he said. "I wrote it in 1594 and in my usual haste. I improved as the century's candle wax waned, but I can also advise you that as I wrote this one, it's better than what you just witnessed. I lost count of the discrepancies between what I set down and what I feign watched." In his need to criticize, he was shifting from lilting poetry into heavy prose.

"Is that so?" I said.

"I' sooth," he said. "It got so I finally had to do something about it. Did you chance to see me speak to one of the actors?"

I acknowledged I had and that everyone else in the theatre also had—the actors as well as the audience.

This had no effect on him. "I wanted to assure," he continued, "that he spoke it as I wrote it and not as any miscreant folio reproduced it. And I was telling him to speak the ensuing lines more trippingly on the tongue than he had the previous ones. I was gratified he took my advice. You heard its musical felicitance."

He'd returned to iambic pentameter.

"'Felicitance?'" I said.

"You don't have the word, do you?" he responded. "'Felicitance,' meaning unexpected and felicitous. The adjective form is 'felicitant.' You don't have either because I didn't give them to you. It gladdens me to hear you have many of the words I coined. I'm sorry you don't have that one, but perhaps now you've heard it, you can pass it along. Although I meant to use it, I could never work it into any of the plays or sonnets. I had it in the first draft of *Twelfth Night* but took it out. I never got 'round to it again."

A light came into his dark eyes. "I mightily enjoyed the game of words and liked inventing them apace. I have a long list I never used. I'm very fond of 'recontrilate.'"

Hard as it is to credit, I realized I wasn't only going along with this, I was getting a kick out of it. I was beginning to succumb to believing I was in the real William Shakespeare's company.

We were now walking along the Embankment, talking like old acquaintances. "What does it mean?" I asked.

"'Recontrilate'? It means what you think it means—as do all the words I fabricated."

"Spell it and use it in a sentence," I said, feeling for an instant as if I were back in grammar school.

He said, "You understand I never even settled on a standard spelling of my own name, and neither did anyone else. Nevertheless, "recontrilate"—r-e-c-o-n-t-r-i-l-a-t-e. Used in a sentence—The gentleman regarded me and longed to speak but only could recontrilate."

"I see," I said but didn't. Well, I sort of saw. According to him, recontrilate must mean desiring to say what's on one's mind but unable to muster the courage to say it. Or something along those lines.

"'Andreony' is another favorite I never got 'round to using," Will said. "A-n-d-r-e-o-n-y. Licentiousness is not my joy in life, but andreony is. Malacious. M-a-l-a-c-i-o-u-s. Yon knave hath a malacious look in his eye. I've got a milliand of them. M-i-l-l-i-a-n-d. A million one hundred thousand."

He paused to massage his goatee, then said, "But disseminating neologisms is not why I'm here." He seemed to have plunged into deep and painful thought.

"If you've got lists of words you never put into the plays," I said, "I'm wondering if you have plays in your head you've never written down."

"Does the queen sit on a gilded throne?" he asked. (I assumed he was referring to Elizabeth I, but maybe he was referring to Elizabeth II. Maybe both.) "I have numerous plays still to write, but why should I write them if they're only to be called the work of someone else, some young pup alive and enerthetically wagging his tail now? I will not. Oh. Enerthetic—e-n-e-r-t-h-e-t-i-c, meaning with excessive athletic energy."

Whatever this folly was had me intrigued. "Then why are you—," I started to ask.

"Why am I here?" he cut me off. "I think I know. I think there's only one explanation." Then he cut himself off. "Do you have time for a drink?"

"Uh, yes," I said, dragging the vowels out to indicate uncertainty and suspicion.

"Good," he said. "I know a pub near here."

He knows a pub, I thought. If he's Shakespeare, any pub he knows is likely to be long gone. But I'd played along this far. Why stop then? After all, any pub he knew might have Falstaff in it.

We'd been walking in the direction of the Southwark Cathedral. He took a right turn and then a left. "There it lies," he said. And, indeed, at the next corner was a Tudor building with a pub on the first floor. "There was an alehouse at this location for years before I knew it. As long as there is ale and men who take their joy in drinking it, I suppose there will be an alehouse on this hallow'd spot."

We reached it. He pointed at the sign swinging above the door in the slight breeze and said, "How felicitant. There. I've used it—such a handy word."

The sign read "The William Shakespeare."

"In my day it was The King's Stallion," he said, "but otherwise it looks almost as it did then."

On entering, I realized it was a working man's pub, and curiously enough the clientele were not dressed that differently from my new comrade.

"Hail, fellows, well met," he said to them and was greeted by a round of hearty "Cheers, mate," which seemed to satisfy him.

"It has not changed, I'm pleased to say," he said. He looked at the other patrons, who'd returned to conversing loudly among themselves and punching each other on the biceps.

We ordered a couple of beers from a bartender who did look Falstaffian to me, but I decided that had to do with the off-kilter frame of mind into which I'd been drawn. I blinked and looked again. He still looked like Falstaff and gave enriched meaning to the phrase "belly up to the bar." (Not a phrase, I think, that Shakespeare manufactured.) Taking the bartender in, I half expected Prince Hal to issue from the Gents.

Will and I carried our beers to an old table into which all sorts of carvings had been made. He rubbed his fingers along some of them and suddenly said, "Clap eyen on this." He was running a thin forefinger along a "W. S." that had been incised. He took a swig of his beer, made a show of enjoying it and said, "I remain amazed to be here."

"I don't doubt it," I said, "seeing as you've been dead for close to four hundred years."

"Time is not a factor where I have been drifting. 'Tis all one."

"What brought you here?" I asked, very much looking forward to the answer I might get.

"I fear I cannot tell you rightly, sir," he said. The iambic pentameter he slipped into frequently was beginning to unnerve me. I'd started repeating the lines in my head and tapping out the measures with the fingers of my left hand. It was like a tic. I worried I might not be able to stop.

What was clear to me, though, was that it was as natural for him as breathing. Come to think of it, he probably breathed in iambic pentameter. I realized I was beginning to.

He went on. "One minute I was hovering. Next minute I was near the slowly flowing Thames. But though I cannot tell you how I am here, I think I can tell you why. You see, my good man, word reached me, as it always does with a man of words, that the authorship of my plays is in dispute.

"In the present age, an increasing number of scholars and would-be scholars are claiming to have amassed evidence that my plays were not from my hand. You can imagine how that grates. I will not claim that all my works are art, but each of them was writ with caring heart and often also with necessant speed. Thus, if somehow my offerings offend, it has not been deliberate, my friend."

I was listening—and tapping so consistently I could have been sending an S-O-S to all the ships at sea.

He caught me at it, and his tone changed. "What are you doing?" he asked.

"Don't mind me," I said. "It's just a nervous habit I have."

That assuaged him, likely because he was envisioning weightier matters, which he went on to express. "How prophetic the title *Love's Labour's Lost* has turned out to be. By which I mean to say the labours of my love could be lost were they to be attributed to others. What misprision! The names they toss about as if they were a juggler's colored balls—Christopher Marlowe, Thomas Kyd, Francis Bacon, Ben Jonson, Edward, Lord de Vere. Lord de Vere! Would that they had spake with him anon, his dithering had disabused them, sure."

He was becoming more agitated. He made fists of his small hands and was waving them. "What gave them leave to t'impute my plays to Kyd, or Marlowe, for that matter? Damn the churls! Did it ever occur to them that I might have written Kyd's plays or Marlowe's or, at the very least, contributed to them? Which devoutly, I did do. We were colleagues. Verily, we made suggestions one t'other. But write each other's plays? Never!"

He was on a genuine Shakespearean jag. He stopped waving his hands and gripped both my forearms with so much force I thought he'd cut off the circulation. He looked me in the eyes. "How much do you know about me?"

I hadn't expected to be asked such a direct question and fumfered. "I guess I know what everyone else knows," I said. "You were born in 1564. You came from Stratford-on-Avon. You were married to Anne Hathaway. You acted with the King's Men. You wrote the plays."

I was trying to remember any other fast facts, but I was drawing blanks. What I knew were the plays. One of the things people do know about William Shakespeare is that there isn't that much known. "There isn't that much known about you. I know that historians lose track of you completely from about 1585 to 1592. It's all speculation. They think you might have been acting with obscure troupes."

My forearms were beginning to hurt. I must have winced, because he let go and gave them each a cursory rub. He was massaging his goatee again and shaking his head. I could tell he was thinking about what I had just said. What I was thinking was that in my hurried remarks, I was making free with the pronoun "you"—as if I'd ceased to have any doubts he was who he said he was.

"Acting in obscure troupes," he said. "That gives my innards a twist. Indeed, I was acting and obscurely but not with traveling players. I was ta'en with learning my trade. Were I to write plays, I knew I had first to live life. Where did these fools imagine I acquired my knowledge of men and women? By doing work where I could observe them, that's where. I became an itinerant. I served on farms, in monasteries, at doss houses and homes of the rich, at sea, on land. I spent profitable hours with courtiers, soldiers, rustics, lawyers, lovers, thieves, musicians, merchants, scholars, philosophers, cooks, astronomers, mountebanks, tinkers, ostlers, doctors, clerics, beggars, necromancers, servants and rulers. I toiled in Lord de

Vere's stables. There's the origin of that rumour." (as stated before with "humour," he blipped on the second-syllable "u" in "rumour.")

He stood up to draw himself to his full height and pounded on his chest. "I wrote my plays," he said. "I had done the research." He said—no, bellowed—"I was fully qualified."

His voice was an arrow splitting the air. He had a trained actor's projection. The men at the bar applauded him. He removed his cap and gave them a low bow, sat down again and in modulated tones said to me, "My outrage is the cause of my return. I see my purpose plain before me now. What my accusers haven't reckoned with is solid evidence to prove them wrong."

I was tapping to beat the band.

"Your nervous habit," he said and looked at me with what I took to be Elizabethan pity.

"Right," I said. "I've tried to stop but haven't been able to as yet." But I wasn't so distracted by my tapping that the phrase "solid evidence" zoomed past me without my taking it in. "Solid evidence?" I repeated.

"Yes," he said. "Do I need to spell the words and use them in another sentence?"

"No, the first sentence will suffice, if you explain what you meant by it."

"I would have thought the meaning was quite clear," he said. "I kept early drafts of my plays. I kept notes I jotted down whenever I got ideas for characters or situations. I kept records of progress I made. My papers are my proof, and you may be intrigued to hear that among them are two nearly completed plays."

"But surely they've been destroyed," I said, by now way past having any gnawing doubts about the identity of the man with whom I was speaking. "Otherwise, they would have been found long ago, centuries ago."

"You cannot find what is well hidden," he said and took a long draft of his beer.

"Hidden?" I said.

"To be sure," he said. "They were my private papers. They were for my eyes only. So I hid them where no one would find them. I buried them, and now I only have to dig them up to establish my authorship beyond dispute."

"Where did you bury them?" I asked. "I hope you didn't conceal them anywhere near the old Globe. It was destroyed a second time twenty-six or twenty-eight years after your death and is now only partially preserved and surrounded by modern flats."

"How you mistake me," he said. "If you know my plays, you know I saw little future for the Globe. I predicted its eventual demise at the end of *The Tempest* when I referred to its having no more durability than a dream. I was far too clever. I buried them where they would not be disturbed until I chose to recover them."

Looking to right and left and behind him to the bar where the patrons were absorbed in their own conversations, he beckoned me closer and whispered in my ear.

That clandestine confidence was how I came to be meeting him after nightfall not two hundred feet from the William Shakespeare publick house, where he had devised a scheme and implored me to join him in it.

Was I going to say no? What if he did retrieve the lead box he claimed he'd sunk into a hole dug in a garden by the St. Saviour parish house that is now Southwark Cathedral?

He'd explained that when in 1610, he was considering leaving London, he decided it was time to inter his papers below ground and reasoned that if there had been a religious edifice of one sort or another at the St. Saviour parish house for a thousand years, there would be a religious edifice of one sort or another in the hallowed spot for another thousand years and more. He reasoned that his belongings were safer there than in any bank.

He'd reasoned correctly. For now Southwark Cathedral, renamed from St. Savior's in 1905, stands there, as does the garden and the ancient tree near which he'd buried the precious lead box.

He hadn't reasoned, more's the pity, that there would be a wrought-iron gate around the garden and that it would be locked at night, which we only discovered when, dressed in dark clothes and furnished with a shovel (his contribution) and a flashlight (a torch—my contribution), we reconnoitered near the garden.

"What do we do now?" I asked after we'd ascertained that no one was near and I'd tried the handle on the metal door with no luck.

He was undeterred. "I once worked as a locksmith's apprentice," he said. "I never made him a character in a play, but I remember everything he taught me." Within minutes he'd located a thin piece of scrap metal, and, Bob's your uncle, we were entering the parish garden, shutting the gate behind us without securing the lock. There were only three trees there, and Will went to the one by far the oldest.

He looked around to position himself correctly. "I was also apprentice to a gardener," he said, "and learned the rudiments of gardening. I put him in *Richard II*—act three, lines 23 to 123, they should be."

He gave me a few seconds to recall the scene before continuing. "When this tree was a mere sapling, I took into account how it would grow. I wanted to make certain that the box containing much of my work would not become displaced by its burgeoning roots."

He walked three paces from the trunk and with the shovel's handle pointed at a spot on the ground. "I surmise the chest of lead lies here," he said.

I was struck by a thought. "After four centuries," I said, "isn't it possible there has been a build-up of earth and that the, uh, chest of lead is much deeper than it was when you buried it?"

"I'd say the possibility is strong," he said, "but full prepared am I to labor long. I cannot think the box is sunk so deep that it will not be found 'fore russet dawn."

With that he bade me stand aside the gate to give him warning should someone intrude. (Now I'm *writing* in iambic pentameter—it's catching.)

So far I may be giving the impression that I was taking this all in stride. If so, it's a false impression. I was shaking in my running shoes— in part because it was a chilly night but mostly because I couldn't see how we would escape being discovered.

Before we had descended the staircase from the pavement above, we had cased the joint—if a cathedral simultaneously elegant and hulking can be called a joint. I had suggested that security guards might be lurking.

(Will was familiar with the concept of guards, although he didn't know the term "security guards.") We saw none. Nor did we see policemen on foot. Only an occasional pedestrian passed near where we stood obscured by night and shadows.

All was quiet on the cathedral's eastern front—and remained that way for an hour or more, during which I must have checked my watch at least fifty times. Almost as often I asked Will if he'd struck anything.

He hadn't, but he never betrayed the slightest sign of worry about his mission. On the couple of occasions when I volunteered to spell him, he took no time telling me he wasn't at all tired and would keep digging as long as needed.

Sometime after three, when the traffic was so light that the sound of an automobile or night bus barely interrupted the silence, I had turned away from the gate to ask Will again if he wanted me to take over from him. He said no, that he liked the work assignments as they were.

So I turned back to cover the gate and standing in front of me, having appeared from nowhere, was a man I figured to be at least six-foot-four or five and weighing three hundred pounds or more. He had broad features which, when I shined the torch on him from below, gave him the look of a heavy-duty bruiser.

Pushing past me into the garden, he asked, "What do you think you're doing?" It was a question for which there was no answer. Yes, there was the honest answer: "That's William Shakespeare over there. He's digging up a lead box in which he's stored papers that will offer so much incontrovertible proof he wrote all his plays that, once and for all, certain contemporary suspicions about authenticity and attribution can be laid to rest."

But in this instance honesty wasn't guaranteed to be the best policy. I did think of something. Stuttering it out, I said, "My friend and I were in the garden earlier today, and he dropped a ring he's trying to find." I thought of something else. "It's not a valuable ring, not gold or anything, no diamond in it. But it does have sentimental value for him."

I must have sounded like a blithering idiot. I certainly sounded like that to myself. The hulking intruder looked at me as if I were a meringue he could crush beneath his huge feet. He gave me another shove and headed towards Will. As he did, Will raised his shovel high and said, "You ask what I am doing here, old salt. The better query is what you might want."

The moving mound of flesh and bone stopped in his tracks and said, "I don't need to explain myself to you. All you need to know is I'm a copper in plain clothes, telling the like o' you to clear out o' 'ere."

That's all I had to hear. I stared at Will with what I hope was a "let's do as he says—and do it pronto" look. But Will wasn't looking at me. He had walked up to the mammoth interloper and planted his much smaller self directly in front of him. Instead of continuing to hold the shovel aloft, he rested on it as if he were a toff with a walking stick.

He bent his head back in order to gaze into the glaring fat, round face and said, "'S blood you starveling, you elf-skin, you dried-newt's tongue, you bull's pizzle, you stockfish. O for breath to utter what is like thee, you tailor's yard, you sheath, you bow-case, you vile standing-tuck, you sanguine coward, you bed-presser, you horseback breaker, you huge hill of horse meat, get ye gone."

When it was clear he'd finished, the man—who had backed off a foot or two or three during the peroration—said, "Hold on, mate. No need to get personal. I was just 'aving a right bit o' fun in the middle o' the night. I'll be gettin' along now. I 'ope you find your ring. I know what them kinds of things can mean to a bloke." With that he did a clumsy about-face, went out the gate, which he then very carefully closed behind him.

Will gave me a knowing look.

"You just took quite a chance," I said.

"No swich thing," he said. "You forget who I am. Will Shakespeare. I write plays. Could I not see into the minds of men, I nothing am and must lay down my quill. Or my shovel."

He held it up and said, "I knew him for a bounder at first glance. His manner and his bearing were the clues. I recognized his cunning, as you see. And now, my liege, I hie me back to work, and you to your watch at the iron gate."

The digging resumed until the mound of dislodged dirt was several feet high and his head disappeared below ground level. It wasn't more than half an hour, however, before I heard him give a cry and then heard the tapping of metal on metal. "'Tis found," he said.

I left my vigil on the instant to peer down at him furiously freeing what was a narrow box about eighteen inches long, twelve inches wide and about six inches deep. When he had unearthed it, he handed it up to me. It weighed perhaps ten pounds, and dirt clung to it. It had a hasp but no lock. I set it down and gave Will a hand up from the hole he'd dug.

I was eager to open the box, as was he, but he only raised the lid to reassure himself that its contents were intact. He allowed me a peek, and what I saw did appear to be old papers tied with old ribbons.

Then he insisted I return to the gate while he filled the hole in. This took less time than the digging had, and it was no more than another half hour before he replaced the grass square that covered it so that it all but appeared it had never been tampered with.

By that time the sky in the east was beginning to get light. It was dawn, but so far not russet. We left the garden, closing the gate behind us, whereupon Will wangled the piece of scrap metal in the key hole and once again the gate was locked.

I held the box while he did that, but when he'd finished with the lock, he took the box back and pointed towards the Embankment, which was only sixty or seventy feet away. He was indicating it was there where we'd examine the contents of the lead box more thoroughly.

What seemed like seconds and a lifetime later, we were seated on a bench with only an occasional early-morning jogger going by. Though Will looked as if he could use a shower and I undoubtedly looked tired, there was nothing about us to make anyone take an unusual interest.

With no ado about much, Will finally raised the lid fully. There lay the papers about which he had spoken. He picked up one sheaf and untied the ribbon. I saw the handwriting—tall, thin, febrile letters leaning towards the right as if running to catch something down the block. I saw a sheet of paper, the writing on which began, "I, Will Shakspear."

He lay that sheaf aside and removed another and then another and then another. After removing a half dozen that seemed indisputable proof he had—as he maintained—written his plays, he picked one up and said, "Here 'tis. The one nearly completed play about which the waiting world knows nothing."

He handed it to me.

I looked at the title—*Love's Labour's Won.*

Just as I did, the first rays of sun shot over the Thames from the east, and something that could be deemed tragic in itself occurred. The manuscript I was holding disintegrated in my hands. So did the sheaves of paper we had stacked neatly next to us on the bench. And so—because Will had unfortunately tilted the box eastward—did everything else therein.

All that was left were grey ashes. My hands were covered with them. So were Will's. So was the bench. So was the inside of the lead box.

Will and I looked at each other. On his wedge of a face was an expression that went far beyond dismay. "But you saw my authorship approved," he said to me as he set the lead box on the bench.

"And did I so and can attest as much," I replied in my own consoling (I hoped) iambic pentameter.

"That is all I need," he said, "someone who can speak on my behalf. And so to you I bid a last farewell." With that he vanished, leaving behind only the lead box and grey ash that was already blowing away in the now-russet early morning breeze.

And leaving me behind to speak on his behalf—to defend him and the authorship of every one of his plays good and bad or, since this is the Bard, extremely good and only slightly less good. Since I see no reason to recontrilate, I'll come out and say what that incorrigible punster Shakespeare might have said were he here to speak for himself: I got it straight from the whoreson's mouth.

What else did I get? The urge to write a play about a playwright struggling with writer's block, who overcomes his problem when he meets Shakespeare at a performance of *A Midsummer Night's Dream.* I'm thinking of including mistaken identities in the plot.

Isaac "Ike" Chafetz's Story

✄ or ✄

Adolf Hitler
and the Dissenting Jew

I bumped into Adolf Hitler on Fifth Avenue. I mean I really bumped into him. Actual physical contact. Impact. At the moment it happened, I hadn't been looking where I was going. My eye had been caught by a window at Cartier's, a store which I'd never actually entered for fear an uppity salesman would openly snicker at me.

Then, suddenly, I felt myself come up against an object I knew was a fellow pedestrian who was also not paying attention to his (or her) trajectory.

Turning with a mixture of annoyance and embarrassment to inspect the wayward stroller, I had to look down several inches. The man—as it turned out to be—was somewhat shorter than my six-feet-two-inches. He was gazing into my chest—tweed blazer, Oxford blue shirt, regimental tie. (For what regiment headquartered where, I had no clue. My people didn't have much to do with these sorts of regiments, as you might guess.)

After only a split second, the man tilted his head upward, and I was peering directly into Adolf Hitler's face—the close-set and stony eyes, the oily hair (under a soiled cap) descending in a taut diagonal over his brow, the sketch-comedy mustache, the all-set-to-bray mouth.

Sure, it could have been someone who looked like Adolf Hitler, but it wasn't. I knew as much. How could I be so certain? Because all my life— or at least since early childhood—I knew that sooner or later Adolf Hitler was coming to get me. Coming to get me, dead or alive. That is, Hitler would come to get me, whether *he* was dead or alive. He was on record about that. He was going down in history for that. He'd scorched the records of civilized behavior over that.

It was only by accident of birth that I had escaped Hitler's clutches so far. I'd done so by being born in the United States and not Germany or Poland or Hungary or France or the Netherlands—and I had the effrontery to be born after Hitler had shot himself.

That was pure luck. If I had been born in Germany or Poland or Hungary or France or the Netherlands, and while entire indigenous populations were still kowtowing to Hitler, I surely would have been rounded up and marched through streets past jeering crowds to be loaded onto a train and sent to Bergen-Belsen or Dachau or Auschwitz or Treblinka or you-name-it for gassing.

This I knew and had often asked myself, "Why me? How, when so many people better than me were exterminated, was I fortunate enough to be spared?"

I could have been born to European parents. Or my parents, but for the accident of their births, could just have easily been older and lived in the old country and had me in the thirties when things were getting bad but when so many Jews denied how very bad it was getting. Even in 1938 when Kristallnacht made it plain this was no passing phase, many remained in denial.

My frequent ruminations hit me as as a form of survival guilt. I suppose that's exactly what it was, and I couldn't shake it.

But yes, survival guilt or not, it was unmistakably Adolf Hitler glaring at me. It was unmistakably Adolf Hitler glaring into my sport coat, undoubtedly checking for a yellow star—or seeing one where one would have been under other circumstances.

My head was so loud with thoughts, it was as if a factory whistle had gone off. This was no hallucination. Hallucinations don't have chunky avoirdupois.

As far as I knew—not that I've ever studied hallucination pathology—hallucinations also don't have aromas. Hitler did. There was a pungent smell rising from him that might as well have had thick, invisible fingers for gripping. That's how tenaciously I felt I was being held by it. The odor was rising from the clothes Hitler wore.

It wasn't the uniform he'd affected as the ranting dictator, as the bellowing fascist, but a workingman's outfit made of cheap fabrics, fabrics a step up from burlap—but maybe not a full step. He had on the loose-fitting jacket, baggy trousers and rough-hewn open-necked shirt of a day laborer with some sort of tatty bandana tied around his scruffy neck.

The stench was so alarming that I looked down at Adolf Hitler's clothes to see what could give off such fumes, the kind of fumes homeless men radiate when occupying subway banquettes everyone else is painstakingly avoiding.

As I examined Hitler's person, I realized the man was also carrying some objects bound with heavy twine. I knew immediately what they were: canvasses—18"x12" (or thereabouts) canvasses bound so that only the backs of two of them faced out.

In no more than the time it takes for an eye to blink, a lip to quiver, a hand to tremble, I realized I hadn't only come toe-to-toe with Adolf Hitler, I'd also encountered Adolf Schicklgruber, the aspiring painter. That explained the dried paint blotches on the dictator's jacket and trousers.

So is this what Hitler is doing now, I conjectured—peddling his amateurish paintings? Is he on his way to or from Central Park where he'd been recording primitive versions of landscapes? Had he been sitting on an Upper East Side stoop memorializing stately or not-so-stately facades?

I wasn't about to inquire.

Why should I? This was Adolf Hitler. For all I knew, the paintings and perhaps art supplies might not have been all the short, compact, odiferous Hitler was carrying in the satchel he had on his back. With his free hand, Hitler could have pulled a Luger from his pocket and dispatched me the way SS guards shot Jews in Berlin and Warsaw streets for the sick thrill of it.

Only a few seconds had passed during which I was processing this abruptly repugnant information, and I felt no need to let any more go by, particularly since it now seemed as if Hitler were about to speak.

To say what? "*Juden schwein*" at the top of his lungs? I couldn't run the risk of that happening. I just put up my hand to wave "No, I don't want anything to do with you" and shook my head so violently in dismissal that I felt as if I might have injured my thyroid.

Then I stepped around Hitler, and as I did, saw the depressing vagrant register a startled, mean look. That's all I saw, for I didn't look back to check if the grubby Schicklgruber was still there, to verify if he was still rooted to the spot or, worse, was following in heated pursuit.

I was so disoriented by the episode that I forgot where I'd been headed. (To this day, I can't remember my destination.) Instead, I hot-footed it to the subway entrance at the northeast corner of Fifty-third and Fifth, and only when I'd pushed furiously through an underground turnstile and had come to a halt on the platform did I look back to see if Schicklgruber/Hitler was on my trail, on my Jewish tail, to see if he was determined Hitler-like not to rest until he overtook my Hebrew *tuchis*.

That grim thought prompted me, unconsciously, to rub my rear—as if I'd already been roundly swatted by the bound stack of canvasses. But Hitler wasn't giving chase and, my good luck, a train was approaching.

Relief, though, was short-lived—sustained for only two days, in fact, during which I convinced myself that the Hitler-spotting (and the Hitler-smelling) had been my imagination acting up. Not that I'd conjured the manifestation from thin air—or conjured the miserable figure from fetid air. There had been something, someone there, all right. I had felt it enough to know it wasn't ectoplasm I could have plunged my hand through. I'd sniffed the being, and for hours afterward the foul aroma lodged in my insulted nostrils.

I hadn't heard the thing speak, of course, because I hadn't afforded it the opportunity. But it had been there, and I had to talk myself into believing what I'd initially dismissed: that it was some pathetic street person who suffered the misfortune of looking uncannily like Adolf Hitler.

I convinced himself—when I wasn't in actual physical contact with
the man—that it had been, must have been, a pitiful soul who didn't
even look that much like Adolf Hitler, or the less well-known Adolf
Schicklgruber.

I concluded, if tentatively, that my long-ingrained, galloping post-
Holocaust paranoia had supplied the frightening facial alterations. I went
over in my mind—sometimes even talking aloud to myself—what I'd
been doing and/or thinking right before bumping into the person I'd
taken for the miscreant Fuhrer. I tried to discern what might have predis-
posed me to hang the Adolf Hitler identity on an anonymous pedestrian.
I bombarded myself with hard-edged comments like, "You couldn't have
seen what you're convinced you saw" and "Why would you want to do
such a thing to yourself?" and "Is an imagined sighting a manifestation of
incipient madness?"

No explanation came to me. Not a blessed thing—or even something not blessed but merely mundane. Near as I recalled of that afternoon, I'd been in a good mood, going along happily minding my business,
enjoying a perfectly fine, ordinary day.

Within hours—many hours—I did get myself back on a nearly even
keel. I'd done some work, talked with friends about nothing in particular—certainly not about literally coming up against Adolf Hitler. I'd eaten
a few healthy and hearty meals. I'd resumed my life.

Most of all, I mentioned nothing to no one. It wasn't the sort of
thing I needed to mention, was it? "Oh," I heard myself practicing, "The
oddest thing happened today. I bumped into Adolf Hitler on Fifth
Avenue. No, really, I bumped right into him. I didn't give him the time

of day, of course. But there he was, just as plain as you or me. I know. I thought he was dead, too. It just goes to show you can't trust the media."

But that's not the kind of thing you say to friends and expect them to sit silently taking it all in without wondering what drugs you're on or how they can gracefully excuse themselves for a minute to summon the men in white suits.

"Look," I sensibly told myself in the mirror more than once, "people go through these things all the time, seeing people who are long since dead. It's an everyday occurrence. I just happened to see Adolf Hitler. No big deal. This time it's just my imagination running away with me. I'll heal but never heil."

The pale man in the mirror had even come to believe it—kinda. Until I was climbing out of the downtown subway at Christopher Street two days later to walk to my Charles Street one-bedroom and, reaching the street, noticed a familiar figure standing on the corner, staring in my direction.

You guessed it: Adolf Schicklgruber Hitler.

As I began crossing Seventh Avenue with the green light, I realized Hitler was also stepping heavily after me and closing in. This can't be happening, I thought to myself, and turned on a dime. (Actually, I turned on a penny that had been pressed into the asphalt, as so many have been pressed into Manhattan streets.) I also thought to myself, "I have to know Greenwich Village better than Adolf Hitler does. I can outfox him."

With that, I began a circuitous route up, down and sideways through the Village's famously non sequitur thoroughfares, moving more quickly than Hitler—still carting his canvasses—was able to. I knew I was pulling away, because from time to time I cast sidelong glances in Hitler's direction to monitor his progress. Gratified, I noticed my pursuer was falling farther and farther behind.

At one point, I saw Hitler stop completely, lay his burden down, put his hands on his knees and take several deep breaths. I took the opportunity to speed up and, at the next corner where I knew Hitler couldn't spot me, begin doubling back to Charles Street. In only a few minutes I reached my building.

I looked right and left, furtively. No sign of Eva Braun's sweetie pie. I'd gotten my keys out along the way and was able to slip inside without—I was certain—being seen. Allowing exhaustion to overtake me, I mounted the stairs to my second-floor apartment and went in.

Before shutting the door, I listened for footsteps behind me. Nothing. No one. Phew. Sigh. I crossed the worn carpet to sit in my club chair for a minute, a chair I'd relaxed in so regularly over the years that the cracking leather seat was molded to my backside.

I remained there for several minutes, trying to think positive thoughts. Then, figuring the crisis was over, I pulled myself from the marvelous comfort of the chair to make a few phone calls I'd been putting off.

On the way to my landline, however—I never used my cellphone in the house—I detoured past one of the living-room windows facing the street. (My apartment was situated at the front of the building—2F, as opposed to 2R.) Glancing out the window, which wasn't decorated with curtains but featured only a tired old shade, I thought I detected movement at the end of the block.

I looked more closely. Oh, no! Standing on the corner by one of the street's thick-based metal lamp posts was—I couldn't even articulate the name to myself: AH. ASH. (And isn't that second monogram a fitting one for this particular person?) And damned if that capped head with those furiously stony eyes wasn't turned upward towards my windows.

I pulled myself back and resumed breathing so heavily I was all but hyperventilating. Now what? Remaining where I believed I couldn't be seen, I lectured myself on control. I asked myself a series of questions, the brand of questions any psychotherapist worth his or her salt would have wanted me to ask.

For instance, I asked whether, given the distance between me and the squat figure at the corner, I was still certain of that figure's identity. I asked whether that person was truly fixed on my windows or was just panning around to orient himself. I asked if—since I was inside, the man was outside and the skies were becoming increasingly overcast—I couldn't wait out the intruder.

That's what I did for the next couple of hours. Two or three times during those slowly passing hours, I edged to the window and, you can bet on it, saw the man waiting, rocking back and forth on his poorly shod feet.

I even had what I thought could be a good idea. I'd call Elsie Abrams, who lived on Perry Street. If she were home, I'd ask her to walk around the block and see if she noticed a strange little man loitering on the corner. If so, could she describe him? Did she think he resembled anyone she knew or knew of?

I called Elsie, to whom I often referred as Elsie A. (To her, I was always Ike, or Ikie—private names being what they were in New York.) She was home and, though sounding skeptical about my unusual request, agreed to honor it. She said she had a few things to finish before she could "reconnoiter"—her word, not mine—but then would "oblige" me by circling the area. She didn't sound overly enthusiastic, moderately tolerant was more like it. Then again, that was Elsie at the best of times.

I waited it out, getting some work done that needed to be done. I was creating a new logo for an ad agency client and tackled it with at least half my concentration. Apparently, I worked up to most of my concentration, because maybe about forty-five minutes later I was jarred from what I was doing by the ringing phone.

Funny how insistent the phone can sound at times and at other times sound merely intrusive or even endearing. This was an insistent ring. It was Elsie. She wanted to know what I was talking about. There had been no man on the corner, familiar to her or otherwise. Passersby, yes, but no one stationary, no one anchored and looking around suspiciously.

"Now I know you're just seeing things," she said, "or people, or whatever it is you see, Bubbie."

Wanting to believe her but afraid to, I went to the window, still standing somewhat back from it. I looked at the corner. No one there. I asked Elsie if she'd passed anyone who looked to be lurking.

"What does lurking look like?" she wanted to know.

"You know," I said, "anyone who looked strange, who looked as if he didn't belong."

Elsie said, "This is New York, Ike. Everyone looks strange. No one looks like he belongs. Or she."

"Did you see anyone carrying canvasses, anyone with a funny mustache and hair slicked over his brow?" I pressed her.

"Manhattan is Art Central," Elsie said. "Every other person you see, especially in this neck of the woods, is hauling a canvas somewhere." I couldn't argue the point. "What's this all about, anyway?" Elsie asked. "You've got to stop this."

I uh-ed and er-ed for a few seconds, deliberating whether I should tell Elsie all. I did enough uh-ing and er-ing that Elsie said, "Are you all right? You're acting odder and odder."

"Well," I began haltingly, "it's really nothing, but…" I trailed off.

"It can't be nothing," Elsie said. "You've made some weird requests over the years I've known you, but you've never asked me to walk around the block to spy on people like a zaftig Nancy Drew. Come on, Ike, tell me."

I swallowed and blurted, "Adolf Hitler is after me."

I both appreciated and regretted the admission.

"What?!!" was Elsie's monosyllabic response, the accompanying exclamation points flying at me like poisoned darts.

"Adolf Hitler is after me," I repeated. "I know it sounds crazy, but—"

"But what? Adolf Hitler—*the* Adolf Hitler—is alive and well and living in New York for the sole purpose of hunting down Isaac Chafetz? Someone hasn't been taking his Zoloft."

"You know I don't take Zoloft," I said.

"Then you should start," Elsie said, "Or Paxil or whatever you can lay your fat fingers on in a big hurry."

"I don't expect you to believe me," I said.

Elsie said in the nasal drawl she'd refined over the years, "That's good. At least you have some semblance of sanity left. If you expected me to

believe you, I'd have thought you'd gone completely, totally bonkers."
There was a slight pause, really the slightest of pauses. Then, "You know
what your problem is, Ikie. You don't get out enough."

"I get out plenty," I said.

"You may get out plenty," Elsie replied, "but it still isn't enough.
What are you doing tonight?"

"Staying home," I said.

"See what I mean?" Elsie said. "You're going to stay home so Adolf
Hitler doesn't pick you off in a crowd? No, you're not. You're going to the
movies with me. We're going to the Angelika to see the French movie
everybody says is great."

"What French movie?" I asked.

"The one about the lovers in Paris," Elsie said.

"All French movies are about lovers in Paris," I said.

"I know," Elsie said, "but don't you get it? The movie is French. Adolf
Hitler won't want to see it. I'm hanging up now. Meet me there in an
hour. And don't try not showing up."

With that the line went dead, the normal kind of dead, not any fishy
kind of dead that might have been caused by an interfering, telephone-
tapping one-time dictator.

What could I do? I changed into running shoes—just in case—and
left the house. But not without looking up and down the street and looking up and down the street again before quitting the front door and not
before looking around me every block or so and at every corner and not
without, when keeping my eyes focused forward, listening for sinister
footsteps behind me.

"Any sign of you-know-who?" Elsie asked first thing when I met her in the Angelika lobby.

"That'll be enough of that," I said. "I'm only telling you what I saw with my own eyes."

"When did you last have your eyes checked?" Elsie said, but then she brusquely waved a handful of long, red fingernails at me to indicate she was dropping the subject.

The whole while we sat in the lobby waiting to be called for the movie, she held to her tacit promise. Only once, when she caught me surreptitiously scanning the large room did she say anything—and then only a prolonged and verbally italicized "Stop it."

Otherwise, she restricted her regularly curled tongue to other matters. She did this straight through to our taking seats in the auditorium, where we were among the first to be seated and whereupon we had to witness the standard movie-goers rush.

Eventually, the later-comers were clogging the aisles, attempting to spot seats together and jockeying for positions. In the flurry, someone pushing past the two people on the aisle directly in front of us was causing a small commotion. He appeared to be carrying an unwieldy bundle with which he was knocking people on their heads or limbs.

These kinds of remarks were salting the air: "Ouch." "Watch where you're going, buddy." "Hey, man!"

Finally, the clumsy patron reached his seat, where, on sitting down, he turned around and looked directly at me with beady eyes ablaze.

"It's him," I said to Elsie.

"It's who?" Elsie said, not sure where to direct her attention.

"The aisle in front of you," I said. I was whispering loudly now. "Next to the couple next to the couple next to the couple on the aisle."

Elsie looked to the left of the three designated couples, but the man was facing forward now, and she could get no clear angle on him. To get a proper look at him, she would practically have had to lean so far forward she might as well have been in the row.

"I'm not going to make a spectacle of myself," she said.

"Forget it," I said. "Let's just get out of here."

"Are you for real?" Elsie said. "The movie hasn't even started."

"Yes, I'm for real," I said. "Let's go." I sprang out of my seat and started up the aisle.

Exasperated, Elsie got up, too, and hurried after me. When we were on the escalator up to the ground-floor level, I said, "I can't look back. Is he following us?"

"No one is following us," she said.

I wished I could take her word for it, but I couldn't. I had to see for myself. Wheeling round, I looked past Elsie and down the escalator to the receding bottom. She was right. No one was behind us.

My heartbeat was slowing. As I was about to tell Elsie she could breathe easy for the moment, I faced front. And there at the top of the escalator—waiting with canvasses in hand and looking like a funhouse dummy—was the Schicklgruber personage.

That was when I knew what I'd known all along: There would be no avoiding my long-awaited nemesis, who at that instant held his free hand out towards me.

Expecting what? Reaching for what? Beckoning for what? My utter surrender? My acquiescing to accept some unimaginable fate? I shook my head no and, swiveling back to Elsie, said, "Now do you see him?"

But Elsie was still looking behind us. "Who?" she said. "Where?"

"At the top of the escalator," I said, pointing behind me.

Elsie A. looked where I was pointing.

"Who?" she said again. "Where?"

I looked at the top of the escalator, which we were rapidly approaching. Again no one. Again nothing.

Elsie put her hand on my arm. "I'm beginning to worry about you," she said. "You're overworked. You're super-stressed. Let's go get something to eat. Or tea or coffee or something really sweet, and you can tell me all about it."

"I just need to go home," I said.

"Maybe that's not such a bad idea, after all," Elsie said. "You can sleep it off."

We walked the quarter-mile silently. Only when we got to Elsie's door did she say, "Maybe I should be seeing *you* to *your* door."

"I'm okay," I said, not wanting to alarm her any more than I already had but also not believing that things were anywhere near okay.

"Are you sure?" Elsie asked.

"I'm sure," I said.

"You don't look sure," Elsie said.

"I'm sure," I said, feeling as unsure as I'd ever felt.

"If you're sure…" Elsie said, unsurely, and slowly opened her door.

I started off, only looking back to see Elsie standing at her open door and giving me a wan smile. I smiled wanly back and set off around the corner, looking behind every car, every tree and every freestanding traffic sign for the least hint of the persistent Adolf Hitler.

My stride alternated between hasty and halting—hasty to cover the three-minute trip without incident and halting to register any indication I was being stalked. That I wasn't, that the footsteps I heard belonged to innocent pedestrians, to neighbors walking their dogs, to exhausted skate- boarders carrying their skateboards, to lovers arm-in-arm did little to put me at ease.

"This is only temporary," I said to myself with doleful uncertainty about Adolf Hitler's inevitable reappearance.

I was so dolefully uncertain that I was not surprised when I walked through the door to my apartment and saw, sitting in the club chair as if there by proprietary right—with the bound canvasses leaning against one of the chair's arms—the man who'd rapidly become the bane of my liv- ing-on-borrowed-time existence.

Had Hitler been sitting or standing anywhere else in the apartment but where he was, I might have had a drastically different—and much more defeated—reaction than the one I did have. But what flashed through my mind was the thought that the seat molded to my own back- side could now be in the process of remolding itself to Hitler's rump.

Mounting indignation trumped all my other impulses. Fight bested flight. Motioning Hitler to get up, I marched to the chair and, as Hitler stood, I said in a voice the forcefulness of which startled and impressed me, "You've got some nerve, barging in here like this. What do you want? Out with it."

At last, Hitler spoke—in the raspy manner I recognized from

Movietone News coverage and Leni Riefenstahl's *Triumph of the Will*. The rasp was somewhat subdued but still raspy.

"Then you know who I am," Hitler said.

"Of course, I know who you are," I said. "Whom else could I take you for?"

"Then if you know who I am, you know why I'm here."

"To get the Jews you missed the first time around," I said, "but you're not going to get me—not in my own home, where I don't have any Zyklon B handy or any valuable furniture you can appropriate for that Berchtesgaden retreat of yours. You're definitely not about to take possession of the chair you've just pulled yourself out of."

Having said that, I looked around for a blunt instrument I might need to defend myself if Hitler got fresh.

"No, no, *nein*," Hitler said, giving his mustache a facial twist. "That's not it. You have it all wrong."

I felt myself becoming more aggressive, less intimidated with every word. I pointed at the canvasses leaning against the chair. "I'm not going to buy one of your lousy paintings, either, if that's what you're thinking."

"I was hoping you'd do that, too," Hitler said, "but I have another, more important reason for being here."

"Not interested in hearing it," I said.

Hitler, now standing with his cap in his hand, continued. "I need something else from you."

I looked at the clock on the kitchen wall. It was 8:17. "From me, you're not even getting the time of day," I said.

"Time means nothing to me," Hitler said.

I felt a twinge of disappointment at not being able to deny Hitler the time of day.

Hitler didn't take that in, though, and went on. "I'm condemned to wander in a nether world until I find a particular person."

"I'm a very particular person," I said. "I'm particular about spending downtime with someone who tried to conquer all of Europe and in the process exterminated six million Jews."

"That's just it," Hitler said, looking as if he'd like to sit down again but not daring to. "The particular person I need to find is a Jew able to forgive me for what I've done to so many of his fellow Jews."

I felt faint. "You mean to say," I said, "you're contrite? You mean to say if you can find one Jew who'll forgive you, you—you'll—what? Get a better hammock in hell? Get into heaven? Get to rest in peace?"

"Something like that," Hitler said. "I was hoping you are that forgiving Jew."

I thought a moment. "Why choose me?"

"Simple," Hitler said, "You have a reputation for being nice. I thought you might be able to find it in your heart to show some compassion."

Nice! Throughout my life, I've been nice. What had it gotten me but an unsolicited visit from—of all unwelcome people—Adolf (Schicklgruber) Hitler.

"In your entire life," I asked, "did you find it in your heart to show some compassion, any compassion?"

"Towards Jews I did not," Hitler said, "towards Hermann Goering, some."

"Surely," I said, "I can't be the first Jew you've asked, the first Jew you've haunted like this."

"No," Hitler said, "there have been many more. I'm always hoping the next one will be the one."

"Well, it's not me," I said, "and now I'm going to ask you to leave, which is more than you asked my people when you could have." I moved to take Hitler by the arm but stopped myself. I couldn't bear the idea of touching him.

Hitler took in the aborted gesture and flinched. Then, regaining a modicum of composure, he picked up his canvasses and, unescorted, walked to the door.

There, he stopped and said, "Are you sure you don't want to reconsider? I can wait."

I pointed at Hitler's cap, implying the man should put it on, and said, "I don't need to think it over. I can never forgive and I can never forget. I know forgiveness is supposed to be divine, but maybe there are times when not forgiving is also divine. I hope this is one of them."

I went to the door and opened it. Hitler left. When I had closed the door, I went to one of the front windows to watch Adolf Hitler step out into the street, the same Adolf Hitler who had rallied thousands to salute him whenever he did so much as step onto a balcony. Out he came with his tied canvasses. He stopped in front of the building. He looked right and left. After a few seconds, he started walking to the left at a halting pace. I watched him until he was out of sight.

I felt no guilt at all. I felt no guilt for the first time since I can't remember when.

Peter Fellowes's Story

✂ or ✂

Oscar Goes Wild

The temporary Paris rental that Con Dooley put me on to for the time away I needed in which to clear my head of several depressing New Haven developments—divorce after a steadily downhill five years not the least of them—was five flights up (the quatrième étage) and included no elevator. The retreat was at the back of a Seventh Arrondissement building and overlooked a small garden with a small stone patio, a white wrought-iron table and two matching chairs. Other than a few chatty birds, no one seemed to occupy it while I was in residence.

Not entirely true. One afternoon, I looked down the five floors and saw a woman seated on one of the chairs, reading a magazine. A small tea service was on the table. From where I viewed her, she looked like Madame Recamier come to life, but she wasn't.

She was just a (presumably) French woman reading a magazine. The view, populated or not, was more interesting than the rental's interior. From the way it was furnished, I assumed the owners never inhabited it but merely derived income from temporary leases. The living room was shabby, as was the bedroom, with a closet containing sheets, pillowcases and towels, all yellowing with age but clean and laundered, I assumed, by whoever previously occupied the space. The kitchen appliances were remnants of an age when French design was in a less advanced state.

Nevertheless, it suited my not too demanding purposes. An inveterate worrier and recent early retiree, I could indulge those constant preoccupations as well as work there as long as relative quiet ruled.

Mainly, it was someplace from which I could depart for more interesting surroundings and to which I could return when my interests or my drearier ruminations on any particular day of the open-ended days that I was in residence held sway.

If I worked in the morning on the family business obligations I'd assumed despite continuing disputes with my contentious younger and still working brother and sister, I could go to the museums or the parks or the sidewalk cafés or nowhere special in the afternoon, which is what I was doing on a reasonably mild, though slightly overcast, November afternoon, a slightly overcast November afternoon typical of the weather since I'd taken up residence.

I was still diligently probing my attempt to take a new control over my life when, having just rounded the corner from rue Bonaparte into rue des Beaux-Arts, a Paris street on which I don't think I'd ever been, I suddenly saw Oscar Wilde coming towards me.

I mean the real Oscar Wilde, who was traveling on his thin legs at an impressively fast clip, walking stick flailing in front of him, scarf flowing in the mildly gusting wind he and November were churning up around him. A green carnation dotted one of the lapels, accentuating his pigeon-breasted chest.

Had this moving image (in two meanings of the phrase) come to my attention in 1899, I might not have taken particular notice. It was widely known that Wilde was staying at the Hotel d'Alsace on the south side of this very street. It's the hotel in which he died and which is now known to parvenus as the luxuriously unprepossessing L'Hotel.

On the other hand, I very well might have taken note of him in 1899, since he was the famous, not to say the notorious, Oscar Wilde. But here it was several years into the twenty-first century. The playwright-poet-essayist-"somdomite" (that's the Marquis of Queensberry's misspelled assessment) had been dead since November 30, 1900.

I'd been sent into the world much later and was still alive and on the self-imposed lam on what I suddenly realized was November 30, nothing less than an anniversary of Wilde's demise. So as the apparently exhumed and reconstituted Wilde passed, I thought to stop him and say how much I admired his plays, especially *The Importance of Being Earnest*.

Yet I stifled the urge. He looked too much like a man on a mission for whom even hastily uttered praise would be an imposition. More to the point, even if this were the hand-to-heart Oscar Wilde, did I want to start with him? Okay, so it's Oscar Wilde, I said to myself. You've seen him. He may have seen you. Now forget it. Go on your way. Honoré de Balzac or Charles de Gaulle could be in the next street. You can look at them, too, and keep walking.

I gave Wilde wide berth—wider berth, considering his girth, than I might have had to give a slimmer personage. He breezed by me like a heifer—I mean zephyr. Only his flowing scarf brushed my shoulder. ("Oscar Wilde's scarf just brushed our shoulder," voices inside my head shouted like a music-hall chorus.)

And that was that—oblong-faced, full-lipped, small-chinned Oscar Wilde surged on.

Or so I thought, for behind me I suddenly heard a plummy voice call in English, "You, sir, hello!" I stopped without turning, certain the salutation, coming from whomever, couldn't have been meant for me, yet slightly apprehensive that it may have been. Again and closer I heard, "Yes, you, sir!"

I assumed it was Oscar Wilde speaking, but I had no idea to whom. It wasn't to me, I continued hoping. Hoping against hope, for just then I felt—and looked down to see—a gloved hand on my arm, tugging me to turn around.

I did. What was the alternative—pulling away rudely? Couldn't do it, much as I wanted. As I turned to face him, Wilde released me. He placed both gloved hands atop his tooled-silver walking stick, now planted firmly on the pavement, and looked me directly in the eye.

Oscar Wilde was, I realized with no small astonishment, addressing me with intent. He said, "My good man, when a stranger speaks to you, it's only polite to listen, even if what you're hearing isn't worth listening to. It's the courtesy the pursued owe the persistent."

I was stupefied. Oscar Wilde—wearing a double-breasted velour jacket, cap at a jaunty angle and knee breeches as out of step with fashion as they were odd in his own time—had, I think, just described me as "pursued" and himself as "persistent." More than that, he'd declared courtesy owed him. The extent of my debt, the extent of his persistence, I had no way to gauge. I was at a loss for words.

He was not. Unsurprisingly. "I had to talk to someone," he said. "I could not look at the wallpaper in that hotel for another minute. I can forgive dullness in my friends, but dullness in wallpaper is thoroughly unacceptable."

I was speechless, thinking Oscar Wilde had just made physical contact with me—actual physical contact. Saying nothing, I rubbed my arm where he had gripped it with more force than I might have expected. To him, my lack of response to the wallpaper sally was unsatisfactory. He gestured with a gloved hand that he expected a reply, was impatiently waiting for it.

I said the first thing that came to me, relieved that something—anything—had formed. "If the wallpaper got on your mind so much, couldn't you look out the window for a while?"

Taller than I had imagined Oscar Wilde would be and making the most of his height, he said, "You must never look out a window. You have no idea who might be looking in."

I hadn't thought of it that way but didn't say as much, nonplussed as I remained at having fallen against my better judgment into brief conversation with Oscar Wilde. Did I say "brief"? That's what I thought then. Ha!

This time Wilde looked to be judging my silence. After a short lapse, he said, "The man who thinks to find diversion in others is peering into the scullery with hopes of locating the drawing room."

I nodded my head to indicate I was in total agreement, not that in my nearly six decades I'd ever seen the inside—or, for that matter, the outside—of a scullery.

"Furthermore," he pressed on, both his hands again on the walking stick, his gaze now directed somewhere above my head, "art is in the eye of the beholder—as long as I am the beholder."

Damn, I thought, Oscar Wilde is talking to me about art. I wonder if he ever talked this way to Aubrey Beardsley.

At that point, he paused and looked at me blankly. I jumped to the conclusion that our more or less one-sided colloquy had drawn to a close. Relief overtook me. Hesitantly, I muttered something like "Thanks for the advice"—if indeed advice it was—"and goodbye."

I thought to leave him but stalled long enough for his gray (Dorian-gray?) eyes to come to life again. He said, "'Goodbye' is the saddest word in the English language—unless you include 'hello.'"

Then he did something curious. He indicated he was about to continue his walk and, with the walking stick, signaled that I should accompany him. I could only assume he didn't recall that when he stopped me, I was heading in the opposite direction.

What was I to do? If Oscar Wilde invites you—even tacitly—to accompany him on a promenade around Paris, do you think it over? Do you graciously beg off? Do you gratefully but firmly bend low and execute a crisp about-face? Do you question whether or not he is Oscar Wilde?

For me, the answer to all those questions was yes, but that's not what I said. Much as I wanted to—or did I?—I knew I wasn't going anywhere special, just taking my own spur-of-many-moments route to see what I might see.

So what did I do, my resolve thawing like ice cubes in hot coffee, I reversed the direction in which I thought I'd been going and fell in step with him. It was a lively step, and sensing—wrongly, as it turned out— the time had come for me to hold up my end of the unexpected dialogue if I was acquiescing to it, I said, "It's a beautiful day, isn't it?"

I wasn't just whistling "*La Marseillaise.*" It had turned into a beautiful day. The sun had come out, the wind had abated. Though the November chill was still present, it seemed less biting. The buildings behind the bare, stretching trees looked as if they'd been incised into a Paris-blue sky across which only a few gauzy clouds floated.

Wilde—looking at me as if to take a measure of my deepest shallow thoughts—said, "Remarking on the weather is the quickest way to reveal an impoverished mind. There's nothing more unnatural than communing with nature. To be at one with nature is to be at odds with the rest of the world. Anyone who prefers solitude to companionship is putting frivolity before wisdom. A man who watches his words sees little and says less. Those who preach morality rarely practice it. Travel broadens the mind, but so does remaining at home with a good book. Modesty is a virtue meant to be admired in others."

This outpouring not only made me feel as insecure as an undergraduate taking an exam for which he hadn't prepared, but I found myself wondering if I should be scribbling notes in anticipation of an impending semester final.

Wilde, whose gaze had again drifted off as he spoke, looked back to me and realized he'd struck me dumb. He stopped walking, placed his walking stick against my right arm with a certain amount of pressure and said, "Nothing personal, you understand."

He bowed his head, almost sheepishly, and confided, "I am compelled to speak in aphorisms." Then the authoritative tone infused his treble-clef voice again and he issued, "Anyone who becomes personal on first meeting will all too soon become impersonal."

We had reached rue Jacob, and he'd continued west for no particular reason I could discern. Also for no reason I could discern, he'd stopped at the southeast corner of rue Jacob and rue des Saints-Peres. He stood there as if analyzing a thought.

People streamed by, some taking us in—well, taking him in, for his garb—others paying little attention. Many of them were students issuing from or hurrying to the nearby Université René Descartes. Others were on the way to or from the facing post office. For all any of them knew, Wilde was wearing the latest retro fashions from the Yves Saint Laurent or Christian Dior or Chanel runway.

Wilde gave none of them more than a cursory glance and an upward tilt of his straight but not narrow nose. You might have thought something malodorous had wafted south from the river.

"I should explain myself," he said, again in tentative mode. "I dispense epigrams as if giving alms to the needy. It is punishment for the sin of my not knowing at crucial moments in my life when aphorisms ceased to be appropriate. The harsh sentence dates from my slander suit against the Marquis of Queensberry. During the first trial, I was asked if I'd kissed a certain youth of my acquaintance. I replied, 'Oh, dear no. He was a particularly plain boy. I pitied him for it.'

"That was not the type of remark that goes down well in court.

Though I did hasten to add—and I quote my usually quotable self—that at times one says things flippantly when one ought to speak more seriously, and vice versa. It was too late.

"I also was asked to repeat what I had said to the Marquis of Queensberry when he said to me and Alfred, Lord Douglas—Bosie—that 'If I catch you and my son together again in any public restaurant, I will thrash you.' I admitted before m'Lud that I had indiscreetly replied, 'I don't know what the Queensberry rules are, but the Oscar Wilde rule is to shoot at sight.

"My verbal profligacy resulted, as you undoubtedly know, in four years' hard labor within the thick and unforgiving Reading Gaol walls. One would assume that was sufficient payment of one's debt to society, and although it was, it has been deemed by higher judges as inadequate payment of one's debt to the universe. I'm paying it now by those same higher authorities condemning me to continue devising aphorisms—as you have witnessed these last few minutes."

He stopped to wave a gloved fist at the bright sky and then to sink into thought. Then, regaining his composure—not to say his imperious glance—said, "Those who live to please others may have a point, but it's a blunt point. Never ask listeners if they agree with what you're saying— it's sufficient that you agree with yourself. People say honesty is good for the soul, but they never specify whose soul."

We had resumed sauntering and had turned on to boulevard Saint-Germain. Walking east, we were in the thick of the passing parade. Wilde maintained his pace, sometimes using his stick to nudge others aside. I did my best to keep up with him and even found myself, on Wilde's behalf, giving apologetic nods to pedestrians whom his Wildean manners had irritated.

Apparently having assessed the contemporary styles swirling around him, Wilde said, "Women dress for other women—men dress for better or worse." I figured that for him the fashions, such as they were on Paris streets, were not so much new as completely foreign.

He switched to scanning the buildings we passed and said, with a toss of one scarf end over his right shoulder, "I understand we must have architectural design but could not someone instruct us how to avoid having to looking at it?"

The throngs by which he blithely sailed must have eventually made some impression, because he blurted, "Other people are necessary to our well-being, but only just."

We were approaching Les Deux Magots, and my cheeks were beginning to hurt. This was a result of the fixed smile I'd been offering that I suspected Wilde considered his due. Vigorously rubbing my facial muscles—a gesture he missed, because he was still looking away from me—I realized there's such a thing as an aphorism-receptor limit, and, while I can't deny my affinity for certain affectations, I'd reached the satiation point. An excess of *bons mots* was the spoken equivalent of an excess of bon-bons.

Furthermore, I recoiled at Wilde's treatment of a thoroughfare about which I had extremely favorable feelings. It was just off the boulevard Saint-Germain—on the block-long rue de Condé—where I'd stayed when I first came to Paris. I liked walking the boulevard no matter what the weather—drizzling, sizzling—to remind myself of the effect the city had on me the first day I was able to explore it. Even the memory of a *clochard* (bum) I almost tripped over that introductory day filled me with nostalgia. He was the first man I'd ever seen napping on a sidewalk.

But how was I to shake Wilde? Even though it was possible he could easily go a few more blocks before he noticed I'd disappeared, I couldn't just walk away from him.

"The only thing wrong with the lower class," Wilde continued, dauntless and sniffing at the crowds surging by, "is that it exists. On the other hand, I have nothing against a lack of beauty as long as I am not exposed to it."

Much as I was—well, flattered, I suppose you could say—at having made Oscar Wilde's acquaintance and by implication to have been found not lacking in beauty, I felt more and more pressed to take my leave of him.

Conflicted and not wanting to be discourteous, I picked up my pace until I was slightly ahead and to the right of him. Catching his eye from that vantage point, I said, "Excuse me, Mister Wilde. I am enjoying our walk immensely, but I really must be leaving. I am supposed…"

I stumbled over what I was supposed to be doing. I could hear the uncertainty in my voice. Making matters worse, I was clenching my hands. They were sweaty.

He said, and with the perspicacity often attributed to him, "I never mind companions dissembling as long as I do not realize they are." He had my number.

I was ashamed and embarrassed. To disguise that, I hastened to say, "Well, perhaps I'm not in that much of a hurry."

He looked at me and said with a silver-spoonful of condescension, "A gentleman never hurries to the world—he waits for the world to come to him."

To emphasize the significance of that observation, he slowed his stride and tapped his walking stick metallically on that particular patch of what I still thought of as the magical boulevard Saint-Germain.

I noticed we'd almost reached the rue Danton, down which were two book stores I knew. I suddenly longed to comb through shelves for anything that didn't have Oscar Wilde's name on its spine. But how to give him the old Victorian heave-ho? My attempt to beg off politely had failed. There must be another way, I told myself unconvincingly. Hoo-ha! A thought came to me as if delivered by wingéd Mercury himself.

"I hope you won't think me overstepping my bounds, Mr. Wilde," I said, "but I've been mulling over your predicament."

"In an intelligent person presumption must be actively encouraged," he mused.

Despite the epigram's coming at me like yet another steel arrow, I figured I should be encouraged by it. I said, "Perhaps I could help you with the aphorism problem."

Halting again, he surveyed me head to foot and back again. "There is a solution," he said, "but it's complicated."

I put on my sincerest expression, so sincere I could feel my raised eyebrows furrowing my forehead. I curled my tongue to say "I'm all ears" but decided a cliché was not called for.

He spoke with deliberation. "My chastising gods have willed that if I can transmit the phrase-making compulsion to someone with whom

I've become acquainted, no matter how briefly," he said, "I unburden myself of the habit for all eternity. I will have passed the affliction on. Then will I utter aphorisms only when I wish to, and I have been assured I will rarely wish to. Ah, but I am chagrined to say that so far I have never met the person." He smiled a half-smile.

It was, I noted, the only time since we'd met that he'd turned up the corners of his mouth even that much. Wanting to offer solace, I said with no forethought, "Hope is the one thing we must hold on to when all hope is gone."

Wilde stared at me as if branding me with his gray eyes. "What did you say?" he asked.

I repeated myself and added, "Defeat always comes from within."

I had barely finished when just there, at the intersection of boulevard Saint-Germain and rue Danton, the man I knew—but only for no more than 45 minutes—as Oscar Wilde disappeared as rapidly as he'd appeared. He evanesced. He went up in a puff (I won't say "poof") of mauve smoke. All that was left of him was the green carnation, falling to a soft, sad landing on the pavement.

"What begins unexpectedly," I said aloud, "will often end just as unexpectedly."

Only then, as I spoke to whomever happened to be within earshot, did I really hear myself. I heard the three observations I'd just made—the one about hope, the one about defeat and the one about expectation—and how I'd shaped them.

That's when it came to me. They were aphorisms. I couldn't deny it. They were epigrams. Having escaped from Oscar Wilde, had I taken him with me? If so, I instantly realized, I'd succeeded in getting my mind off my consuming troubles. I'd succeeded in settling my mind on a new one.

Once a worrier, always a worrier, but now perhaps I could at least convert my worries into deathless turns of phrase. Let's see: There's nothing wrong with worrying that additional worrying will not ameliorate. Or: When other people are worried, they undoubtedly should be. Or: It isn't love that makes the world go round, it's worry.

Say, this is fun. I'll keep it up, and eventually I'll have my own collection. I looked up and down rue Danton. The sun had come out. Paris was smiling at me.

My Second Story

※ or ※

Homer Is Where the Heart Is

Ever since I watched Marilyn Monroe as Hamlet, I kept waiting for something similar to happen to me. That's all the while I was collecting the other, preceding stories. Nothing ever did happen—nothing, that is, until many years later when I'd been in Manhattan for several decades and knew parts of the city better than I knew the back of my hand.

Truth to tell, I don't know the back of my hand—either hand—very well. They're nice hands, but I don't study them frequently, much less think about them often. I know the front of my hands, my palms, even less well. I've never had fortune tellers look them over. I'm not interested in whether I'm going to take a trip on a boat or whether someone with the initial "S" is going to give me a hard time.

Nevertheless, one part of town I know very well is Central Park. I've rollerskated through it, biked through it, strolled through it, sung through it. Always only to myself. It has never lost its big-city charm, its promise, its ability to relax, its ability to inspire when I need it most. Central Park in the spring when the lilacs are in bloom is my favorite time, although there are several others that run a close second.

Recently, after getting a lengthy whiff of this year's lilacs, I kept going to Sheep Meadow and, while contemplating what I needed most—something, anything to write about next—I passed a group of bearded men and a lone woman sitting in an untidy circle.

Many others were passing them, not taking them in, as if they weren't there, which is the way it goes sometimes. I was in the process of doing the same when I heard one of them say something I mistook for the name "Odysseus."

That stopped me not quite in my tracks, but it slowed me down. I was intrigued. What could they have been talking about? Whom could they be talking about with a name that sounded like Odysseus?

So now I'm ambling around them more slowly, and I hear another declare a rather cheerful sentence that this time distinctly included the name "Odysseus." I was even more intrigued. I thought to myself, Who wouldn't be fascinated by a group of old folks who had a friend—I assumed they were talking about a friend—called Odysseus who was up to this and that? No doubt a Greek, although outside of the epic poem, I'd never encountered a Greek called Odysseus.

Hearing mention of this Odysseus, I, for one, was definitely fascinated. I decided to—let's be honest here—eavesdrop on them. I didn't want to be too obvious about it. So I sidled near them and sat down on the spring grass, though not so close that I'd appear to be interloping. I made a point of looking anywhere but directly at them. I looked at the blue sky and the birds wheeling there. I looked at the trees coming into bloom. I looked at other passersby.

All the while, the old men and the one woman bantered on. I couldn't hear what they were saying with total clarity. I only heard "Odysseus" repeatedly and then snatches of sentences about what this Odysseus character was up to. Once or twice I also heard the name "Ulysses." How odd, I thought. How literate.

As I continued sitting and listening, I noticed that one of the men had gotten up and was heading my way. There was no doubt about it. As he threaded through strollers paying him no mind, I could see out of the corner of my slowly panning eye that I was his destination.

"Young man," he said, when he was standing in front of me, and I could no longer pretend I was occupied elsewhere, "You seem to be interested in us." The "young man" was generous. I'm no longer as young as I was when I first moved to New York City, but I was younger than this chunky, bearded man whose eyes, while they sparkled, also held something deep within them suggestive of true understanding. I was also markedly younger than all of his white-bearded, flowing-mane male compatriots.

"Perhaps instead of sitting here trying to catch what we're talking about," he said leaning over, his grizzled beard nearly grazing my forehead, "you might like to sit with us."

My first impulse was to deny all charges, but there was an air about this man, who may have been seventy or eighty or ninety, that told me I'd be foolish to lie to him. Anyone energetically discussing Odysseus, or Ulysses for that matter, would recognize feeble mendacity in an instant.

Coincident with my first impulse was the urge to stand up and hurry off, but that, too, hit me as foolish. The man was looking at me not as if he were looking through me but as if he were looking into me, and with benevolent acceptance.

Something about him indicated that if I blew him off, I'd regret it. As I'm thinking this, he looked back at his pals for a second. I turned that way as well and saw they were all looking at me with the same glowing expressions of kindliness.

Feeling myself in an inexplicable thrall, I stood up and mumbled that I would appreciate their company, if only for a short time.

The man's smile broadened and he said, "My friends will be happy to know that. Come with me."

He took me by the arm—all this, while other park goers passed us—and began to lead me over to the other bearded seventy- or eighty- or ninety-year-old men and the unbearded seventy- or eighty- or ninety-year-old woman who I could see had sat themselves on beach towels and newspapers.

They were all shapes and sizes. Two of them were tall and thin. Three of them were short and squat. The other two, including the woman, were somewhere in-between. If they shared any other outward characteristics, it was their ruddy cheeks, ready smiles and bindlestiff clothes. A couple of them gazing off into the distance appeared to be blind, but I couldn't be certain. They might only have been concentrating.

"What's your name?" my guide asked as we approached. I said I was Paul Engler. "And what do you do, Paul Engler?" I told him I was a writer but didn't mention that I was a writer who at that moment was between books and didn't have the foggiest idea what to write about next.

"That's what we suspected," he said as we reached his elderly gang. "It's a pleasure to meet you, Paul Engler." To them he said, "Friends, this is Paul Engler. As we thought, he's a writer."

A second man said, "Welcome, Paul Engler."

A third man said, "It's a pleasure to meet you, Paul Engler."

A fourth man said, "It's always a pleasure to meet a writer."

A fifth man said, "Another writer."

A sixth man said, "You probably want to know who we are."

The seventh—the woman—said, waving a chunky forearm at the others, "We're Homer." At that, the other six shook their heads up and down enthusiastically so that their beards bobbed, and said things like "We sure are" and "And proud to be" and "That's the name we like to go by." One of the short and squat ones who spoke above the others said, "A storyteller is forever."

The man who led me over to them gestured for me to sit down. He said, "We're not all of Homer, of course. There are many more of us who couldn't be here for one reason or another."

One of the other Homers said, "There are many, many more of us."

Another Homer said, "Even we aren't certain how many."

"Over several generations," another one said.

"But we're the ones," the Homer who'd initially come to me said, "who agreed the world needs a continuation of Odysseus's story."

"You know," another Homer said, "the story of what happens to Odysseus and Penelope once they are reconciled."

"And Telemachus, of course," another added.

"That's what we're doing here," the Homer who was my guide said, "hammering out the story of what happened to the family after it was reunited."

A different one said, "Because why would the story end where we, the dozens of us—"

"Perhaps scores—" another inserted.

"—ended it—"another added.

"—after many, many years," yet another said.

A different one said, "We thought it should end there at the time."

"But really," a different one said, "why would it? In some ways when Odysseus and Telemachus killed Penelope's suitors—"

Another interrupted, "—and peace was ostensibly restored in the household—"

And another, "—and Odysseus and Penelope repaired to the marriage bed—"

The one who interrupted continued, "that was just the beginning."

Another said and the others nodded, "With all those slain suitors littering the halls, there were bound to be repercussions."

"Weren't there?" another one said, excitedly, and the excitement proliferated.

"There had to be," another said even more excitedly, and the excitement proliferated again, accompanied by the occasional elderly cough and wheeze.

They all joined in as if tossing out words and phrases like slogans in a preview of coming attractions.

"More travels."

"More terrifying monsters."

"More obstacles."

"More temptations."

"More battles."

At this point, the eight of them quieted and fixed me with sweetly stern (or sternly sweet) looks, waiting for my reaction.

But how do you react to such a formidable disclosure? I certainly wasn't prepared and sat with what must have appeared to be a comically nonplussed face—so comical that their reaction to mine was a round of belly laughs. Not, I could easily tell, at my expense but in appreciation of my wonder.

Finally one of them said, "That's what we've been hammering out for some time now."

"Any ideas?" another one inquired. They all turned to me expectantly.

"You're a writer," another said. "What do you think?"

I thought for a second and said, "I don't know how far you've gotten."

They all chuckled at that, and one of them said, "Of course, you don't."

"We had better fill you in," another said with an idiom I wouldn't have thought was common to Greek troubadours.

They did. Fill me in. They outlined what they had come up with to date, much of it based on their knowledge of Greek history and Greek mythology as far as Greek history had been recorded (not reliably, a few of them suggested) and Greek mythology had been established—and then added to by the time the first Homer, or Homers, had originally begun compiling *The Odyssey*. (A couple of them mentioned *The Iliad* but not in detail and only, really, to concur that it was an epic to which the sequel had, of course, already been provided.)

Their new saga not only included poetic set pieces focused on the revived Odysseus-Penelope-Telemachus home life, in good part given over to the reawakening of their romance, and the introduction into it of a love interest for Telemachus, but followed father and son as they became entangled in regional campaigns with countries whose warrior sons had been slaughtered in Odysseus's court. As well, they'd preliminarily shaped chapters involving tantalizing (though not Tantalus) new figures diverting the heroes from their forced travels.

I won't go into specifics for a very specific reason. As the Homers took turns spinning their draft in what I can only call true troubadour fashion, they often stopped to check the effect they were having on me.

At first, I just listened, as if I had slipped into a time warp that landed me in, say, 800 BCE. I nodded that I liked what I was hearing. After a while, though, and with their tacit encouragement, I began to offer reactions, proposing that they rethink a particular development or description.

Even as I was offering them, I was thinking how god-almighty presumptuous I was being, but they must have liked what I had to offer, because as they revisited more of their composing to date—each picking up from the previous one—they nodded more pointedly for me to keep chiming in. Even the ones I thought might be sightless turned my way with the shared ready smiles.

This went on, I realized, for hours into the early evening when it was time for them to go their separate ways and for me to go mine, which I did before they did. But none of us had departed before they invited me to join them the following week. I did so for the next nine weeks, at the end of which and with great jubilation we reached the twenty-fourth and final chapter.

The accomplishment enables me to announce, firstly, that my new collaborators disbanded (to where I don't know) and, secondly, that next year will see the publication of *The Odyssey Redux*. And because the Homers judged it expedient in the twenty-first century, I am both proud and humbled to say the new epic poem will be published under only my name. What a way finally to surmount my writer's block!

www.ingramcontent.com/pod-product-compliance
Lightning Source LLC
Chambersburg PA
CBHW031233120726
47905CB00002B/577